HOLLYWOOD HAVOC *Fat Boy*

I0553366

HOLLYWOOD HAVOC

The Trouble With Fat Boy

John Klawitter

DoubleSpin

DoubleSpin

Book Layout and
Cover Art by Deron Douglas
www.derondouglas.com

Covers produced for DoubleSpin
By Bronco Bradley Merville
www.creativeroundup.com

ISBN-10: 1-938674-01-4
ISBN-13: 978-1-938674-01-3

Lynnie, we hit the ground running
We dodge
We turn
We make it through.
And let's not forget fun…
We try our best to make it fun,
for what is life
without a warm smile
and a bit of wonder
at the absurdity of it all?

AUTHOR'S NOTE

Those of you who remember me from the studios, the indy production companies, the post-production houses, the location and equipment services, the casting sessions, rehearsals, scouting and pre-pro meetings, the Director's Guild of America, SAG & AFTRA, the Writers Guild of America, ASCAP, Disney, Warner Bros, Hanna Barbera, Universal, Paramount...you, who yourself have gritted through the long nights in post bays and laughed it up at the old Hollywood places like Musso Franks, Chasens and The Tin Horn Saloon...you may find moments you recognize like an old dream or nightmare. You may see between these pages some heroes, heroines, scamps and wenches you might suspect you have known in your own lives and careers. You may even think you see some reflection of your own image in the well. But in this I must assure you are paging through a work of fiction, and all the incidents, events and characters here are made-up situations and imaginary rascals and fine faux ladies, created from pixie dust for the purpose of telling this fictional story of heart-stopping action and non-stop adventure. You in real life are far more clever, tricky, aspiring, unpredictable and wonderful than any of the pale imitations cavorting through these pages could ever hope to be.

Chapter 1

The icy black water hit me like a cold body slam. I rolled over and over, panicked in the dark with blind-folded eyes and air bubbles frothing around my ears. Which way was up? I had no idea. You know, the experts always tell you the bubbles go up, but in the inky blackness it's all up...or down, or sideways.

My hands were tied, but I could kick some with my feet. One foot struck the hard edge of a slippery ledge. Okay, maybe that way was down...or sideways. I felt for the rocky ledge, crouched, gathered myself in a ball, and pushed off.

I'd guessed right; the surface came with a rush. I managed to suck in a quick gasp of air. I shook off the bath towel the bastards had taped around my head for a make-shift blindfold, and saw the dark line of the shore directly in front of me—and the black outline of my two assailants standing there, laughing like I was some new electronic sports game and expectantly hopeful I would sink out of sight, never to be seen again. I kicked desperately and shook my head, an attempt to clear the water from my ears.

"What shall we do, do you think?" I heard the one on the left say, as if they were discussing dinner plans or who might take out the garbage. Yeah, that's me, the garbage.

"I say pop him," the one on the right replied.

"No, no, no. He's too close to shore. He'll just drift back in."

"Well now, old chap, I could not disagree more. After all, he'll drift, either way."

Wait a minute. What the hell was I doing here? Me, Matthew Havoc. Okay, they call me Hollywood Havoc, but this is way past some of the minor schemes and scrapes I get into. I am a small-time Hollywood movie producer. Small beans, very little sauce. I work for Berger Royal, and we do schlock movies. We don't even own our own stages, for Christ's sake; we rent space on the Raleigh lot below Sunset in what is affectionately known as 'Old Hollywood'. And I certainly wasn't here to star as the drowning man in my own movie.

"Wait," I gasped in a bubbly, confused shout. "It's not my fault. I don't really pick the scripts!" That was a lie, of course. At least, part a lie. I do help pick the scripts. Okay, I'll admit it. If anybody deserves to be shot for producing imitative, cheese-ball movies, it is me.

Oh, oh! I see a yellow flash and the sharp bark of a pistol. Jesus H. Christ! The crazy-ass *mudder-humpers* are shooting at me! Why can't they just get their refund at the box office? Yeah, I know. This isn't about the movies. This is too serious. This is attempted murder. Hell, this is about to *be my murder.* But making movies has been my life and I can't figure out what else it could be. I pay my taxes, I don't do dope, I don't have any powerful enemies. Another quick gulp of air and I kick down and away. The dark water wraps icy fingers around me, and I do my best to put distance between the shore and myself. My arms, of course, are useless, bound the way they are. By now, I'm desperate for air. I force myself, I kick, kick, kick, giving it that old Havoc try, even though I can feel the burning pain surge through my lungs.

But the gods are smiling on me, at least to the extent that there is a favorable undertow, and this time when I come to the surface there is about ninety feet between me and my two friends, the nonchalant shooters making a game out of taking me out. Just ninety feet, the distance from home plate to the pitcher's mound. Still, better than nothing.

"Oh, sporting chance!" the one waving the pistol says.

"Allow me. I'm the better shot," the other replies, and they grapple for it.

"No, idiot. I am."

They're wrestling over the pistol, and I judge that to be a good thing. I gulp air and pump my feet while they amiably wrestle for the right to kill me.

I shouldn't have to repeat that I don't deserve this. But they're not listening, and my complaints aren't true in the first place. Off-hand, I can think of a dozen reasons you should find some slow and horrible way to kill me. Look, if you're going to shoot me for anything, it should be that doomed scene in Dragonfly Madness where the fake model helicopter (possessed by demonic influences) comes down on Metropolis like a limp beetle. On the other hand, I didn't have the budget to do anything better, and we had to finish the picture or lose a payment, and we at Berger Royal never miss our play dates or our pay dates. Or maybe you might want to send me to the torture chamber for that rotten tomato film we did called Klish Clash, with its garbage can lid musical numbers, one of our few attempts at social parody. The miserable failure of these individual productions aside, I stand accused—and rightly so—of living for my job, but there have been times when I've thought it's a great job. I'm assistant jack-of-all-trades to the great Hollywood mogul of crap B-movies, the one and only Vincent Berger, known in the trade as Slick Vinnie or Vinnie-the-Cheap. To me he's just Vinnie, a skin-flint at spending money on his pictures and a heart of gold for every sob-story starlet who comes his way.

I'm Matt Havoc, Hollywood Havoc, the solver of all problems cinematic, the *sho-biz guy who gets things done*. They should give out an honor like that at ShoWest. Maybe they would from now on, in honor of me and my watery death.

Flashes from the pistol are starting up again, so I gulp more air and head back down to my bad ending. My enemies in the business will tell you I deserve this.

They say the life I lead is crap, and that the movies I help turn out are basically stupid and unwatchable. I will admit this much: At Vinnie's shop, Berger Royal Pictures, we create nothing but low-budget exploiters. Yes, that's what we do, and we're the very best at it, and there's a market for it. Come on, I'm supposed to be ashamed for making a living? As Vinnie's fond of saying, *Art, schmart, who gives a fart?*

As I am down there underwater thinking these and similar thoughts, I somehow come out of my confusion long enough to allow the immediate panic to subside. My lungs, I realize, aren't actually bursting and I can probably go a ways before I have to surface again. Yes, it is dark and cold and scary, but as I kick along I try to review how I could possibly have gotten into this mess. How did I, the cleverest low-budget guy in Hollywood, a guy who can create budgets as if by magic, dodge location fee cops, satisfy cast sexual appetites (My black book is legendary), find free parking and feed a cast and crew on the run, ever allow something this stupid to happen?

Earlier in the afternoon, just a few hours before, I'd been in Little Saigon looking for locations for a new picture that wasn't even green-lighted.   I didn't find anything half-way decent or even exciting enough to snap a digital, and I'd driven back south to Newport Beach where I lived. I was returning to my condo, absent-mindedly ambling along the short gray cobblestone walkway that I share with my long-time neighbor Bertrand Burke, semi-affectionately known as 'Old Bertie' or 'Old Grampers,' when out of the corner of my eye I noticed the shattered frame of the old coot's front entrance, the opening where his sturdy door used to be. For a moment the image didn't compute, and then I had what the Hollywood story guys call the *bad inkling*, the hero's first hint that things are not quite as they should be.

Let me move this along and try to sum it up here for you before I drown. I'm a thirty four year old journeyman Hollywood producer. I can do—have to do—everything. I know how to write and direct. I've been called on to shoot film when the cinematographer gets the runs or the flu or doesn't come back from a hot weekend in Acapulco. Yes, I am the complete film maker, a MacGyver of the silver screen, the guy who pulls off the impossible shots with bubble gum and a ball of yarn. You know, *My mind is the secret weapon.* Well, enough of that. Obviously, it isn't, or I wouldn't be here, sinking to the bottom of the bay. Let's get back to more Hollywood gossip about me.

I am divorced, a half-dozen or so years ago, from a self-absorbed, gum-chewing, teenage vixen…at least, that's who she was when we took our vows. I guess I knew. Like the country-western ballads lament, *What was I thinking?* Actually, I wasn't thinking, at least, not with my brain. It was one of those spur-of-the-moment Hollywood weddings doomed to failure from the first…well, read the gossip rags while you're standing in line at the supermarket, you know how it goes in flickerville. Still, ours wasn't your usual bang-and-run story. We were actually destroyed by success…hers, not mine. Soon after our wedding, the career of the lady of my affections began to blossom, and she forthwith lifted herself like a gaudy hot air balloon right past my cheapie movies to her present rarified altitude as one of America's most ogled and highly paid set of tits available on the silver screen, that is, short of triple-X. Today she's known as Joy Benefeté, but when I first knew her she was Madge Sacknall, an auburn-haired theater and drama major with a great body and a wicked grin, a gorgeous starlet who couldn't sing a single note on key. Not that she didn't try, but it was painful. I affectionately called her Peanuts, and in the beginning I was glad of the singing because it meant she wasn't perfect. The other cracks in the dam showed up a little later.

Okay. Another gulp of air, another glimpse at my story. About the time Peanuts married me, fat, bald, Big Vinnie introduced her to fat, bald, little Super-Agent Harry "Horny" Hyatt. It was Christmas, and Vinnie was in one of his magnanimous moments. However, since Berger Royal Pictures had been the kiss of death for many a young starlet, Horny's HHH Agency repaid the favor by christening her Joy Benefeté and moving her out of our shop.

Of course, Vinnie resented the move. He thought of Berger Pix as one of the few training grounds for greatness, and maybe he was right. If Steve McQueen could rise above his performance in The Blob, Peanuts ought to be able to gain artistic recognition with the lead role in Mission 998, a hot babes in wet T-shirts in outer space spectacular we had planned for

her. Vinnie was moved to righteous
indignation. He would have loved to squeeze
another picture or two out of that magnificent
set before she moved them on to the silk and
caviar mob.

I'm not the best judge of these things,
having lived too close to the feisty fact of
Peanuts in person, and there may have been a
certain sense in which you might call my ex-
wife morally weak, perhaps lacking in strength
of character—but you would never call her
weak-willed or without purpose. Strong as iron
comes to mind. Relentless and even reckless
in pursuit of her career, certainly. She knew
what she wanted, and she knew how to get it.
That made me something of a way-station on
her golden path.

When Horny Hiatt told her she was
ready to walk around the next bend, she
believed it. And the rest of our relationship
was Extra-Extra history, that is, food for the
paraparazzi, Extra Extra and The Insider.
Madge Sacknall emerged from her cocoon as
the beautiful, generally nearly-naked butterfly
Joy Benefeté. Her exit from Berger Royal
Pictures and my bedroom was followed by her
steady and relentless climb to a sort of lower
rung stardom. Cheap, that is to say, because
my ex-wife became known and appreciated for
the lift, weight and luminosity of her perfect
breasts, rather than for her acting. And frankly,
I believed that was unfair; I knew her better
than most, and I saw that, somewhere inside
all those curves, that wicked smile, and her
devious, unrelenting thirst for stardom, my girl
Peanuts really had acting ability.   How much, I

wasn't sure. But the director in me sensed something there that went considerably beyond the luminosity of the flesh.

I told her just that, a time or two, but by then it was too late. She said things like, *I was just trying to hold her back. I was cruel, uncaring, selfish.* And, to tell the truth, after a few months of that, I gave up trying to make a go of it. I had my own grueling schedule. Schlock films wait for no man. Things having become what they had, the two of us were less and less an item around town. Busy lives, separate directions. We drifted apart and separated after a year or two, but we didn't seem to get around to the divorce until a half dozen years later, and when it finally happened it was almost an afterthought. She'd been about to dive into matrimony in the classic Hollywood manner, tying a hasty knot (not unlike we ourselves had, but this time) with some dark-haired and flashing-eyed Italian cinematic heartthrob. And then the Enquirer took an interest, researched the files and found out she was still technically married to me. As they say in the turning-point scene where the complication becomes clear, *Oh, oh.*

Give me a moment here; oxygen seems to be at a premium. A few kicks, another gulp of air, a few more flashes from the now receding shore. Okay. Better now. On with the narration: Long time before, my father, Jack Havoc, was in the film business, too, but he worked for the studios, and he had better credits than I do. Vinnie had known him, and that's how I landed my first job, running myself ragged as Vinnie's go-fer, back when I was just out of film school.

Let me tell you about Vinnie Burger. Yes, he's that important. Vinnie, himself, is a larger-than-life personality. He tops over six foot five inches. He carries an enormous girth, and an ability to be amused in the direst of circumstances, and an even bigger talent for squeezing production money out of hitherto untapped sources. Greece. Romania. South Africa. A giant used car dealership in Pomona. All this, combined with a huge appetite for spending his production monies on Bentley sports cars, big sailing boats, and lavish gifts for wannabe starlets he finds…well, everywhere. Yes, he spends on those splendid luxury items rather than on the production itself, and with my help, he manages to hide the financial drain. Our movies look decent on paper but for these and other reasons turn out to be potboilers that play in the last three or four drive-in theaters in Canada and Mexico and then ship directly to Hong Kong, Seoul and Jakarta. Vinnie's a rogue—but he's got a sense of honor, life alternately outrages and amuses him, and, as had my father before me, I have the bad judgment to like him very much.

I guess I am drifting here, things getting a little fuzzy. I don't see the light yet, though. Jennifer Love Hewlett, the lady who wears those skimpy negligees on Ghost Whisperer, says that when you see the light you are to go for it, and then I guess you pass through the veil or something and you're dead but happy. I was thinking maybe you don't see the light if you're headed to hell, and, after all, only dogs and Oscar Winners actually go to heaven.

Right, right, my story in a martini glass…let's see if I can gulp it down, get through it before I'm fish food. After over a decade of doing hard time as Vinnie's right hand man, I've arrived to where I'm pulling down the producer or co-producer credit on almost every miserable, rotten film we do. It's a little strange, because I always thought the producer's title would be the end of the world for me, my golden ticket. But when you do successful B movies, that isn't necessarily so. Lately what the literary novelists call *malaise* has set in on my normally indomitable spirit. I find that more and more I want to write, not just screenplays but short stories and novels. *Less crap, more meaning.*

I even daydream of retiring from my career as the clever slave-laborer who cleans up Vinnie's messes. In my dreams the serious people, those who make their way in the world of real ideas and literature, take me seriously. I don't have shouting matches over putting the key light at boob level, I have conversations about literature and art, and a New York agent who doesn't always ask *Okay, guy, how many sex scenes we got here?*

I know you're not asking, but in case you were, Sure, Hollywood agents love me, at least the lesser known ones do (Dogs are even attracted to guys who have smaller yummies to hand out). But in my dreams, I'm a long way removed from here—no, not underwater—far removed from my current position as co-captain at the helm of inconsequential Berger

Royal bubbles of action/adventure and pot boiling sexual fantasy. You've got it by now—I'm lost in what Vinnie calls the Fairyland of Tits & Ass, the land where sex, dope and even blurbs in the Hollywood Reporter can be negotiated for a screen credit. That means, of course, the immortal soul (or at least the carefully hoarded life savings) of a famous used car dealer in Pacoima may be sold for a name above the title. I know where I want to end up, and this is not it.

Enough about me. After all, I'm drowning here. You can read the obit in The Hollywood Reporter. On the other hand, I'm sure Bertrand Berke, my neighbor, is the one who got me into this. Old Bertie's your ordinary, garden-variety, querulous semi-retired old fart living on a fixed income of maybe slightly larger than normal proportions. I would cast Walter Matthau, if he hadn't already walked happily into the light. I may sound cruel, but I like Bertie too, more than I will ever admit in his presence. In a way, for him it's all over, his life is a finished history rather than any blank new pages to be filled. At least, that's what I thought, up until this afternoon. Ironic, isn't it? I'm the guy drowning here and I'd been thinking Old Bertie was the gone goose.

A widower for the last five of his 80 years, Bertrand's backed away from his middle-aged twin sons, who nearly simultaneously decided to go for the gay life, though not with each other. Not that they didn't fool around, but they never made it official. That would have killed Old Grampers on the spot. The twin pervs, Bertrand calls them, trying for light-hearted malice. Back when he first got the bad news, he recoiled like a man with a couple of spiders in his soup. Today, the twins are out of range, both drifting quietly along in long-term relationships somewhere on the East Coast. Or at least that's the going story, and as The Man Hemingway would say, it would be pleasant to assume so. You wouldn't think Bertrand was a person who could get himself tangled in a dangerous and deadly mess and then pull me in with him—but real life has an enormously unpredictable plot-line, have you noticed?

I cannot recall how many times in the early morning I'd be staggering in from pulling a post-production all-nighter at MatchFrame or Pacific Video, and Old Bertie would be out there in front of his condo in his multi-colored Bermuda shorts and Wall Street Journal T-shirt, the one with the spotty white bleach stains. Like as not, he'd be staring up at the gutters, cursing the pigeons or the bats. Some decades before, he'd invested in a clothing company appropriately named Crazy Wear, and he had stacks of cardboard boxes in his garage crammed full of gaudy clothing you couldn't even sell for profit in third world countries that had never heard of Ralph Lauren or Hugo Black. Lord knows he'd tried.

"Paper in the banana tree again?" I'd ask. But no, this time it was the bats.

"Bats are filthy creatures, Matthew Havoc. Pestilence. Spawn of the devil. And it's not a banana tree, it's a bird-of-paradise gone wild."

"You think all plants would go wild if you didn't drench them in Miracle-Gro."

That's all it took. Old Bertie would launch from there, selecting from his list of the many things large and small that provoked him, sputtering about cruel and unusual property taxes, the growing hordes of greedy wetbacks up from every province in Mexico to take California back, and the inferior quality of the potted plants the condo gardeners—notice the sneaky bastards all speak Spanish when nobody is looking—stick in our front flowerboxes to mark the passing seasons (Coral, cream and light-purple geraniums in February and orange and yellow-and-brown chrysanthemums in August, Southern California being a two-season place).

"Right, Bertrand," I would say. "You got a point there."

"Jesus-God-Damn right, I do," he would agree, grumbling as he moved off to water his spindly over-fertilized citrus tree with a garden hose.

I'm too busy to be Mister Nice Guy, but I found it impossible to ignore the crusty old fellow who, in all fairness, had to walk around the heavy stacks of film cans, video cassettes and scripts that FedEx dumped at my doorstep on a fairly regular basis. I don't think Bertrand minded, because it was some proof that I did real work, though I think he assumed I was more responsible for the shipment, rather than the creation of, the films and videos inside the parcels.

And, yes, I knew him to a greater degree than I'm saying. At Bertrand's insistence, we had a procedure in case of his business emergencies, and once I'd even had the chance to put it to the test. He was in Mexico City when a man called from Brazil, desperately needing a bid on a mobile X-ray unit. I tried to get through to Bertrand, but you know the South-of-the-Border telephone system. Hey, the guy needed a bid, and he needed it right away. I made up a page of numbers, figuring a piece of machinery like that being mobile and all might cost about as much as a six or seven minute Willie Nelson music video or a short but highly sensuous promo film for my ex-wife's latest ode to nubility.

I must have been in the ballpark, because the guy gave Uni-Amer Industries that particular piece of business, though for the next six months Bertrand was griping about the size of the kickback. I guess he was grateful—he gave me a watch that told time in three zones, something he got for Christmas from a Norwegian shipping company.

"Set it for Tokyo and Singapore," he advised, "any hour of the day you could know what those tricky damn foreign skunks is up to."

Before he left town this last time, he'd switched his incoming faxes over to my machine, so all I had to do was glance at them...that is, when I remembered, and for a long time it was mind-numbing stuff about the functionality of the AZ-37 desktop radiation mode, or the exact dimensions of the trundle bed carrier, that uncomfortable cot-on-wheels that people laid down on before they got swung under Madame Curie's invention for peeking at bones.

And now somebody had broken down his door. I suppose I should have quietly tiptoed inside my own place and called the gate guards the minute I saw it, but curiosity got the best of me. That's the problem with us movie guys. We always want to know the whole story. I walked up to the door and gave a little push. But, instead of opening, it came off its remaining hinge and toppled over with a crash. There was a sudden rustle from the spare bedroom that Bertrand had converted into his office, and before I could retreat, two men came out and surrounded me with their extremely persuasive selves.

Their complexions were black as midnight onyx. They wore shiny business suits that I would have chosen as wardrobe for the successful gangster-businessmen from Hong Kong in Klish Clash, one of the countless Vinnie Berger chop-sockies, that is, the cheapie martial arts films that were among the Berger Royal staples. These black-as-onyx guys had broad shoulders and a collective scowl on their faces.

"Are, perhaps, you Bertrand, himself?" the one on the left said, giving me a little push for emphasis.

"Noooo..." I said uncertainly, pressing for time to think of something clever, or at least get my gears in reverse so I could motor on out of there. I started babbling as I tried to back out the way I'd come in. "Bertrand, himself, is an octogenarian with a bad temper. That's obviously not me. I'm not even 35. And I'm fairly even-tempered. You have to be, in my business. Say, did you guys see who broke in here?"

I thought I'd leave them an out, they could say they'd seen a white guy in a funny hat running away, but even that last was the wrong question, at least, coming from me. As it would turn out, there were no right questions.

Skin tones on Negroes in America tend to shades from light peach to cherry red and various shades of chocolate brown. Not on these guys; these were blue-black men from the old country, men so dark there was a depth and a luster to their skin that made it shine like polished hardwood. Really, although it is quite beautiful, skin like that will give a lighting director the fits. Even the newest fine grain 35mm can't stand the contrast between an ebony sheen like that and, say, the whites of the eyes and teeth, and no matter what the film schools tell you, video isn't any better.

"No, why do you say that about breaking in?" The first one asked. The annoyance was apparent in his voice.

"This door was hanging open from before we happened here," the other said with a sly half-smile. He looked like the wolf about to jump Little Red Riding Hood.

"Ahh, yes, right. We thought our dear friend, Mr. Bertrand Burke, might be injured," the first added helpfully. "So, of course, we entered this domicile to come to his aid and rescue."

"Bertrand isn't here," I said. "He's away on business."

I don't like crowds in the first place, and these unpleasant refugees from GQ Africa were pressing in too close for my comfort level. Heavy scent of Old Spice trying unsuccessfully to overcome body odor, and all that. Nothing an occasional shower couldn't handle, but that wasn't the point. Far worse for my particular situation, the shared entranceway to our condos was isolated from the general view.

In hindsight, I see I should have been a little more concerned a lot sooner, but Sea Garden Cove is a quiet, gate-guarded enclave. We don't encounter real trouble, situated as we are, a half-mile inland from the spangled neon glitz of the Coast Highway. Our gate guards aren't much, but in general their obdurate presence is enough to discourage the garden variety of local evils like Jehovah's Witnesses and grade school kids selling overpriced milk chocolate bars with almonds.

"Can you tell us, perhaps, where Mr. Burke has gotten himself off to?" the guy on the right asked. They both were broad-shouldered and athletic looking, but shorter than I was, and I'm barely six feet in my stocking feet.

"Well," I said doubtfully, "He said something about Budapest."

"Budapest!" They gave each other a startled look and then glared at me. I could see further conversation would be required.

I brought it on with a rush.

"Come to think about it, guys, I'm not sure he actually went to Europe...Bertrand is an import-export guy. He goes everywhere, but, as he works for himself, he doesn't report to anybody, and when he does say where he might be going he's not very big on the details."

That explanation didn't really seem to satisfy, either.

"So, then, inform us. Where are the actual business offices of Mr. Bertrand Burke?"

What a snappish little dictator! We could have used this fellow in Klish Clash, where we'd been panned for lack of authenticity. There was a big scar authentically indenting the bridge of his nose. I wondered how he'd gotten it. The only explanations I could come up with were unpleasant. Of course, there I was again, type-casting.

"Yes. Yes, precisely where are they?" the other added like an evil echo. "The offices of Mr. Bertrand Berke of Uni-Amer Industries?"

Maybe it was my overactive imagination, but I sensed an arch indifference and the hint of a foreign accent in their voices. *I was just meat to these guys—they were treating me like I was playback from the dead.* I thought their speech pattern might be French Colonial rather than German or English, but I'm not really an expert in that sort of thing. In the Berger Royal school of low-budget filmmaking, we go for broad impressions rather than literal accuracy.

"Here." I replied simply. "Right here, where you're standing. This is the broken doorway of Bertrand Berke and these are the offices of Uni-Amer Industries, LLC, *Excellence in X-ray Exports.*"

"Impossible!" The wide black man on the left looked around skeptically, as if Old Bat-brain Bertie might be hiding under the fallen door, or in the nearby hall closet. "I say, I mean to ask you, *Where are the actual offices of Uni-Amer Industries?*"

It's always hard when dreams come crashing down to meet reality. I don't know what these guys expected, but Bertrand's little shell of a company certainly wasn't it.

"I thought you just asked that?"

The fellow gave me a glare that would have crushed an ordinary mortal, but, of course, I'm on the low end in show biz and I take a lot of crushing. But I didn't need my directorial genius to recognize the increasing coldness in his voice and the dark granite set of his chin. He wasn't asking, he was demanding.

"Hey, don't shoot the messenger," I said.. "This is Uni-Amer, and it's not my fault they don't have a pretty secretary, but with cut-rate shipping, this is what you get. Bertrand works out of this condo, right here where he lives."

I suppose I should have been more on my guard; after all, tricky and unexpected things are always happening in our flicks, which are invariably full of heart-thumping action even if they come up lacking in motivation or real meaning—not that Big Time Hollywood does much better with three times my crew, four times as many shoot days and a hundred times my puny budgets. But the point is, I don't expect adventure in my own pathetic little mess of a personal life. *Adventure* is something Vinnie and our cheap pack of writers and hack directors and I invent and then present to the forgiving masses as entertainment.

Still, in the back of my mind, something about my present situation reminded me of the time in Dragonfly Madness when the corrupt Harrigan Matre's henchmen (who were themselves the Demon-spawn of the Dark Chop-man)—anyway, I was reminded of the time these guys had surrounded brave Tran Le just before they jumped him. Not a good sign, and then, just about when I decided I'd better be doing something about that—oops, it was too late.

I never had a chance. I'm nearsighted and, even with my Calvin designer eyeglasses, I have terrible peripheral vision. So I didn't actually see the cold and heavy object that struck me on the side of the head. And after that, I suppose I slumped to the ground without saying anything significant or even out loud. Suppose, but wouldn't really know.

Chapter 2

What followed the rude thump on my brain was a fuzzy-headed period of cramped, cold darkness. You may find it hard to believe, but you shouldn't read the weather from the network television shows. They just don't want you to know that it gets unpleasant here. It's bad for business at Disneyland and the Universal Studios Tour.   Southern California can be disgustingly cold and damp in late November, particularly at night near the coast. My head ached and the comforting rumble I heard wasn't comforting at all; it was the thrumming diesel engine of a big Mercedes-Benz motorcar, and I was trussed up like a turkey and locked in the dank and smelly trunk.

Lucky for me, I always carry a pocket Handicrafter's tool, one of those combination pliers and knife tools that I've found comes in handy for cutting open packets of film gels or fixing obdurate camera lens caps. Even better, my wrists, although bound tightly, were tied in front of me. I figured maybe I could work my way around to getting my hands in my pocket so I could get that old Handicrafter out to free myself. But here again, the way Vinnie and I would have written it into an escape scene wasn't the way it actually worked in real life. Even with my hands tied in front of me, in my semi-dazed frame of mind, I couldn't reach that stupid little tool.   I kept trying, but I went in and out of consciousness until the car stopped…after which I became aware of an unpleasant silence.

But that didn't hold them back at all. They swung me and let go and I turned over once in the air and hit the icy water in a graceless belly whopper. No points for Matt Havoc on that one. My fancy Calvin glasses were lost forever. Naturally, it went without saying that, if my new acquaintances had their way, I wouldn't need them any more.

The quiet was too brief for my tastes, much less my ambition to free myself. In another moment the trunk was flung open, and I found myself blinking like a dazed owl, staring directly into the bright blinding glare of a flashlight beam.   The two men from Africa grabbed me hand and foot and easily tossed me to the side of the road.

At least, I thought it was to the side of the road. Actually, that would have been a pretty good deal, compared to what I got. But, unfortunately for me, my abductors had backed close to a high stone jetty.

"Hey, wait!" I yelled in helpless protest.

But that didn't hold them back at all. They swung me and let go and I turned over once in the air and hit the icy water in a graceless belly whopper. No points for Matt Havoc on that one. My fancy Calvin glasses were lost forever. Naturally, it went without saying that, if my new acquaintances had their way, I wouldn't need them any more.

Incredibly, I knew where I was. We hadn't been driving more than ten minutes and the only nearby location that fit this description was the man-made jetty that protected the

Newport Harbor inlet from the rare but violent Pacific winter storms that occasionally batter our choice little bit of California coastline. Yeah, storms. The tourist bureau doesn't want you to know that, either.

I knew this location well. I'd stolen many free sun-setting-over-the-ocean pickup shots by pointing a 35mm Panaflex off to the west from right here, on this very spot. You know, *steal the shot and run?* It's a rush; you open the sliding door on the van and the camera is ready to go. Minimum crew. Flog the cast into some rough approximation of a matching shot, roll film—one take only—pack up and be scooting out just in the nick as the local law enforcement swoops in for the kill. After a year or two, once I honed my game, they never had a chance. You can't catch Berger Productions stealing a location shot if all you've got is a couple of bikes and a dune buggy.

Call me an optimist, but at the moment the black guys threw me in that water, I couldn't get it through my head that I was in an absolutely impossible situation. After all, in Keg's War, our imitation Rambo Movie, the incredible Horace Keg, ex-army ranger and mercenary with a too-kind heart for the ladies, was tied hand-and-foot by the Viet Cong and tossed into the Mekong River. And, being in that situation, he was able to survive for hours by swimming with a dolphin movement he'd learned as a U.S. Army Ranger. There actually is such a training; I had researched it for Kevin Doobler, our lazy-bum Keg's War director. (Vinnie bounced him after the first three weeks for non-performance and got me to shoot the rest of it, sans Doobler. The Director's Guild says that's not allowed, but Vinnie does a lot of stuff that the rule makers frown on.

However, that's not the point. Here, in the icy chop a few yards off the coast of Newport Harbor, I quickly realized that flopping like a fish in a cheery aqua colored swimming pool was nothing like trying to raise my head above the moiling and frigid ocean water for a gulp of air, and this in watery darkness while my jacket and pants were pulling me down like a sodden stone.

The one thing I had in my favor was the evening tide that was swiftly pulling me out to sea. While an off-shore tow would eventually pull me several miles out, where sharks would devour me and my body would never be found, at least for the moment that same evil tide was drifting me away from my two black friends and their obsession with using me for target practice. The Lord giveth and the Lord taketh away.

I knew how to act, at least how to pretend I was a limp fish. When you do a Vinnie Berger picture, you get to be an actor as well as a member of the crew. So I did my best to look listless, wilted and punctured, and even to get a sly gasp of air in the same moments.. The evening swiftly thickened into night as the dark tide gathered around me and began to drift me away to my watery grave. Either I was good enough at playing dead, or they ran out of bullets because after a few turns at plinking away, the amateur shootists got back in their large and expensive car and drove away.

And so there I was, bound hand and foot, and heading out to sea, and it seemed a toss-up whether I would drown, freeze to death or perhaps poetically be eaten by a very large fish like some poor fool in a Hemingway novel.

And what of me personally? Who was I to find myself at the unlikely end of my life before the story, at least from my point of view, has scarcely begun? I am Matt Havoc, admittedly somewhat of a scamp and a traditional loner, a self-made filmmaker whose parents left the scene tragically and unexpectedly before I was out of high school.

After the loss of mom and dad, if noted for any one thing, I was tenacious about my own survival. I had to be, to stay out of the clutches of the system. I managed to dodge social services for years, living alone in my parent's condo while slowly draining funds from dad's unexpectedly large bank accounts. Dad had a huge notebook with the phone numbers of his show biz contacts. After I worked my way through UCLA film school, I started calling numbers from that phone book until I got to the "B's" where I made a call that landed me a starting assignment as a junior production assistant with Burger Royal, one of the larger of the hundreds of indy companies in Hollywood that fed chop-sockie, blood-and-guts and horror movies to the international film distribution market.

When you work for an independent production company, you do it all; one moment you're using Budget Master to fake up budgets, then the director runs away with the makeup girl and you get to direct until Vinnie can convince somebody with a credit or two to finish the picture, and the next minute you're demoted to go-fer, on a run over to the Arco station to buy gas for the generator and a pile of powdery sugar donuts for Vinnie. For over fifteen years I'd been making my steady climb from doing absolutely rotten films to some that were merely pretty bad. Maybe I was making a difference. At Berger Royal Pics, there really was no way to tell. The weekly paycheck from Vinnie fell like welcome rain in my checking account, and for a long while that had been all that really mattered to me, a clear case of survival trumping art.

In spite of my feeble contributions to the history of the silver screen, flailing around in the uncaring ocean while dozens of couples dined on lobster and crab at seaside restaurants just a few hundred yards or so away seemed an odd and pathetic way for me to die. I decided to do my best not to allow it. I made a concentrated effort to get at the Handicrafter, still deep in my pocket. But flailing in the dolphin way took up all my time, and I nearly drowned before I had the clever little tool in my hands, and by then my fingers were so numb that I let go.

Adding to my troubles, a stinky rumbled past, close enough to tumble me over in the relentless black water. It was probably one of the small, private sports fishing boats that was returning late to the docks. I came to the surface sputtering and gasping, the Handicrafter lost forever in the watery depths.

Well…! That was it, then. There was nothing to keep me from drifting out to sea—except for the sudden jerk that spun me over on my back and set me dragging through the water behind the stinky, which proved to be a 35-foot sport-fisher. Now I couldn't get my breath at all, and I was being dragged along like a hooked mackerel. May the Gods of Complicated Story Plots be praised—the guy who ran the boat had a trolling line out, and he'd snagged me on it! I was being rescued, but I was also being towed underwater where I couldn't get my breath. Chances were, I'd be drowned dead as a Bonita before anybody even realized they had a big one on the line. You know that old joke about being run over by a tiny Volkswagon bug? Maybe it is better to be eaten by sharks. What do you think Hemingway would say about that?

I came to lying on the deck of the sport-fishing boat. I could sense water was dribbling from my mouth, and I should have been coughing it up, but I was too far gone for that. I heard a dim murmur of voices. I was grateful somebody had cut the electric wire that had bound my wrists and feet. And then I heard somebody say something I understood all too well.

"I say throw him back," the voice said. "This is just more stinking trouble. And we're in deep enough crap, as it is." It was a young woman's voice, high-strung, nervous and edgy. I guess it was a little too soon for me to be showing the normal gratitude, assuming I could get the spunk to drain my lungs.

"Now, Mindy, back off a minute," a deeper voice said. "Suppose this poor, soggy lump was you lying here on the deck?"

"Aye, aye, Sir Mister Captain," the female voice replied with a heavy dose of sarcasm. "Suppose it was me? Would you save my sorry ass? I'm thinking not!"

"I'm going to dump a body overboard? Use your head, bitch—that's the U.S. Coast Guard giving us the eye."

"Okay. Tell me what you're going to do about that, Admiral Genius Boy Wonder?"

Oddly enough, it is at moments like this when I'm at my best. They don't call me *Hollywood Havoc* for nothing. Havoc the Scamp, that's me. It didn't take much to fill in the blanks of what was going on. My head was lying next to a clear plastic garbage bag filled with gray-green weeds and my teeth were chattering. I tried sitting up but I felt numb and fuzzy and barely managed to roll over on my side. I coughed and tried again with no better luck. *Come on, Havoc,* I told myself, trying for a rally. *Time for lights, camera, action!*

"Get...get a blanket" I managed to blurt out through chattering teeth.

"It speaks," the bitch replied, not very impressed.

"For Christ's sake, give him a blanket."

She threw me a worn Coors Lite beach towel. I did my part for the California Free Marijuana Movement by spreading the towel over the bag. Then I staggered to my feet, making the short distance to the side rail before throwing up.

"Oh, pretty," the girl said.

"Ahoy, Starfollower," a megaphone voice boomed over from a large white boat not thirty yards away. "Stand by while we prepare to board."

"Wait," I shouted—bubbled, really-- waving my arm in their direction. But at that moment my rescuer, the captain gave me a shove, and for the second time that evening I tumbled headfirst into the icy ink-black water.

I suppose I did all right as a diversionary tactic. While I fell back into the sea, my former rescuer fairly leapt for the wheel, hammered the gas and spun the Starfollower about in a 180, heading back out to sea.

This time it seemed like forever and a day until I came up out of the watery blackness. But when I did, someone in a uniform rolled the water out of my lungs and finally put a bowl of hot broth in my shaking hands. Saved by U.S. Coast Guard, the standard Berger Royal Pictures happy ending. I felt sick and stupid and like I wanted to puke all over the concession stand, but I was alive.

Chapter 3

The U.S.S. Vinnie Berger steamed down the hallway at the Coast Guard Station like a battleship, leaving a string of protests in his wake. "Sir, you're a civilian...Military only...You can't go there...restricted area...Sir!!"

They'd left me in an empty room lined with desks while they were trying to figure out what to do with me. The sergeant in charge figured I could be a good source of evidence, and while they were arguing about it, I retreated to the furthest desk and called Vinnie. It was easy, just punch nine and dial the number.

"You're where....?" Vinnie's grumpy, unbelieving voice came at me over the phone. "Yeah, yeah, be right there." He was at his downtown nest-o-love, so it took him 45 minutes, but once he got there he wasted no time, and that was a good thing because my rescue quickly deteriorated into a surly interrogation.

It seemed the Starfollower, the small sport fishing boat that had snagged me, had been under surveillance for months, and had been stopped several times in the past. Their routine was to head out to sea, supposedly chasing the elusive albacore tuna runs. But it was suspicious because they rarely took along any fishermen, and seldom caught any fish.

The Coast Guard suspected they were pulling into some small port like Castro's Landing, half way down Baja, where they took on some freight, and, incidentally, a few hundred pounds of frozen fish. They'd been tracked by radar and pulled over at sea a half dozen times. But, as it was their custom to weigh down their cargo with bricks and leave ample holes in the bags, they had yet to be caught with the goods.

The Coast Guard saw me as a lucky accident. I was a member of the gang who had fallen overboard. It did no good to explain I'd spent the last several months posting Chop of Death, and the last two weeks location scouting. I couldn't convince them I was a film guy; I was a dope guy, and they were sure I knew all sorts of secrets. If only they could get me to sing.

I could hear Vinnie coming from half a building away, "You're not the military, you're the fancy-pants Coast Guard," he was shouting. "How come you're not out there patrolling the dark waters?"! Dark Waters, our horror flick about aliens rising from the deep to enslave all of mankind.

He boiled into the room where they were interrogating me, shouting "Rinky-Dink Assholes! What the hell are you doing with my man?!"

The sergeant, who had been leaning on me with the threat of thirty years to life for transportation of narcotics, looked up in amazement.

"Is this your man?" he shouted. "*You're* man? You admit this is *your man?!*"

"Of course he's my man!" Vinnie yelled back.

"So you're the leader of the gang!"

"We're not a gang!! We're creative artists! We make motion pictures, you idiot military cretin!!" Vinnie looked ready for another heart attack. The card he carried in his wallet informed whoever needed to know that he'd already had three.

"How'd you get in here?" the sergeant roared, jumping to his feet and waving a finger in Vinnie's face.

"Fuck you, lifer-loser," Vinnie barked back in his face. He took me by the arm and hoisted me to my feet. "What's the charge, sarge?" That was a line from Keg's War. Vinnie had dialogue from over 30 pictures at his beck and call. He had snappy comebacks and one-liners for most situations one might encounter in B-movies, if never in real life.

"*Your man* was transporting narcotics. We caught him in the bay."

"Yeah, I can see that, him being wet and all."

"We'll have you arrested, too!" the sergeant thundered. He was a bald, round man, and had to look up a foot or so when he talked to Vinnie.

"Right. For being an American citizen." Vinnie started for the door with me in tow, but the sergeant grabbed my other arm. Vinnie pushed me the other way, using me to cram the sergeant into a wall.

"Son," Vinnie said to the sergeant, "Let go his arm before I hammer you into the floor."

That was Horace Keg at his best, just before he took down a half-dozen vicious Viet Minh interrogators and made his escape from the secret North Vietnamese prisoner of war camp. It was Vinnie's last quiet comment, the lull before the storm. The next moment all hell broke loose as a squad of six enlisted men, led by a top sergeant, stormed in. They pushed us back against the wall and swung their long flashlights, using them like black nightsticks.

Vinnie took the blows on his chest and shoulders. He wasn't trying to protect himself or me. He was holding his cell phone high, recording a video of the scene.

"Stop! Men, stop!" The top-kick shouted, holding his men back like a dog-trainer. "Sir, hand me that cell phone!"

But Vinnie was the tallest man in the room. He held his phone high, and swung it in a small circle to make sure everybody was in his shot.

"Too late, ass-wipes," he said. "My lawyer's looking at you right now. Aren't modern electronics a marvel?"

"You're not talking to your lawyer," the top-kick said.

Vinnie held the phone to his ear, listened for a moment, then spoke, "She wants to talk to the guy with all the stripes. I guess that would be you." He handed the phone to the top-kick."

"Yeah, what?" The top sergeant screamed into the phone. But whatever answer came in reply calmed him down considerably.

"Well…no actual evidence, Ma'am, but the circumstances…"

There was another period of listening, and now the top-kick wore a concerned look on his weathered face. Vinnie snatched the phone from him, took my arm and began pushing for the door..

"Come on, Havoc. We're out of here!"

"Now just a frickin' minute, buddy!" the duty sergeant yelped.

"Where's your commanding officer, sergeant?" Vinnie roared.

"Well…he's off duty right now, sir."

"Right. And you're holding an innocent American citizen without evidence on American soil. You're in deep crap up to your eyeballs, son."

By now, Vinnie had me half way out of the office, headed for the front door.

"Stop!"

The top-kick had worked himself up into a wild-eyed lather. Vinnie had a way of doing that to people. The sergeant was standing in a crouch, barring the door with his bulky presence. His right hand was poised over the .45 automatic nestled in his belt holster.

Vinnie's voice deepened into a growl. "You going to slap leather on me, sonny-boy, you better be ready to go all the way." Straight out of Keg's War. Vinnie never forgot a line, at least not one of his own. The sergeant dropped his hand to his side, and Vinnie made for the door.

He softened enough to scrawl his name across some paperwork at the front desk, and then he was steering me through the parking lot toward his Bentley Sportster. He took off his windbreaker and tossed it to me.

"You look like a wet cat of death warmed over." Vinnie could do one-liners all day, but on his own he was a master of the mixed metaphor.

"You don't look so good yourself."

Under his jacket he was wearing a nightshirt that he'd stuffed into his pants.

"Hey, I was tucked in for the night. Holly is the one, going to be pissed at you." Holly Sweets, Vinnie's latest short-time stand, the new wonder in his stable of starlets. Vinnie has a wife back East, a fancy home west of Beverly Hills, a steady mistress in Malibu and his high-rise in downtown L.A. for what he calls his *condo rondos*.

"That wasn't your lawyer, was it?"

"Naw. Gloria can do a good feminist prick lawyer with that deep voice of hers."

Gloria was Vinnie's steady squeeze from his place in Malibu. When he gets in trouble, he doesn't call his wife, he calls Gloria. Vinnie's personal life is complicated and unpredictable. Sometimes even I need a scorecard to keep track of the players, important, because I end up having to pay the bills from our production budgets, under the category of *out-of-pocket expenses*.

In no time, his machine was purring south along the Coast Highway, Vinnie driving with two fingers the way he'd heard Steve McQueen did it. After impatiently waiting out a few stoplights, he gave me a bright look of anticipation.

"So, where's the dope?"

"Nowhere, Vinnie."

"Can we sell it? I got plenty of contacts."

"I'm sure you do."

He was eager as a schoolboy in heat.

"Did you get enough so we can do Carnage Days?"

"Vinnie, there is no dope."

"Okay, I believe you."

He didn't say anything more for a while, and I had to break the silence.

"You weren't going to actually sell dope to finance a picture."

"Naw," he shook his head. "I'm already in too much trouble for tax evasion and philandering."

"Philandering isn't a crime."

"No...expensive hobby, though."

"Flirtations have their consequences." He eyed me silently, both of us thinking about Peanuts, or maybe I was thinking about my ex-wife and he was reviewing the long, muddy mess of damsels he'd marched into his bed.

"Okay," he said. "So what actually happened tonight?"

"Late this afternoon, two guys broke into Bertrand's place, kidnapped me, threw me in the harbor, shot at me and left me to die."

"Yeah?" In the light from the dash I could see he was eyeing me dubiously, like we were in a late-night story session and the plot was spinning out of control. "Then what?"

"Then I got snagged on a drag line, and pulled into this stinky loaded with bales of hemp."

"Jesus, you got more lives than a raccoon."

"Cat, Vinnie. More lives than a cat."

"Right," he agreed. "I think raccoons are a type of cat. And then?"

"Then the Coast Guard came. My rescuers pushed me in the water and took off."

"Jeez, Havoc—nobody's going to believe that. You're the cat who serenaded the canary. Lucky I bullshitted you out of there."

Vinnie's metaphors were mixed as ever, but he was probably right. His instincts were telling him we had a case of what the gurus in film school called implausible possibility. In movies, you prefer plausible impossibilities, that is, you look for things that are exciting but could never happen in real life, and you shy away from less interesting things that could happen but probably wouldn't.

"It doesn't matter, Vinnie."

"No dope, huh?"

"No dope. At least, I didn't get any."

"Who's Bertrand?"

So I had to go through all that, and by that time it was close to one in the morning and Vinnie was laying a ten-spot on the gate guard to let us into Sea Garden Cove without any fuss. Which, of course, he did.

It would take me a week or so, but I finally sent the Coast Guard a stack of Keg's War T-shirts, a token of our gratitude at Berger

Royal Pictures. I figured it was best to stay on their good side, if they had one. You never know when you're going to need a shot of a Coast Guard cutter churning through the harbor waters to intercept a load of dope, or maybe a horde of illegal aliens from Guadalajara, or even the ones from outer space.

Chapter 4

In Hollywood there's *above the line* and *below the line.* Stars and directors and producers are above the line and they make a lot of money. I guess, after years at BR Pix, you could say I was *above the line*, but just barely. It's a hard life. The truth is, most of us creative and crafts types who actually make the shows don't have regular jobs, and so we don't have regular vacations. We have what we in the profession politely refer to as *going on hiatus.* It means we're between pictures, we're marking time, we're like kids scuffing dirt in the play yard until the bell rings. At the time of my abduction, I myself had been *on hiatus,* and I considered myself luckier than most because I was on half-pay. I'd finished the final posting on Chop of Death two weeks before, and we'd shipped it off to Hong Kong, Singapore and Manila. Chop of Death, as it sounds, was our latest tribute to the skills, bravery and lusty sexual encounters of the Oriental fighting man. And we hadn't yet started our next picture, a filmic venture titled Carnage Days. This one, though it was running with blood and gore, seemed an odd choice for us, in that it proposed to teach a moral lesson, maybe something you'd read in the Bible or The Farmer's Almanac, *What you sow, so ye shall reap.*

Vinnie wouldn't give me a firm start date, which led me to the conclusion his latest funding difficulties still hadn't been overcome. My guess was, if there had been any dope on the Starfollower, he'd already have the BR Pix crew regulars out hawking it on street corners. And, because he wasn't any good at anything but conning unknowing investors and making shlock B movies, like as not, by now he'd be in jail or running for his life from some mob guys who thought he was cutting in on their turf.

On one level, Vinnie's career was one long quest for money, a continuing hunt for new investors. One pure and shining truth I'd learned about Vinnie; he wasn't going to spend his own money. *What, you crazy? Does Madonna play with herself?* I'd told him before, that was a bad analogy, but you get the point. That's the prime rule of indy producers, *Always spend somebody else's dough.* Then too, with his expensive lifestyle, if Vinnie actually had any money of his own, it had to be buried very deep. Meanwhile, I was on half-pay, squeezing the last nickels out of Chop of Death and Vinnie was hopping back and forth across America, skulking around convention centers and trade meetings like a fat duck hunter in the marshes. He had that cunning, slit-eye look, the carnivore on the look-out for the next successful shoe manufacturer or rich banker from the Cayman Isles who wanted his name up on the big screen.

"You never know where you're going to flush out the money dingos," he told me. "My first picture was funded by the rabbi at our local synagogue. This was Angie's Dilemma, in Brooklyn."

"What was that about?"

"Broad gets knocked up by a mob guy or a cop, she doesn't know which. Mob guy's dirt poor, he hasn't made his bones yet, but he treats her nice. Cop is on the take, plenty of dough, but he treats her like shit. You know the old story."

"Did Angie's Dilemma fund a new rest home for the Jewish community?"

Vinnie gave me a long, sad look and turned away.

"I never steal bread from a man of the cloth," he said over his shoulder. "And it's not my fault we got swindled by greedy distributors in Bombay. Always get your cabbage from the front of the turnip truck, I learned that lesson!"

I didn't have to be anywhere in particular on the morning after my damp misadventures, so I started the day in my kitchen with do-it-myself waffles and a hit of home-made latte. I fretted over recent events without coming to any conclusions other than the obvious one; as Vinnie kept saying the night before, I was lucky to be alive. Multi-tasking, I ate big, syrupy bites of waffle, sipped my latte and allowed my fingers do the walking through the Yellow Pages. Every handyman or carpenter I called either was on vacation, out on a call, or out of business. If we'd had a production going it would have been easy to enlist somebody to bang up a new door on Bertrand's place, but our regular guys were scattered to the winds. *On Hiatus.* I finally contacted a laconic personality who said *Yeah, mon, he'd come right out to Sea Garden Cove to replace that there door.* He sounded a little loopy, but beggars can't be choosers.

"Okay, mon," I replied. "Come right out as soon as you can."

"Yup, okey-dokey," he replied, hanging up before I could tell him how to get here.

Yet, perhaps I have too little faith in mankind, because, somehow, he found it on his own. He drove up the little hill from the guard gate in his small, dusty pickup truck. The hand-lettered sign on the side said *WILLIE The Wood Dude*. There was a surfboard in the back, some sweats, a wet-suit and a pair of dark green swim fins. And I saw there was a box of tools thrown in, looking like a last minute afterthought.

The wood-dude, himself, was outfitted in ragged surfing cut-offs and a faded Hawaiian shirt with a monster gardenia print in saffron and fuchsia, and he sported corn-bread braids in his artificially kinky blond hair. I could tell it wasn't going to be love at first sight, or even respect.

"So you're the nail-banger," I said, leaning into our relationship and aiming for casual command. He sized me up with a sneering look that made me suspect he hadn't read my credits on IMDb, and we had a thing going.

He eyed the splintered mess that had been Bertrand's door.

"They sure don't make them like they used to," I said.

"Give me a couple hundred," he said, cutting right to the chase. "I got to go buy a door, and that messed-up molding there."

"You didn't even measure it."

"It's a standard door," he said. "And that there mess-up is standard molding. What, you don't got no money?"

"I got money," I scowled. "I got plenty money."

"How about half my fee up front?"

"Pushing our luck, are we?" I gave him for the door and the molding and ten extra for breakfast.

` He took the money and retreated down the hill and out the front gate. He was gone for hours, returning in the early afternoon with damp pants and a surfboard with a small puddle of water in the bed of the truck.

"Surf up, huh?" I said.

"Oh, yeah!" he said with a cheerful smile that faded when he saw I wasn't really happy he'd been gone so long.

"You scavenge this door from some demolition site?"

"You didn't say you wanted a *new* door. Once paint's on it, it looks new. Just go bury your head and let me do my job."

It looked solid, and it was the same style as the others in our complex, so I didn't argue about it. I went away for a while, grumbling that it had better fit. There was a fluster of sawing, sanding and scraping, but the door was finally looking respectable. He had some beige paint in a can on his truck, and was busily slopping that on when I dropped in to see how things were carpentering along.

"You want I should replace the locks, too?" the Wood Dude asked.

"No. Why would we do that, Willie?" By that time we were on a first-name basis. I'd memorized his name off the truck, and, though he wasn't going to say it out loud, he was thinking of me as *Optimus Asshole.*

His lip curled. "Think about it, *mon.* It was a *break-in.* Think about it. What's to keep them from coming back?"

"Willie. If the bad guys had to break in, they don't have a key. Your powerful and strong new door is supposed to keep them out."

"So now you're a break-and-enter expert." He scowled as he threw his tools into a big plastic bucket.

"What do you care? You getting a kickback from the locksmith?"

Willie The Wood Dude gave me a dirty look that told me I had scored bingo, but he could see I wasn't going to relent on the lock business.

"Fast dry paint," he said, screwing the door handles back on. I noticed he was careful not to touch the door, which I assumed was a little tacky and would probably dry shut.

I didn't say anything, and Willie collected his check and went away. I kept the door open a crack, the way he'd left it, hoping it would dry before nightfall.

A few minutes after The Wood Dude had tooled back on down toward the beach, a squad car casually pulled into the Do Not Park space in front of Bertrand's garage. Two cops sauntered over like it might be the only exercise they'd had in many a day.

I gave my report without going into my personal adventures. That meant I deleted my kidnapping, being dumped in the ocean, rescued by the trawler, thrown back in the briny deeps again, and rescued from the Coast Guard by Vinnie. Those things only happen in schlumpy, low budget flicks, anyway, and I didn't want to strain their brooding investigatory imaginations. Everybody doesn't get to be smart cops like one sees on television and in Berger Royal pictures..

As it was, even with my abbreviated version, the officers of the law eyed me skeptically. The older one with the bigger paunch was taking notes, "So, two gentlemen in expensive suits jumped you, hit you on the head and took your wallet."

I tried to keep my voice level. "Right. Like I said, they broke in my neighbor's place," I indicated Bertrand's door. "I interrupted them and they turned their attention on me."

"*Interrupted* them." The younger cop put his finger on my chest. "How do we know you didn't just break in yourself?"

I wondered how he'd feel if I broke his finger like Horace Keg always did when some pirate or pimp tapped his chest, but I couldn't see how that would further our relationship in a positive way, so I took a quick Zen breath and a short step backwards. This was nice because he was expecting me to move the other way and it made him stagger a little.

"I have my own key," I said. "I can get in any time I want."

I saw the next question coming and answered before he could get his accusatory finger back to burrowing into my chest. "I take care of the place when Bertrand's away."

That was about when Dim Eddie showed up. Dim Eddie was one of our pathetic, dim-witted gate guards, and he'd been on duty the night before when the two black guys had come calling for Bertrand.

"That right?" the cop said, turning to Eddie. "This cheese-ball telling it straight?"

"Well, ahhh, I guess so," Dim Eddie shrugged. "Everybody takes care of everybody here at Sea Breeze Gardens. It's a nice place."

"Sea Garden Cove, Eddie," I said.

"Whatever," he said, looking around as if they changed the name of the nice place on him just last week. But then, that's why he got his nickname.

"So you don't know for sure if this guy broke in or not," the cop asked.

"Uhh, now, geeze…" A glazed look came over his face. Eddie was suddenly nervous, like a kid who forgot it was exam day. I could see he was stalling for time, mulling his options, probably envisioning himself in a striped outfit, breaking rocks with a big mallet because of the fibs he told that time over at The Cove.

"Dim Eddie," I poked him in the ribs and my voice went up a notch, "didn't you see two black guys come past the guard gate in their big Mercedes?"

"Well—sure…" He didn't want to get in trouble, even though it was common practice for the guards to open the gates and let anybody in who looked like they could afford it.

"I don't know," one of the cops shook his head, looking at his partner. "That's leading the witness."

"And when you talked to us you didn't say they were *black* guys," the other said, giving me a hard-eyed stare.

"That's withholding evidence," the first added, as if he was reading off of cue cards.

"You guys aren't very good," I said.

"What do you mean?"

"Well, it's not just the script. You have to work on it or you won't even make it in a TV cop-o-matic series."

"Like we couldn't be cops in one of your Berger Royal shoot-em-ups?"

So, you see, they knew who I was, the guy who steals shots around town and never hires the local cops to stand around on the set.

"I didn't mention the black guys because I didn't want you to think I was racist," I replied.

The older policeman glared at me, figuring I was taking an oblique shot at their sometimes vow of political correctness. Knowing me, you'd have to agree he might be right. I was getting nowhere fast with these guys. It was Havoc time—camera, lights, *action!*

Taking the dunce by the horns, as Vinnie might say, I snatched the clipboard from Dim Eddie's limp hands.

"Hey!?" he protested, grabbing around like somebody had taken his favorite toy, but I held it away from him while I ran down the list of the previous night's entries until I found the right one.

"Here. California license plate EYJ 643. Dark green Mercedes. Seven fifteen. They came in twenty minutes before I did."

I handed Eddie's clipboard to the cops, pointing out the right line.

"Doesn't mean nothing," the younger one said, giving me his stare of professional cop awareness. "And you're sounding more and more like somebody who has something to hide."

"I know actors and I know acting," I said. Meaning what?"

"It takes lots of effort to hold a mean-cop look like that."

"I should arrest you for inappropriate big mouth. You could get at least a couple months for that. Inmates could teach you some deviant sexual practices."

"Yeah, or or you could hit him with your night stick," Eddie encouraged him.

"Why take it out on me? We all have something to hide," I said, clipping my words neatly as my man Keg, who had been thrown out of several of the finest Ivy League schools, himself might have phrased it. "Look around you. Dead bodies everywhere. In the cupboard, the garbage cans, everywhere. There's crime here, I can smell it. Officers, start arresting people."

Dim Eddie was looking uncertainly at the garbage cans, which were out on the street for the weekly pickup.

The cop with the evil stare gave me another poke in the chest, "Hey, funny-fellow, we can take a hard case like you down to the station."

"Let's go," I said. At that moment, I wasn't thinking too clearly. I guess I was figuring I could at least get some good dialogue, but my willingness had the opposite effect.

"Naah. You're no fun. We got real scuff-laws to admonish."

"Admonish. I admire your vocabulary."

"You should be admiring our restraint." They wrote everything down, tossed a copy of their report in my general direction and strolled in a leisurely way back to their patrol car. But they didn't drive away. After five minutes, finger-cop beckoned me over with his busy digit.

"That license plate is a dead end," he said. "It belongs to a car leased by the Nigerian embassy."

"But—that's a good lead!"

The older of the two erupted in an amused snort. "Right, it leads us to a fricking truckload of Nigerians. And, as you've pointed out to us, their skin is black, and that's surely another clue, or at least some sort of suspicious coincidence. What else you got?"

"You're not going to follow it up?"

"Yeah, sure, soon as we get done here we're going to put out an all-points bulletin for an Embassy!"

"A big dragnet," his partner added, nodding in serious agreement. "A full-court press. You just wait and see. We'll bring the whole fricking Nigerian nation to justice."

They waved and slowly pulled away, voicing suggestions for calling in the SWAT team and the California National Guard to clean up the dangerous situation at Sea Breeze Cove.

"I told you it was Sea Breeze Cove," Dim Eddie said, frowning like I'd tried to pull one over on him.

I pointed to the header on his clipboard. "Sea Garden Cove, Eddie."

"Ahhh, maybe somebody made a mistake there," he said. But, by the way his voice trailed off, anybody could see he wasn't sure.

I was glad I hadn't gotten any further into what happened after the bad guys clipped me on the head. I don't have much respect for the local gendarmes, and my ill will was already starting to show.

It wasn't just a stolen shot or two at the harbor. I'd made a career out of shooting around Southern California, *from the mountains to the sea,* as the newscasters used to say, without paying location fees, a hit-and-run game with the cops that was necessary for survival in my world of skimpy budgets. We had so little money we often printed the first (and only) take in any scene, and shoot-and-run setups were up front in my book of how to produce on the cheap. The Newport street-cops I'd met could always be bought, but they had to catch me first.

What kind of name is Havoc, anyway? A made-up name, actually. Our ancestral name isn't Havoc. My dad came from a respectable, potato-eating Irish family with a name that filled over 24 pages in the greater Chicago Area phone book. But dad gave up his semi-respectable career as a copywriter in the ad business and launched himself in Hollywood as Johnny Havoc, would-be novelist and screenplay writer.

He almost made it, too. After a decade of churning out episodes for Saturday morning kiddy fare featuring happy Neanderthals, clever Yellowstone Park picnic bears and big, slurpy dogs, he'd finally started to connect with the big time. His first novel was about to be published by a big New York house, and just about the time he finished adapting it as a screenplay he took a fishing trip south from the tip of Baja. Problem was, it was monsoon season and his boat never made it back to Cabo.

Mom, heartbroken, died soon after. No apparent reason, the saw-bones said. He was an old guy with a philosophical bent to his practice.

"Sometimes they just give up," he said.

And that left me alone in the small two-bedroom condo next to Bertrand's big place. I had enough money in the bank to limp along as if nothing had happened. And that's the way I played it from day to day, living alone even though the state said I was legally too young to do that.

I got away with it because I pretended to live with a crusty maiden aunt who signed the social security checks over to me from Milwaukee in return for my promise that I would never come anywhere near the Midwest. So I owed old Bertie, who could easily have turned me in when I was still in high school.

When I mentioned it in later years, he'd always grumped, "Better the devil you know…", his voice trailing off into the dangerous land of unforeseen consequences. For a guy who'd happily dealt business hands all over the globe, it seemed to me he was strangely paranoid about a lot of little things. But that was before my rough handling at the hands of the Nigerian thugs. I was going to have to reevaluate my assessment of Old Bertie.

Before Dim Eddie could get away to his guard shack I lured him into my kitchen, where I zapped up several slices of pepperoni pizza to distract him long enough so I could copy down the license plate number of the Mercedes. There was at least some chance my lost wallet was in the trunk of that car rather than logging moisture under 40 feet of murky water in Newport Harbor. And if there was any way, I was going to find out. Matt Havoc, master sleuth, detects a license plate number that leads to an embassy that leads to a Mercedes that leads to his very own wallet. I'd done a few murder mystery flicks for Burger Royal; I knew how it worked.

`Twenty-four hours later I was watching nightly news while I squirmed around on my dad's old Victorian chair, the uncomfortable one with the howling spirits carved in oak on the armrests. He'd nicknamed it Soul-sucker, probably because it was so uncomfortable to sit in. I liked it because it had been his. If I'd wanted comfort I'd have snagged a recliner from one of our shoots. When I was a little kid,

I'd wanted to grow up to be just like Dad, and with him leaving the scene early, part of me had never grown out of my adolescent hero-worship. I never got to hate my dad in the usual teen-age way. Jack Havoc was the greatest. My movie-guy, super-star dad.

The image of him that I most cherished was from the time of his big success, just before he'd gone missing in the Pacific. I remembered him looking at me with his steady gaze, studying me from his throne, seated easily on Soul-sucker. Crazyhead, his first novel, was due for release and he'd just gotten a big check for writing some Saturday morning episodes of Ninja Turtles. Our small condo was filled with the peace and tranquility that comes with those rare moments of prosperity in the life of a domesticated creative person.

"Dad, some day I'm going to be a writer, too." I bubbled.

"You fly as far and as high as you can," he said. "No reason why you shouldn't."

Well, it was over a decade later and so far I'd been flying for Vinnie Berger's Berger Royal Pictures, which I was coming to feel was about like trying to take off down Runway Hollywood with fifty pound weights strapped around my ankles.

I found myself thinking back to that brief time of prosperity. There was Mom looking at him with what I now know was a sigh of loving resignation. The life of a freelance writer wasn't easy, particularly if you were trying to raise a family. She didn't say anything, but you could see the affection shining in her eyes.

She never said I shouldn't follow in the old guy's footsteps, either.

I snapped out of my reverie in time to hear Dallas Raines explain why the local newscasters had all gotten the weather wrong for the fifth straight night. And that was when Julia blew in through my front door like a classy hurricane, exhaling her own clouds of exasperated indignation as she stormed around my kitchen. She was looking for her grandfather, and, of course, the first and only place she looked was my condo.

Chapter 5

"Somebody has changed grandfather's door!"
sweet Julia
yelled, glaring at me as if I'd done it.

"Oh, how do you know that, Julia?" I
asked, treating her with the usual air casual
dismissal. "You never know anything."

"The color's all wrong! And he's
missing!"

"You're right about the door. The condo
committee's already been after me to change
it."

"I'm right about everything! Gramps is
missing!"

"Well, I'm not old Bertie's keeper."

Julia was the sole child born of a brief
and furtive liaison between Herbie, the eldest
of Bertrand's twins, and some missing
missionary woman. This was back before both
sons found out they liked each other better
than women. I used to call Julia *The
Accidental Accident*, in those adolescent years
when she came to live with Bertrand and his
now deceased wife. The things Julia called me
in return are largely unprintable. I don't know

where she ever got that vocabulary; certainly, not from me.

The pert young lady charged past me and blasted through my living room, bedroom, study and finally the bathroom.

"Julia," I complained. "You think I have Old Grampers trussed up in the tub for safe keeping?"

"Well, crap-meisters, I wouldn't put it past you, Matthew Havoc!"

Julia and I had a history of kicking each other around that went back a ways.

Easy to see, this wasn't going to be one of our rare joyful times. Inspired, I thought to make it worse with a little banter.

"Julia!" I bubbled, in a bad English accent, all full of false good humor and blathering joviality. "Just catching up? Good of you to stop by. How are you, my lady?"

I couldn't remember our relationship ever being on what you might call good terms. We'd been on shaky ground since I'd asked her over to do some Trig homework and persuaded her to a game of strip poker. That was when she was a Senior at Newport High, and she finally figured out that my bad reputation wasn't entirely based on false rumors. I had her down to her T-shirt and panties before she caught me palming the jack of clubs. The thing about Bertrand's family, they tend to be long on vengeance and short on light-hearted humor.

"Matthew Havoc!" She thundered. That brought me back to the present with a start. Julia could really crank up the volume when she wanted to. "Will you stop your jabber and sit up and pay attention to me? *Where is he*, Matt!?" She yelled so loud I had to slap my own ear with the palm of my hand to un-pop it. I was still feeling the effects of my dunking in Newport Harbor. I didn't suppose it would do any good to appeal to her sympathetic side, as she didn't seem to have one.

"Ouch! You should be arrested for extreme loudness!" I glared back at her, "How do you know Bertrand is missing?" Since she couldn't answer that one, I figured I'd have a little fun. "You think he's still pissed about that time I put the remote mike in your purse?"

"I'll put your dick in a vice, Matthew Havoc—" Her voice had dropped an octave. Her lips thinned and the small rosy blotches started on her cheeks. I waved my hands in surrender and retreated from the familiar signs. I could see she was really worried about her grandfather. And I had to admit, if only to myself, that there were enough reasons she should be.

Over the years since his wife had died, Bertrand's two scattered and largely uncaring sons, Herbert and Philbert, had made a few half-hearted runs at putting him away in an old folk's home. They claimed to see, in his mad dashes after a shrinking business, all the warning flares of approaching senility. I couldn't make a call on that one, but I knew Julia was the best ally Bertrand had left. She still cared whether or not he was okay. But the old man, in turn, was so thoughtless and rude to her that you had to wonder if his brain really was melting into waffle batter.

As I may have already said, Hurricane Julia had developed into something of a knockout. Radiant puffs of light blond hair illuminated a heart-shaped face and pouting red lips. There was about her a lithe and yet full-bodied gracefulness and the airs of a Nordic princess, but when it came to her opinions, her comments were rough and mean as a truck driver's. About that tape I'd recorded, I hadn't meant for Bertrand to hear her frank and pithy description of his wandering trip through Israel, what he thought of as his *Search for The Meaning of Jesus* and she blithely called *Fruitcake of Destiny Meets Pimps of the Desert.* But it just turned out that way.

"His door used to be sandy beige," Julia said, giving me a charged look that would have wilted a medium-size frog. "And now it's Navajo tan."

"Oh, picky-picky," I said. And you shouldn't do a full body frown like that. You'll get wrinkles on your love handles."

"I don't have love handles," she said, her voice dropping another octave or two.

"Did you try the lock?" I suggested. "Not the one on your chastity belt, the one to Old Gramper's door...?"

I followed after her pert figure as she stormed out of my door and raged across the short stone walk to try her key and, of course, the door to Batty Bertie's place opened right away.

But her quick and intense search revealed no nutty old geezer peering disapprovingly at her over his spectacles. Yes, disapproving. Among the many things Bertrand didn't like was Julia's career as a junior Oriental Antiques and Art Specialist at the Getty. He'd thought she should take her Harvard Doctorate and go make babies in the interest of continuing the Berke family lineage.

There was a brief time when I might have agreed with him, so long as she manufactured the babies with me. But real life had intervened in that little rainbow daydream of mine before it came to anything. And Julia had made it clear to Bertie and me and one and all that she would run her life as she saw fit. That meant a lot more Miyamoto Musashi and a lot less Matthew Havoc. In fact, these days when she dated she seemed to go for cultured types with polished nails and from all indications Matt Havoc, himself by this time a marital retread, wasn't even in the running. I sometimes wondered how she'd learned to control her potty-mouth, but apparently she'd tamed her savage native spirit.

"He isn't here," she said, the exasperation clear in her voice and her body language down to the way she tapped her attractive foot and glared at me.

"I could have told you that," I said politely. "He's in Budapest."

"You flabby-brained idiot, Bertrand is not in Budapest," she flatly contradicted me through clenched teeth. "And you could have had the common courtesy to tell me he wasn't home."

"Well then, where is he?"

And that was when Julia the Oriental arts expert, one of the most determined and forceful young woman I had ever met, began to lose her composure. She slowly sagged against the nearest brick-and-mortar wall and sobbed as if the world had come to an end.

"I-I don't know," she wailed, "A-a-and I'm worried about the miserable, cranky old fart!"

Will wonders never cease? Julia Navarra (she had taken her mother's maiden name, not wanting to be associated with her dad, the gay blade) Miss Julia Navarra had a heart after all. Too bad it didn't beat for me. The peaceful moment of revelation only lasted for about 30 seconds. In fact, I was about to declare a truce with a consoling arm around her shoulder when we were interrupted by a taut and bristly dude wearing tailored black jeans and a tight black polo shirt over his buff chest and pumped-up arms. He had silvery hair cut in a short crew cut and it offended me somebody his age couldn't act a little more...well, ancient, or something.

"Julia," he cried in a phony *basso profundo* like the soggy hero out of Love Me, Love My Boat, or maybe an old Owen Wister Western novella. The minute Julia saw Mr. Perfect approaching, Miss Proper came back out and the real woman went away. And that was the end of our brief entendre, over practically before it had begun. The frosted-hair guy gave me a look like I was dog poop and moved his carved six-pack between Julia and me, placing his own arm around her shoulders.

I guessed he'd been waiting for her in the car, probably grooming his impeccable later-middle-aged good looks. He was closer to sixty than forty, but some men just age better than others. Actually, he looked like he had less worry wrinkles than I did. Show biz can do that to you. There was expensive and highly successful written all over his close-cropped gray hairdo and, yes, he had polished nails, and I wanted to step back from the heavy scent of newly applied men's perfume. A civet of a guy, I thought, all quiet lurking and positioning for the pounce. I told you I'm not a nice fellow, but I'm allowed my own snap-impressions, and I knew right away I didn't like him.

"No, Robert," Julia replied like she was trying to calm a lap dog on steroids. "It's just the neighbor. Grandfather doesn't seem to be anywhere around." Just like that she had it back together again. I felt vaguely disappointed, and annoyed beyond reason. What the hell did I care? It was only Julia, a small and bothersome thorn in my side, lo, these many years.

"Well then, let's be going," he said. Mr. Perfect Boy-Wonder wilted from his half-karate stance to something less silly, scarcely bothering to give me a second glance.

Now I was just the neighbor. "Julia, where are your manners?" I asked peevishly. "Aren't you going to introduce me to your latest—err, male whatever?"

"Oh, shut up, Matt," she growled through clenched lips. She could look pretty even when she was annoyed, but I'd shamed her into going through the formalities. "Robert, this is Matt, my perverted childhood chum from the old days when I lived here with grandfather.

He has a big mouth, he thinks he's smart, and we should have moved years ago."

I shook my head sadly, "But you couldn't afford it. Daddy ran off with an interior decorator named Jimmy and Mommy drained the family piggy bank and headed south to save all those pagan babies. You had to live with Old Grampers."

"You called him 'Grampers'?," Robert asked, clearly wondering where any of this came from. It was great, seeing her worlds collide.

"That's his nicest name," I piped up.

"Shut up, Matt," Julia repeated.

"Robert," I said with the briefest of nods in his direction, "My pleasure. And, yes, I'm the reason she lost her virginity."

"We never--!" She started to shout, but I interrupted her.

"I never said we did. But perhaps we should have. You'd be better off now."

"Better in what way?" Her voice would have freeze-dried a spring sparrow in mid-flight.

"Less repressed. More a real woman."

Robert reverted to his odd little martial arts stance. "Shall I teach him a lesson, Julia?"

"That would be a real mistake, Robbie," I said, amused at the thought, "You should stick to interior decorating or house painting or whatever you do."

After my dad disappeared, the members of his old army unit had adopted me in the unofficial way they seemed to do everything. The Old Spooks & Spies they called themselves. I had been taught to defend myself by people who chatted about Uzi's and ice picks over morning bowls of Honey Nut Cheerios. Maybe I wasn't good enough to take out two black dudes from darkest Africa, but I felt I was more than enough for a guy who used avocado face peels and modernized his chest with ladies hair removal systems.

Julia moved quickly between us, probably remembering the night four unfortunate members of the high school football team had tried to feel around with her in the back seat of a car in the Newport High parking lot. It was the only good timing in our entire sad relationship, the fact that I happened along just then with my trusty baseball bat. But the lasting impression may well have been *Matt Havoc gets the job done.*

"We don't have time for this!" she said.

"Well," Robert responded peevishly, "I'm not the one making us late for Boris Gudinov!"

"Oh, right," I said, more and more spoiling for a fight when I heard he was a ballet guy, "Musorgski's men in tights can't wait."

"Matthew, you're just showing off. You wouldn't know Gudinof from goulash!"

"Oh, let me pop him a good one," Robert said.

"Stop whining, Robbie," I said. "If you want to take a shot, just haul off and lay one on me."

It looked like things might get sticky between the two of us amateur warriors after all, but just then old Bat-Brain Bertie did in fact show up. Bertrand in the flesh—crusty, cranky, and mean as ever. He tolerated Julia's teary-eyed hug, the entire time looking at me over her shoulder with his hard-eyed, steady gaze.

When she finished, he patted her shoulder and asked me, "Anything needs immediate attention?"

If Bertrand was going soft in the flinty part of his grey matter he reserved for business, I couldn't see any indication of it.

"Nothing that can't wait until morning, Sir," I said with a shrug. If I had spilled the beans about the two black thugs who had tried to kill me and were probably still combing heaven and earth to find him, Julia would have gone into hyper-drive, never a pretty sight.

"Hmmmm. Good, I guess."

My reading was, he also figured it wouldn't do much good to open up in front of his granddaughter. He separated himself from her hug and went into his condo, dragging his heavy suitcase behind him. He closed the door and we heard a click as he manually locked the bolt. And that left the three of us on his doorstep, staring at each other.

"He just locked us out," Julia said, looking startled and out of sorts. "Grandma must be rolling over in her grave."

Bertrand's wife Leigh Anne had been a lady with high style and impeccable manners. When she was alive, Grandma Leigh Anne had always been able to smooth over his rough spots. They had been together over fifty years, but since her death it was obvious that none of her graciousness had stuck. Always a business dynamo, Old Grampers seemed to have an increasingly large blank spot when it came to civility or common decency. I wasn't sure Julia was more offended by her grandfather's lack of manners or disturbed that he might be off his rocker after all.

To me, Bertrand seemed more or less his usual grumpy self, so I tried to calm her down.

"Maybe things were rough in Budapest," I suggested. "And, after all, he did find his way home all by himself. It isn't like we had to pick him up in a nut-house in Marseilles or a chicken ranch in Pahrump."

"He wasn't in Budapest, you limp-dick peabrain!" She glared at me while Robert gaped at her, seeing a new side to the sweet little lady he was escorting to the ballet.

"Why are you so sure, stink-head?"

"His passport lapsed. He can't leave the country any more."

"What, been snooping around Old Gramper's desk again?"
I stepped back almost before I'd finished speaking. I knew that look, the vicious female raptor just before she strikes.

"Okay," I added quickly, "I'll grant you locking us out might be strange behavior, but he's always been a bit odd."

"You should talk, Mister Small-time ShoBiz!"

"Yeah, me, sure…" I had to agree with her. "But…come on, Jules, give him a little slack…Bertrand hasn't been the same, you know…not since Grandma Leigh Anne died…"

Julia thought it over and finally nodded in agreement. I knew we both were thinking back to earlier times when the business dynamo had been on his track, happily dispensing X-ray machines all over the world to eager third-world nations, and his wife had been there to cleverly save and wisely spend his money and to keep his thinning hair dyed and combed and his trousers zipped and make sure he put on the shirt without the pizza stains.

"Say, it's really cold out here," Robert interjected, hugging himself with his bare arms. I found myself wondering if he did that a lot because it made his pecs show through his thin cotton shirt.

"You should dress more warmly," I advised. "It is November on the coastal plain, and the cold winds duth blow."

He turned angrily toward me, but Julia held his arm, restraining him.

"Havoc does that to everybody," she said with a tired tone in her voice. "That's how he got his name. He's a disaster."

I didn't know exactly what to say. I did feel sorry for her, getting upset at old Bertrand and all, so I decided not to go for the usual incendiary bait that lay between the two of us. "You want to come in for a bit?" I waved a negligent hand at her beaux, "He can come, too."

"Well…" It seemed for a moment like she was going to relent, but then penis-head interfered again.

"Julia," Robert said with a little cough, reminding her of her pressing obligations with high art or whatever the fuck. *Time to suck it up and get back to real life.*

"Maybe some other time," I said in a tone that meant *Sorry I asked.* I know it was stupid, but sometimes I just can't stop myself. Forget Bertrand, there were times when I could be my own runaway train. "You can still catch Act II if you get your wayward butts in gear."

He gave me a look that was a combination sneer, glare and snarl, but Julia tugged him away before I had a chance to disrupt his particles. And that was pretty much that for the evening.

Chapter 6

The next morning old Bertie shuffled in while I was making a latte and warming a jumbo bran muffin in the toaster.

"Bertrand, old bean," I said. "Where have you been, my *mon*?"

I was pleased to see he had his T-shirt on right side out and his socks were a close enough match to get by so long as nobody was looking.

"Matthew, don't talk like a black street person from Jamaica." His lips curled into a frown under his thin moustache.

"And your socks are close enough, though the one on the left has those little yellow polka-dots, while the other is just plain blue. On the islands, of course, we don't wear socks, mon."

"Stop it!" he commanded. "You're not a black person!"

"Is that a racial remark?"

"Crap, no. I got nothing against niggers. White, black, red, brown, yellow. We are all of us niggers, each and every one, in God's eyes."

I nodded gravely, showing I was impressed by his wisdom, and shifted my accent to a bad imitation of the French Colonial English, the accent the two black thugs had used when they decided to thump on me and throw me in the bay.

"Where have you gotten yourself off to, Bertrand? Where you been, and what have you been up to?

He frowned, not able to pinpoint my new dialect, but, of course, being a low-budget schlock-meister at Berger Royal, my accent was more a mish-mash than anything specific.

"Uhh, Montreal..." he lied, his watery old-man's gaze wandering around the room in a weak attempt at innocence..

"Right. Sure. Without your passport. Tell me about it."

He firmed up on that one. It didn't mean he was telling the truth, just that he knew a lot of facts he could throw into the mix.

"You don't need a passport to go to Canada."

"Do, too.

"You do not, Matthew Havoc! You show business people don't know everything. And anyway, why do you want to know? Your little pumpkin sweetie-pie princess Julia put you up to asking?"

"Okay," I sighed. "You went to Canada. What exactly went on in Montreal?"

He gave me a bright-eyed stare and reached for a nearly empty bottle of Robertson's Lemon Curds on the counter and started smearing it over my bran muffin with his finger. "Client was supposed to show up with a big check for a deal I'm putting together. Client didn't show. Big check, phooey! Big waste of my time."

"What sort of a deal, Bertrand, old bean?"

"A really big deal," he mumbled. "And don't call me an *old bean*." I could see he wasn't going to say any more. He wolfed down big bites of the bran muffin that formerly had been mine. There was a pale yellow glob of lemon curds on his upper lip under that thin Clark Gable moustache of his. He hadn't used hair color for over a week, I could see a quarter inch of white hairs next to his skin.

"Nigerian client...?" I asked calmly.

He didn't even bat an eye; but then, I hadn't expected him to. After all, Bertrand had taught me to play poker. It's no wonder I ended up knowing how to deal from the bottom. I saw I was going to have to use bigger bait.

"You might as well come clean, you octogenarian screw-up. I read your faxes."

It was true. While he'd been away, a whole pile of faxes from Lagos, the Nigerian Capital, had showed up on my machine, everything from merely interesting queries to totally outrageous demands for cash. There was one from the Nigerian embassy acknowledging his claim for the return of twenty four thousand dollars in fees he'd paid for something or other that seemed unclear. They had acknowledged his claim, but didn't seem to be taking any action to pay it back. And another written under a big fancy seal from The Central Bank of Nigeria:

IN OUR CAPACITY, WE WRITE TO INFORM
YOUR COMPANY THAT YOUR FILE IS
RECEIVING URGENT ATTENTION WITH
TWELVE OTHER COMPANIES SCHEDULED
TO RECEIVE PAYMENT THIS QUARTER.
SINCE THE APPROVAL OF THIS
EXTRAORDINARY LARGE PAYMENT ($36
MILLION DOLLARS U.S.A CURRENCY) BY
THE PRESIDENCY IT IS IMPERATIVE THAT
YOU MAKE ARRANGEMENTS TO ARRIVE IN
LAGOS IN PERSON FOR THE
TRANSACTION.

I read that part out loud and then tossed
the faxes on the table in front of him, but
Bertrand was intent on devouring the rest of
the confiscated bran muffin. He paused briefly
to scan the top transmission.

"Hmm, Shamseen Usudman, Deputy
Governor." His gaze wandered to the
refrigerator. "Got regular milk?" he asked.

"Yeah, and this fax is carbon copied to
the Presidency and the Federal Ministry of
Finance. Nigeria has the reputation of a land
infested with rodents, Bertrand, and it looks like
you're dealing with the big rats, here."

He shook the milk carton in my face, a
sip of whole milk apparently more important
than the fate of nations.

"No," I said. "All we have is two
percent."

"If God meant milk—"

"I know, Bertrand, but some cows can't
give whole milk. The farmers who own those

cows have to bottle it and sell it as skim milk. Now what the hell are you up to?"

"Smart ass," he said. He took a sip straight from the carton, watching me as he drank, his head tilted sideways and eyes peering like a bright-eyed old crow. With the yellow lemon curds smeared on his lip and milk dribbling down his chin he looked like the village idiot on Percocet. Still, as Horace Keg always admonished his sidekick Bucky the yellow lab, *Appearances can be deceiving.* (that is, when he wasn't telling Bucky *There are no coincidences.*)

"Alright," I said. "No, it wasn't Julia putting me up to anything, though she is worried about you. And she was never my pumpkin sweetie-pie. Lord knows I tried, but I couldn't even get to second base."

"*Second* base!?"

"First base," I sighed. "I meant first base."

"Good to hear it," he said with a brief nod. "I would have turned you in to social services in a flash. You would have spent the best years of your life in the Home for Young Punks, just like all them other Hollywood bastards, instead of your endless lazy surfing days with the potheads of Newport High."

"Bertrand, while I am grateful, that was ancient history. However, barely one or two days ago a couple of Nigerian thugs broke down your door, banged me on the head and tried to drown me. And for that I think you owe me an explanation."

That last caused him to blink once and drop his last lump of muffin on the floor.

` "What were you doing by my door?" he asked.

He picked up what was left of the muffin and stuck it in his mouth without a second glance, risky business when you consider I did my housekeeping more or less on an annual basis.

"Bertrand, I *live* next door! I'm supposed to look after your place when you're gone!"

"Tried to drown you?" he asked, his voice like a distant echo to something I'd said ten minutes before. There was a momentary flicker of concern and then he gave me the wide-eyed stare that with Bertrand passed for a humorous look. "Didn't realize what a good swimmer you are, did they...?"

"It's not funny, you crazy old coot! They just about had me under for the big soak, or whatever you call it. And now I've got to go down to the Nigerian Embassy and try to get my wallet back."

I explained my theory that there was a good chance my wallet had dropped out in the trunk of their car when they tried to kidnap me.

"Can't do that," he said, shaking his head after I'd finished.

"I sure as hell can."

"Can not, neither," he asserted. "There's no Nigerian Embassy in Los Angeles."

"But the police said—"

"Flaaaa!" he razz-berried, with that one syllable reducing the Protect & Serve Mob to a band of idiots and incompetents. "I know exactly who those Hottentots were and where they are right now," he declared. "I'll go with you, Matthew. We'll retrieve your wallet."

He was a devious old rascal, and there was no way I could trust him. What's more, there was something half-hearted about his delivery. Misdirection was a way of life with him. On the other hand, I didn't have any other offers and I was on hiatus. I figured I might as well tag along and see what he was up to.

"Go where?" I asked.

"Bel Air. Them damn skunks live in Bel Air. I was there, once." He was talking about one of the more exclusive enclaves in Southern California. I knew it well; it happened to be where Vinnie Berger lived, at least when he wasn't at his downtown pad-o-love or the ranchette among the oaks in Malibu where he stashed Gloria.

"And what are we going to do, assuming the armed patrols let us in?"

"You got a crowbar?"

"What the hell do I need a crowbar for?"

But Bertrand was already heading for the door. "Don't you show biz people know anything?" he called back over his shoulder.

The people like me whom Bertrand lumped together in what he called *the show biz gang of thieves, crooks and rapists*, were among his more serious pet peeves. When my folks had originally applied for the condo in Sea Garden Cove, his was the only dissenting vote on the reception committee. Julia had told me, ammo in one of our running verbal battles, and he'd never denied it, but that was because I'd never had the courage to bring it up. I also knew his inner character was more than a little conflicted, because somewhere in his tiny, twisted, black soul he actually liked me a little bit, or at least had learned to tolerate me more than most of the other people in his sorry life.

"Come on, let's go!" His raspy voice bounced back in through my open front doorway, "Or are you going to spend all day eating your lousy breakfast?" One thing I had to say for Old Grampers, once an idea sprouted in his head, he was quick to give it plenty of fertilizer.

I called after him, "You are going to put on some Bermuda shorts or something over those jockey briefs before we head for Bel Air, aren't you?"

There was no answer. The bang and clatter from his garage seemed to indicate he was already collecting our burglary tools.

"You might wear the butterscotch ones," I added, getting a little bolder now that he was out of hearing range. "I think the color goes good with your eyes, bloodshot and all from the strain of telling me all those fibs about your adventures in Canada."

Still no answer. I sighed and made my way to my own front door. I stopped at the Victorian antique oak coat rack that mom and dad had inherited from my Great Aunt Clara. It was hard to decide between my Chop of Death baseball cap or the floppy old khaki number Horace Keg had worn in Keg's War. I took off my glasses and gave myself a nearsighted squint, pretending I was John Wayne looking for distant smoke signals. I was getting too thin again. I always lost weight when working on a picture, and hadn't had time to fatten up. I took stock of myself in the mirror, staring critically at my own light gray eyes, dark brows and long dark lashes under the wave of dark brown hair over my forehead and the crow's nest of wrinkles starting at the corners of my eyes. I decided I was maybe a cut or two below leading-man star quality, but still more than your ordinary bauble on the chain of love.

And there, for no reason at all, I found myself having a reflective moment. I wondered why Julia had never become my pumpkin sweetie-pie princess, and why it should be, now after it was too late, that my long-lost hopes in that direction should mean anything at all to me. I finally decided Keg's hat would look more like a disguise so I pulled it down low over my ears and slouched off after Bertrand like the felon I was about to become.

Chapter 7

The sad tale of How Bertrand and I Became Crooks began with an hour of bump-and-crawl on the freeway. I was behind the wheel as we headed north on the 405. I was driving, but Bertrand was driving me crazy with a game he invented called "Name That Tune." He claimed it had been a radio show in the 1940's out of WLS in Chicago. There had been a band called Captain Stubby and The Buccaneers, led by Stubby himself, who was something of a populist musical genius. People called in and gave the first three notes of any song, and Captain Stubby and his band of marvels would instantly guess the song and rush into their own triumphant version of it. Unfortunately, Bertrand's gaping front teeth allowed him to whistle two notes at once, both of them badly off-key, and so far I hadn't gotten anything right, including "My Country 'Tis of Thee," "Oklahoma," and "Camptown Ladies."

"You look a little dented," Bertrand poked at me with that whiny tone in his voice. "Don't be a quitter. Everybody hates a sore loser. Here, I'll give you an easy modern one." He started in on a new song that was a bit like the call of some trumpeting bird in heat. I had no idea three notes strung together could be so unpleasant.

"What is it?" He said, his eyes bright with anticipation.

"Christ, I don't know. *The Devil Came Down To Georgia*?"

"Matthew, I would not do a song glorifying the devil. Don't you know nothing? That was "Sergeant Pepper's Lonely Hearts Club Band"! The Beatles!"

One thing I was sure of about Bertrand; when he got chatty, he was hiding something.

"I'm not too good at this game," I said. But he rushed right on, reinforcing my suspicions.

"Aww, come on, Mister Showbiz Guy. Don't worry. You'll get one sooner or later." He did three new notes—Uck! Uck! Uck!

"A duck hit by three golf balls off the sixth tee at The Riviera Country club?"

"Now you're just being silly! That was the great and famous Peggy Lee singing Fever!" He grunted out a few bars, and I still didn't recognize the song.

"Full of passion," I said. "I don't know how you do it."

"Some folks are just born to tunes," he replied.

"That would explain it," I said, but I was already too late. He was working up a trio of clacks that sounded like he was trying to spit and toot at the same time.

By the time I took a rough aim for the off-ramp at Sunset, my teeth were aching from the sonic discord.

"Hey, Sunset, already," I said, hoping to distract him. "Shouldn't you be filling me in on your Nigerian buddies?"

"Get this one," he said, puckering his wrinkled old lips for another three-note song opening.

I didn't guess that one or a half-dozen others as I drove my dented Range Rover the curvy half-mile east on Sunset. I caught the red light at the Bel-Air entrance, so I pulled into the left turn lane and waited. Bertrand had quit his "Name That Tune" game and was gaping at the high, presumptuous gates that had always reminded me of imitations of the beige gray mortar and curly wrought iron Paramount Studios entrance, the Paramount gates themselves being some 1920's movie set designer's deco imitation of Spanish imperial gates. Imitations of imitations—now that's the real Hollywood!

I executed my turn, brilliantly cutting off a self-important scuz-ball in a black Porsche, and pulled up to the guard station.

"Havoc for Vinnie Berger," I growled at the guy who popped his head out of the nearest castle window.

The snappily uniformed gate guard was surprised to find my license plate on the list of people Vinnie said were important enough to come and go as they pleased. And if he was surprised, Old Bertie was astonished.

"They going to let you in here?!"

"My boss lives here, and he loves me like a true son. Plus he knows I'm the only one who will drop everything to schlep him to the hospital for his next heart attack."

Bertrand gaped as the guard waved us through. Suddenly, he wasn't as chatty as he'd been on the expressway. I was beginning to suspect he hadn't believed we'd actually get past the castle moat. A truly devious fellow, as I've already noted.

But Bertrand did seem to know the way and, true to his word, he showed the directions as I pointed my Range Rover up and down the hilly streets past the finely clipped hedges and brushy rock outcroppings of Bel Air. The roads were narrow and cut into the hillsides. Back there in the steep and rocky tan hills away from Sunset, there were hardly any front lawns, the land being mostly dynamited flat to make room for the large homes and the mandatory swimming pools and maybe a tennis court in the back yard two hundred feet or so below.

Bertrand whistled, but it was only two notes to get my attention.

"Wheee-up! Wheeuu-up! There," he said. We had already made five or six turns and curled our way up and over and down, always heading deeper into the enchanted forest.

I was beginning to believe he was lost, but I looked to where he pointed, and saw the dark green Mercedes of my recent misadventures.

"That's it!" I said.

"I know that's it," he grumbled. "I told you, Matthew Havoc. Now let's get out of here."

"Not so fast, Bertrand, *my mon*."

"Matthew, don't talk like a grass-head."

"A who?"

"You know—them Bob Marley Rastafarian reggae hop-brainers."

"Oh, them. Okay, *mon.*"

It was parked on the downhill side of the street we were on, across from a large house with huge squared columns of a distinctly Sumerian or perhaps Tinker Toy origin, the columns spaced between carefully pruned cones of Italian cypress.

"Matthew, I *said--!*

"You've got some explaining to do, here, Old Grampers."

"N-n-noooo. I think we better mosey on out of here."

"I'm plumb out of mosey, Bertrand," I said.

The Mercedes was parked on the narrow brow of a pull-off that looked out over a pool and a back yard that was hundreds of feet below us.

I pulled up behind it. It was the right license plate. So here we had Matt Havoc, ace detective, and his sidekick, old Bertrand Badtooth, about to commit some sort of crime or maybe even a felony.

"You ever pop a trunk?" I asked. I was feeling oddly elated, considering I had no idea if my wallet was in there or not.

"What do you think I am?" Bertrand wailed. "Come on, let's go!"

"A dim-witted old crank," I said. "But enough compliments. Give me the crowbar."

Bertrand threw up his hands as if he'd left the gas burner on or the pizza in the oven overnight. It was the worst case of acting since my ex-wife had wiggled her way through

California Climax. Of course, she hadn't really had any lines to work with...just her curves, but that's a bad pun, and not really fair.

"I forgot it back at my place," he lied, trying for as much wide-eyed innocence as his ancient, droopy eyelids would allow.

"Bertrand, this was your idea!"

He'd lost his cool, or whatever you call it that keeps an 80-year-old habitual liar stoked. "Well, I-I think it was a dumb one," he stuttered. L-Let's just forget about it and get out of here."

"Okay," I said. And I really meant it. But then I remembered what had happened and how I'd felt. "Bertrand, those guys tied me hand and foot and dumped me at night into the dark and murky Pacific for shark bait."

"This isn't getting us anywhere good," he muttered, shaking his head.

"I'm thinking back on that moment when I was hitting the icy water and sure I was going to die. And now I'm seeing that same car, the one in which I was held a captive like a piece of meat."

"You're talking nonsense, Matthew. You're alive, that's all that matters."

"No, Bertrand. Honor matters, too." Spoken as only Horace Keg could, in that moment before he stepped into the North Vietnamese torture chamber. "We actually find the car and now you want me to turn around and drive away like a meek little lamb?"

"Lambs don't drive cars, Matthew," he reminded me.

"I think something more is required of this moment," I said. I shifted into low and popped the clutch. My trusty Rover lurched forward and smashed into the back end of the Mercedes. Nothing happened. You have to hand it to those Germans, they built a stout motorcar.

"My God, man—what are you doing?" Bertrand threw up his hands in a panic.

"Calm down, *reggae mon*. You don't even know what a Rastafarian is."

Before he could disagree, I backed up enough to give myself a running head start and then rammed the Mercedes again.

"That's the thing about the Land Rover," I said. "Built like a tank...or maybe a garbage truck."

This time we collided with a touch more force. Dust erupted from under the rear fenders, the Mercedes jumped forward a few feet and the trunk flew open. I hopped out and ran over to have a look.

"There it is, Bertie! My wallet!"

"Come on, come on, come on, COME ON!" he muttered impatiently, his eyes flicking around like darting insects, his wary brain imagining all sorts of bad things that might pop out of the brushy hillsides and get us.

It took a moment to get my wallet out, but in spite of the sound of the two ramming incidents there was no response from the house. I walked around to the front of the Mercedes and looked over the edge of the hill.

"Hey, Bertie, *mon!* You think our black friends might be down below sunning themselves by the pool? Or mayhap snorting coke as is the custom among the local gentry?"

"Matthew! We got to go—now! These are dangerous people!"

"Tell me about it…say, Bertie, maybe they're not even home. It's not just the movies…I've found there is such a thing as serendipity in real life, too."

"Are you crazy?" he wailed.

"Of course not, Bertrand. It's just not a frequent enough occurrence on which to hang the turning point of a screenplay. Keg's rule: *Accept no coincidences.* And am I not wearing Keg's authentic cap?"

I took the cap off and waved it at him. Then I returned to the rear end of the Mercedes and did a quick scan inside the trunk. There was a thin black carry-on travel case, so I took that, too, and threw it in the back of the Rover.

"What are you doing?" Bertrand asked. He didn't see me take the travel case because he'd ducked his head below the window on his side of the Rover and his voice was sounding faint and muffled. Actually, it probably was for the best that he wasn't witnessing what was going on.

I shook my head.

"I'm disappointed, Mr. Bad Tooth. I've always assumed you're on the shady side with your taxes and your liberal passing out of kickbacks."

"Stop talking craziness!!" he shouted.

"But you certainly have odd scruples when things get even a little serious." I got back behind the wheel of the Rover and turned the key. "Of course, I'm not one to talk; when you're on the low end of the film business you end up greasing everybody's palm from local politicians to the guy who mops up the toilets."

"What are you--?" His eyes widened and he grabbed the overhead handle for support.

"Hold on to the family jewels," I said. "Come *on*, Matthew Havoc, let's get the Be-Jesus out of here before we get caught!"

I jerked on the 4-wheel drive and made sure we were still in low.

Bertie's eyes, already wide, looked like they were ready to pop. "Wait...what...No, my God, what are you doing?"

"Working on healthy ways to vent my anger," I said, gingerly nudging up behind the sprung trunk of the Mercedes. The big German car's wheels were locked in park, but the rubber tires slid on the gravel roadside and it wasn't much of a strain at all for good old Rover. Just a few healthy nudges and then the Mercedes took off like a large green bird, practically, it seemed to me, on its own volition. After turning over in the air in a graceful dive, the plunging German automobile took out a fancy hexagonal gazebo with a glass roof that was next to a beautiful slate slab pool decking.

"Nooo, NOOOO! We'll get caught!" Bertrand wailed.

"They don't always explode and burst into flames," I told him confidently. Blowing up cars was one of my areas of quasi-expertise. "We mostly have to rig them for the effect."

But I was wrong about that one. A few seconds after I'd given my opinion, the Mercedes came apart with a tremendous fiery roar that rattled our windows.

"Of course, you never know, sometimes they do," I added quickly. That's one thing about me, I can generally admit my mistakes and move on.

As we exited Bel Air and retraced our path along Sunset back to the 405 South, Bertrand spent the trip worrying about terrible people and dire but certain consequences that he wouldn't name and said he couldn't talk about.

"No one can trace us, Bertrand. Those are movie plates on the Rover. We bought them from a junk yard guy."

"I'm not buying that, Matthew Havoc! You've gotten us in terrible trouble."

"No," I said, eyeing him carefully. "But I may have complicated your secret deal…right?"

He gritted his teeth and wouldn't say another word even as we passed LAX.

"Want to play three toots and I can guess your song?"

"No, I don't!" he shouted.

When we got to Jamboree, I pulled off the 405 into a Del Taco for some burrito specials.

"What's making you so antsy, Bertrand?"

I couldn't figure him out. After all, we weren't talking about Mr. Sainted Person here. This was devious old Bertie. Like most people in the scrambling bottom of the import-export biz, his life was a constant stream of quietly crooked little deals. I remembered a few years ago when the shabby looking guy showed up at Sea Garden Cove with the special black boxes that allowed one to bypass the cable TV company and get it for free, Bertrand had the first one that fell off the van. If anybody ever needed a grey-market car from Europe, rubies imported from Burma in a secret compartment or an illegally imported rare tropical bird or venomous snake, Old Bertie would be the purveyor of choice.

He'd enjoyed his free pirate cable for a month, and then the system shut down throughout our entire complex. Charter Digital Cable had some way of knowing what he was up to. They'd sent a technician knocking on every door, but Bertrand, who had nothing better to do, had seen them coming a block away and had his black box hidden well before they got to his front door. After that, he blew the system six or seven more times when I was home, and Lord only knows how many times when I wasn't. The second time he got a free week before they got onto him. After that, Charter fine-tuned their detectors so they could cut off Sea Garden Cove in a few minutes. Unfortunately it would cut off my broadband internet service at the same time, and they would take their own sweet Jesus time about turning it back on, too. We could be down for an entire day or two. I finally got so disgusted I switched over to DSL.

The point is, Bernard himself was a scofflaw beyond repentance, so why was he so worked up over me getting my own wallet back and a little vengeance on the side? I figured he had some kind of scam going, but all I had was my hunches. I didn't have any of the specifics, and, Keg's Rule #23, *It's generally some little, forgotten detail that kills you.*

I ordered the little shredded beef soft tacos *carboné* and a few Del Classic Chicken Burritos, and while we were idling in line for the quik-mex, I hopped out and took the gaffer's tape off the fake license plates I had left over from California Climax. That one, starring the nubile Madge Sacknall, was Berger Royal's blood-and-lust flick about a USC couple who went mad after a football defeat at the hands of their hated UCLA cross-town rivals and started a crime-and-sex spree that used up a hundred and fifty thousand stage bullets without killing, wounding or even scratching anybody on or off screen. Sometimes, I, myself, wonder how we do it.

I thought a half dozen chicken wraps in the soft taco shell might loosen Bertie's tongue, so I threw those in for good measure, but Old Grampers wasn't going to reveal any of his deep, dark secrets for a chicken taco. He grumbled about the expense of what he called eating out, but I noticed the mex-wraps disappearing in his direction at an impressive rate.

Chapter 8

So much for Batty Old Bertie's help in solving the mystery of the two goons who jumped me and tossed me in the brink. If I was going to get to the bottom of The Bertie Badtooth mess, I was going to have to do it on my own. We got back to Sea Garden Cove and I waved him in through the new front door of his condo and retreated to my own place.

My first move was to lug in the black carry-on travel case that I'd taken from the Mercedes. *What a disappointment!* It turned out to be one of Bertrand's own business cases, and it was stuffed with old invoices and orders for shipments of X-ray tubes, lead isolation wall packing, operator shields and starter switches for radiation machines and a dozen other things of little consequence. My guess was the bad guys had lifted it when they broke into his place.

Having a thorough grounding in cheap detective movies (that I myself had worked on), I glanced through the contents of the case, looking for clues. Unfortunately, I didn't find anything I thought might be useful or even mildly interesting. A hot porno magazine or even a California Scratcher ticket for $5 would have been nice. From the invoices and business letters, I could see the old geezer was selling replacement parts here and there, but it had been a long time since he'd sold an actual X-ray unit, and that's where he always said the real money was.

Bertrand was a constant complainer, but if this was the sum total of his recent business activity, he was doing even worse than his grumbling. Okay, so in bad times, a businessman can get a little greedy, and maybe take chances he wouldn't in ordinary times. *True, but oh so generic!* I didn't see anything useful, and no light bulbs went off in my head. I remembered Bertrand had left his garage door up; I walked over and set the carrying case on a shelf on the back wall next to his garbage cans.

After that, I went back to my own humble digs and called my buddy Ken, the telephone guy. Ken, who had taken me for a ride with several slick trades in our Fantasy Football League, wanted to gloat.

"You actually traded for a wide receiver with a broken leg," he chortled.

"That was last season, Chump Boy. And he broke his leg the week after I got him."

"Yeah, yeah, yeah. He was an accident waiting to happen…sort of like you, Mister Hollywood. And, talking about that, when do I get to star in one of your movies?"

"How about when you get a new face?"

"Ouch. That's brutal."

"I do need your help, however, Kenny-boy. It's worth a couple hundred..."

I explained what was required.

"That's a little bit illegal," he said.

"It's for a good cause. And I'll get you a bit part in our new movie, Carnage Days."

"When's it start?"

"So you can be bought."

"Of course. I'm finishing up a job in Orange County. I'll be right over."

Ken was good as his word. While he was busy under my desk, wiring away and stringing lines through the walls, I went to the kitchen and sliced some dry salami and gouda cheese.

Just abut the time he finished and washed up I cracked open a few cold Beck's beers. He sagged into a chair opposite me and took a grateful sip.

"Okay, Havoc-man, you're spliced in to Bertrand's phone, his fax and his computer. It's line three on your phones."

"I already have access to his emails because he gave me his passwords."

"Be careful not to pick up line three."

"What if I do?"

"Well, if he picks up at the same time, he'll hear you."

He wrapped a slice of salami around a hunk of cheese, washed it down with a gulp of beer, gave out a contented burp and flashed me his show biz grin.

"So I get the lead role in this Carnal Days flick?'

"No, but if you promise not to burp on camera and not to get any starlets pregnant until completion of principal photography, you can be a crazed telephone man who wants to cut down all the wires and go back to nature and living in the woods."

"Do I get the girl?"

"No, not *the* girl, but you get laid a lot." I lied about that part. Keg's motto: *Tell them what they want to hear.* I knew he'd be happy just to hang around the set, and if he didn't end up on the cutting room floor, that would be a big plus.

"Hey, works for me. When do we start?"

"Pretty soon. We don't have a start date yet."

I didn't want to explain about Vinnie out there fishing for money. I liked my friends to believe the financial fantasy that Berger Royal was on a rock solid footing. Ken nodded his satisfaction and managed to rag me a bit more about my loser Fantasy Football team, the Dancing Bears, before he made his exit.

He paused at the front door.

"There were a lot of extra wires and old stuff under your desk," he said, hesitating for a moment as if something was bothering him.

"What? You need more money?"

"No, no, no." He waved me off when he saw I was reaching for my wallet. "Maybe it's nothing, but it almost felt like somebody might have done to you what we did to Bertrand."

"What? Bugged my phone? Why would anybody do that?"

"I don't know. You tell me."

"You sure?"

"Well, no, that's the thing…actually, I'm not certain of anything. It's just a feeling.

There's nothing there now, just old tape where there might have been wires. Whoever spliced in…if anybody ever did splice in… it had to have been a long time ago. How long you lived here?"

"My father and mother lived here before me…" My voice trailed off.

"It could have been twenty years ago," he said.

"Yeah, I guess today the bad guys wouldn't need wires." We shrugged.

"Want to trade wide receivers?" he asked, winking and shooting me with his finger.

"Next year," I said. "The Dancing Bears *are gonna dance all over you*."

"In your dreams, Mister Hollywood."

I stood in my doorway, watching as he got in his truck, took the turn and made his way down to the guard gate.

But my mind was no longer on Fantasy Football. I was thinking about my dad. *Jack Havoc, former military guy, former spy…Would there ever have been any reason for someone to bug his phone? And after 25 years, who would even know?*

As evening pulled the orange globe of the sun into the fog out over the ocean, I sat back on the swivel chair in my study and looked at the neat rows of screenplays lined up on the shelves over my desk. There were three groupings: first, the half dozen screenplays written by my father, including Crazyhead, the one adapted from his novel about war, drugs and corruption. The second bunch consisted of 26 screenplays, all of cheapie low-budget films that Vinnie and I had done since I signed on at Berger Royal. There was a third place, but that was just a big stack of loose pages. That was my dream pile, the unconnected bones, tendons and flesh of my own great novel, the truly significant and meaningful piece of crap that I myself was going to finish one fine day.

For dinner that evening, I thought I'd make Eggs Benedict, but a quick search revealed I didn't have any ham, English Muffins or Hollandaise sauce. Not to worry. I did have some spicy turkey kielbasa sausages and a loaf of peasant's wheat grain bread from the Neighborhood Bakery, and I had plenty of Mexican sauce. I sliced two of the sausages and nuked them on high for two minutes in the microwave. At the same time I poached two eggs by spinning them for a minute in a deep pot of boiling water. I toasted two slices of the rough brown bread, buttered them lightly and added a thin layer of mild Southwest Salsa, a layer of sausages, placed a poached egg on top and poured another spoonful of sauce over the egg. At first glance they seemed a little incomplete, so for a finishing touch I threw on a spoonful of Miracle Whip and stuck three black Kalamata olives on top of that. *Some fine goop, huh?* We know how to live here in Tinseltown.

I sat at a corner of my black granite kitchen top divider and wolfed my eggy delight down. My new recipe may not have been recognizable in a fine gourmet restaurant, but that just meant nobody was going to steal it. The yoke from the egg calmed everything down just enough to make for a civilized meal. I was feeling good about myself. I had created a mutant distant cousin of Eggs Benedict...I was of a mind to call them Eggs Viva Zapata.

After that, I wandered into my study and put in a call to the only one of my father's old friends that I had stayed in touch with. Halliburton Rooks still worked in military intelligence somewhere back on the East Coast, though said he was a civilian now and that he had semi-retired five years or so ago.

Rooks had come out for the funeral service after my dad, Johnny Havoc, was lost at sea. I'd spent a few summers back East, before I'd flung myself full-tilt into the meat grinder that was the low-end movie business. He'd sent me a tattered Viet Cong flag when I'd graduated from Newport High and a worn army .45 automatic when I got out of college. He claimed to have watched the videocassettes I sent him of all my movies, and I, in turn, had followed his pattern of broken marriages and relationships through lengthy emails that he composed over late night gin and cold hamburgers. He'd even helped us at Berger Royal a time or two when we needed help with the inner workings of secret agencies.

Rooks picked up on the first ring.

"Rooks," I said. "Ever the insomniac."

"Havoc," he answered, the pleasure evident in his voice. "How goes the war?"

"You're supposed to know the answer to that one."

"About all I know is it never ends," he said. "War is a process rather than an event. You have a question for me?"

He'd developed into my expert on spooks, spying, military drops, guerilla warfare, secret plots, explosives, arcane and complicated military machinery and a myriad of other subjects of interest to the low budget schlock moviemaker. Vinnie always was good for $500 a pop, and Rooks occasionally got his *nom de plume*, Arthur Alabastardo, on the credits.

"Actually, I do…do you have any idea why somebody would have bugged our phones?"

"You mean recently?"

"No. When dad was alive."

"Ohhh…complicated question, Matthew. He did have a lot of people didn't like what he was doing…with Crazyhead."

"Why?"

"Nobody knows why. Secret service is like that. Secret, you know?"

I could see I'd run into a dead end. After a quarter century, it was probably just as well.

"I have another matter," I said.

"Shoot," Rooks said.

I spent the next five minutes outlining the little I knew about Bertrand's adventures in darkest Africa.

"He takes strange trips chasing money…" I added.

"Fairly normal in the import-export business."

"Right. But lately he's been secretive about some dealings with Nigerians. I've seen faxes from The Central Bank of Nigeria, one where he's trying to get some fees back that he paid."

I heard Rooks sigh on the other end of the line. "Sounds like the standard money-laundering stuff."

"How does it work?" I asked.

"There's a thousand variations, all of them playing on good old fashioned American greed. Sometimes the good men from Africa say they want to get a chunk of money out of their country. It's usually a big number, maybe $20 million or so. They offer to cut the sucker in for 10% if he'll open a bank account in the States so they can transfer the money. Hey, two mil for essentially doing nothing."

"Why don't they just do that themselves?"

I heard the faint clink of ice cubes on the other end of the line.

"Because they can't. You have to be a U.S. citizen to do that kind of banking in this country. But that's not the real scam."

"Okay, then what?"

"Well, for starters, there is no $20 million. But the guys like Old Bertrand, they get so eager for their take, they don't think about that part. They dive right in and swallow the hook. And that's when the requests for fees start."

"Fees for what?"

"Electronic bank wires. Permits. Right-to-work. Lawyer's fees. Official authentication. Anything the Nigerians can think of. They always give a broad wink right up front; they make no secret that the deal is illegal. The mark is told the big loot is under-the-table money."

"But you said there is no loot."

"Exactly. But the marks don't know that. So the story goes down that the fees are for kickbacks and bribes to intermediaries. I mean, their story is that getting this big chunk of money out of a corrupt country like that involves a grand plan and plenty of complications."

" So, nobody's really clean, here."

"Well, sure. The sucker knows from the start there's dirty business going down. He just thinks he's on the clever side of the scam. And he doesn't stop to think that, when they put the screws to him, he's got nowhere to turn to."

"How do you know this?"

I heard Rooks' sardonic chuckle. "Scamming is the second-largest business in Nigeria."

"Ohhh…" I couldn't think of anything brighter to say, so I asked, "And what's the largest?"

"Oil," he replied without hesitation. "But they've got scams for that, too."

"Why don't they put a stop to all this?"

"Who? Our state department gets over a hundred complaints a week. What are we supposed to do about it? After all, Nigeria is a sovereign nation."

"Stop giving them foreign aid?"

"Dreamer." Rooks' soft chuckle came at me over the miles. "What else you want to know?"

I told him how I'd caught two black thugs breaking into Bertrand's place and how they'd tried to kill me.

"I'm not surprised, chum," was all he said. "You be a little more careful. These are not nice people. You still have that sidearm I gave you?"

"Sure."

"Maybe you could start carrying it around with you...?"

"I can't do that here in Southern California."

"Oh yeah, I forgot. Land of the touchy-feely people."

"I guess I probably could lug it around."

"Well, it's either that or you can rent-a-cop to watch your back. I'll send you a hideout holster. Behind the belt. .45's too big for an ankle...or maybe something smaller...how else can I help?"

I was running out of ideas. I realized I didn't know enough about Bertrand's business to ask the right questions.

Rooks spoke into the lengthening silence. "Send me the faxes you have, along with any names," he said. "Maybe I can track the bums from here. But I've met old Bertie, and you've told me lots over the years. I won't be able to pound any sense into him. You're on your own there."

I thanked him and hung up. I opened a bottle of Chilean wine that I'd picked up earlier that week for half-price at Costco. Not exactly the harmonic symphony of nutty berry flavors they'd promised, but better than the average red swill that came in the big two-liter bottles. I was still hungry so I went back to the kitchen and fixed myself a small plate of English Stilton cheese on Ritz crackers. I felt good about the day's work. In a few short hours I had gotten my wallet back, destroyed an expensive car, stolen a black travel case full of Bertrand's old papers, and hotwired all the communications leading in to the offices of Uni-Amer Industries.

I didn't really know why I'd gone through all that trouble to spook out Old Gramper's office. Maybe I was still angry about my abduction, or maybe it was for Julia, or maybe I was more worried than I'd care to say about cranky old Bertrand of Nigeria. No matter my reasons, I did what I did and you can write me down as Hollywood Havoc, producer of crap flicks and unrepentant electronic scuff-law.

I went to sleep that night with my mind on Julia. You would think a guy like me who'd enjoyed of ecstasy and madness with some of the hottest hungry young babes in town would have other shapes and forms on his mind, but I was tired of sharp-eyed girls with augmented boobs, puffy fish lips and tiny vocabularies.

First time around, I'd married an actress and that had resulted in a decade of anguish. Somewhere in all that emotional pain, I'd come to the simple wisdom that I'd rather be tolerated for whoever I really was than fawned over because I was the next rung up the ladder. Still, even a dating game retard like me should have known it was too late to make a move on Julia, and if I did head in that direction, there was a very good chance I would screw it up. Julia would scan me through to the bone in a cheap-shot minute. She knew the difference between a person of real talent and some fool who'd simply fallen into a lucky Hollywood gig.

Another thing, Julia and I were as much opposites as Bertrand and me, or as I'd been with my first wife. It was hopeless. I had my lonely bed and my crash-and-burn history with my celluloid goddess, and Julia had her garbage mouth, her career in Oriental Art and the slick and manly (albeit middle-aged) Robert. *East is East and West is West, and never whatever*, I thought. Still, my mind kept drifting back to the way Julia had looked standing in the doorway with the sunny halo of hair around her bright, intelligent face.

Too bad, I thought. I found myself wondering why opposites never actually did attract in real life. I mean, sure, they flirted over the fence when there was nothing else to do, but why didn't the schlock filmmaker ever get to ride off into the sunset with the beautiful princess? Huh. I took another sip of wine. Actually, I'd already done that exit into the setting sun bit, but Peanuts had proved to be an imitation princess. She even turned out to be something of a frog-princess, at least in the emotional department. Somehow it didn't seem fair and yet I knew that if I was writing the story myself that isn't the way I would end it.

Vinnie would agree with me, too, about the ending. My boss may have been one of those guys who reduced everything to the least common denominator—*How much did we make on that dog?*—but he knew story and he knew people. Just thinking about it, I could almost hear that big, hearty laugh of his echoing in my ears. Yeah, sure, he would say, the underdog can get the girl, but he has to be a *likeable* underdog with some *shred of redeeming social value.* What's the Havoc

claim to social value, California Climax? Keg's
War? Hump Day? Dragonfly Madness?
      It took a couple of hours but I finally
drifted off into dreamland with a last sigh for
the lost glorious days of laughter and the nights
of wondrous and tender passion that I might
have shared with Julia in another life or
another time. Too bad, too bad, too bad...

Chapter 9

The phone rang at three o'clock in the morning.
I glanced over at the cartoon hands on my
authentic and classic 1938 Mickey & Goofy
alarm clock, thinking vague thoughts about
how maybe Rooks had come up with a bright
idea, or Vinnie had another heart attack and
his wife or his girlfriend (depending on where
he was spending the night) would be wanting
me to bring the Rover down and lug him over
to the emergency room at Cedars-Sinai. I
picked up the receiver without really thinking
about it.

    "Soul's Midnight," I growled. "Hollywood
Havoc, Keeper of Hell, here. What can I do for
you, Oh Master of Evil?" My voice was hoarse
with sleep or maybe too much Chilean red and
I probably sounded like a grouchy
octogenarian because the man's voice on the
other end of the line said "*Hallo?*" with a slight,
possibly French inflection. The caller paused
for a moment and then continued, "Bertrand?"

    That brought me around. I'd tapped
Bertrand's line, but I'd just intended to listen. I
wasn't really supposed to pick up on his calls.

Still, that old Horace Keg saying about *Never complaining about the mud on a gift AK-47...*

"Uh, huh," I grunted, hoping to keep the charade alive.

"Bertrand," the voice continued. "Do not pretend you're asleep."

"Right," I growled. "Sorry. What can I do you out of?" I ran the words together as my foggy old neighbor might if it really was him on the phone. I felt sorry for Bertrand. Three o'clock in the morning and his callers wanted bright and cheery. Low-end show biz may be close to the bottom of the pit, but it was clearly better than the export-import racket.

"You're playing a dangerous game, my friend," the voice said.

I tried to jar my wits awake. I needed a few hundred thousand more brain cells to come online, and right away. *What dangerous game?* What moves had my old-fart neighbor made that strangers would threaten him? To my knowledge, the most controversial thing old Bertie Bat-Brains had done in ten years was to send petitions around when he disapproved of the new fawn beige color the housing upkeep committee had proposed for Sea Garden Cove. (I'd never realized there were so many shades of tan, or that they could have such meaningful significance.) I couldn't think of anything serious and what was coming across with the quietly menacing voice on the phone didn't fit any of the scams that Rooks had outlined. The silence lengthened until I finally realized it was my turn to talk.

"We...we had a deal..." I protested, stammering in a low voice. That seemed safe.

There was some sort of a deal, and I knew one of Bertrand's principles was never trust anybody, always hang back until the money was in the bank.

"Yes. But first, I get what I want and then you get what you want."

"No," I growled again in a low voice, "Money in the bank first."

"Bertrand, we will start by killing everyone you love," the voice on the other end of the line said. "And then we will take away your own pathetic little life."

"The money…" I said in my best imitation of tough, bad Bertrand.

"First the truck, then the money…" His voice paused in mid-sentence. Maybe I hesitated a moment too long or I was losing my hoarse Bertrand-voice, or maybe he realized entirely on his own that he'd said too much. Whatever the reason, there was a brief pause followed by an electronic click and I found myself listening to the cold static of a long distance line.

A truck! Bertrand's top secret deal was something about a truck! I hit callback, and the number that illuminated the green screen was an overseas one. I probably should have disconnected, but the auto dialer was already beeping its way through the sequence, so I let it ring.

"Hello," the same cold voice said from the other end of the line.

"This isn't Bertrand," I said. "And what the hell is your game?"

"I know who you are."

"Fine. It's no big secret. Why don't you leave the crazy old coot alone?"

"You're the crazy one, Matthew Havoc," the calm voice replied without a moment's hesitation or a hint of alarm. "Quite mad for calling me back. I thought it might be you, but I wasn't sure."

"What kind of scam are you pulling?"

"I know what you're trying to do," the voice said with an irritating confidence. "You hope to keep me on the line so that you can trace where I come from. That is such foolishness. You should know I can talk to you for as long as I should wish. Yes, I am a Nigerian fellow, a *scamster* as you might say. Just one of the horde of evil savages who will drag you stupid, greedy Americans to your doom. But too bad for you, your pitiful little sleuthing game ends here at the edge of the jungle, in the coastal swamps of Lagos, the Nigerian wilderness you might call it. Would you like to talk about the weather? It's afternoon here, and fairly hot and muggy."

"Tell me more about the truck," I said. "Maybe I can persuade Bertrand to turn it over to you."

"Beware, beware, the Bight of Benin," the cold voice recited. "Few come out, though many go in."

"The truck," I repeated.

"Do you find me pleasant?" he asked. "Are we having a good conversation? I am, after all, a civilized man and I do try to be cordial."

"Don't want to talk about the truck, huh?

"There is no truck."

"Fine. But I'm telling you to leave Bertrand alone," I said. "I may just be another schlock film guy, but I'm warning you, I have some very powerful friends." I was hoping Vinnie and Hal Rooks counted as moderately powerful.

"I am sure you do," he replied politely. "Let me assure you, your friend Bertrand is a very, very stupid and stubborn man. I wish we could get him over here for about five minutes."

"If he's so dumb, how come he's got you over the barrel for your precious truck?"

"Goodbye, this time forever," he said, with not even the faintest hint of warmth in his voice.

There was only the faint crackle of overseas long distance static in my ear. I dialed back, but this time no one picked up on the other end, even though the phone rang over and over. There was no chance I was going back to sleep. I threw on a pair of jeans and a Keg's War T-shirt. Bertrand and I were quite the odd couple; he had cartons of colorful and zany Crazy Wear in his garage while I was the proud possessor of 500 T-shirts from a variety of movies nobody in the U.S. had ever seen except maybe a handful of late night TV junkies. Hardly collectors items, though you never knew with EBay on the rise.

I was too burned out to make my own coffee so I drove the Rover on over to the Starbucks on Macarthur Drive. I sat alone with my tall percent no-foam latte and listened to lonely nighttime jazz. A few cars hummed by outside, early morning travelers heading to the airport. The gay barista saw my mood and left me to my gloomy thoughts. Time passed, and I was no closer to figuring out my batty neighbor's troubles. *Beware, beware, the Bight of Benin. Few come out, though many go in.* I knew the old rhyme because we'd researched Africa for a slave trade picture that Vinnie had finally dropped as a *dog movie that wasn't going to make back it's nut.* A thoroughly mixed metaphor, but you get the idea.

The morning dawned bright and early, but by nine a dense fog had moved in and Johnny Mountain was forecasting cold rain sliding down the coast from Oregon, a strong front he said was destined to move into the Southland just in time for the evening commute.

The two big glasses of that Chilean red I'd had the night before had given me a headache that wasn't about to go away. By that time, I was back at my place nursing the grandee latte I'd gotten to go. And I hadn't been back ten minutes when Julia walked up the stone path and started banging on Bertrand's door.

"For God's Sake, woman, have a little pity!" I yelled through my open front window.

That was a mistake, because after that she made her way in through my front door and began yelling at me.

"Where is he, idiot boy? Where is he?"

I had to smile, wondering how the wildly unlovable creature in front of me could possibly have been the object of my previous night's lonely heart musings. I had unwisely drunk a second and maybe a third glass of wine in her honor, and now here she was looking as fetching as a raging badger.

And yet, I had to confess, seeing her standing there with her arms akimbo and filled with a passion that might have been the beginnings of rage or even fear, in that moment I felt an almost physical tug of attraction for her. Lust, even. I wanted to reach out and take her in my arms. Unrequited love was so unfair. Or untamed lust, or unbrindled passion or whatever the johnny-nobber's uncle they called it these days. *Johnny-nobber's uncle?* Ask Horace Keg, or better yet, Vinnie Berger. But about Julia; it made no sense reaching for the impossible dream; look what happened to Don Quixote, Cyrano de Bergerac, the Hunchback of Notre Dame, Clark Kent, Dudley Do-Right and that crazy guy who fell for Jody Foster.

So, instead of saying something endearing, I threw my arms out wide in a gesture of helplessness, "Sweet Julia, I'm not the keeper of Old Grampers. And, by the way, you're not either."

"Yes, but we care for him, you loony, stupid—film person! I know you do, and nobody else around here does and he's getting too old to think straight all the time and I'm worried about him and…and…and…"

The words tumbled out of her and for the second time in as many days she looked like she was going to burst into tears. And against every instinct and every warning and everything I'd been telling myself about how great my unattached single life was, I took her in my arms and gently stroked her curled golden hair.

"Now, now, Julia, there, there," I babbled, saying the same senseless and stupid things men like me have said to women when they were upset since the beginning of time, or at least The Ice Age, when this man-woman thing was supposed to have advanced past mere lusty carnal sport to meaningful sex and even that vague area women always bring up in conversations, that stuff they call relationships.

Sweet Julia didn't seem to mind that I held her, and it felt so good I had to remind myself that she was emotionally upset and it didn't really count as a *special moment.* Still, this wasn't going to support my resistance movement. I had to get back to my sardonic old self or I was going to be Matt, the Fool For Love.

"I'm blubbering on your stupid Keg's War T-shirt," she said with a little laugh.

"No problem. A few tears will go good with the ketchup and beer stains. I'll get you some Kleenex."

"You have Kleenex?" she asked, pulling away from my embrace and seeming grateful to slide into the teenage banter that had gone on non-stop in the days of old, even after the strip poker incident.

"Sure. You have to have something when you run out of coffee filters."

"I thought your back-up was toilet paper."

"Hard-case Hollywood types like me don't use toilet paper."

"Oh, blah…dare I ask?"

"Kleenex," I said, triumphantly whipping out a six-pack from under the sink. "We have cases and cases left over from Beam Me Up, Bernie."

Beam was Vinnie's failed attempt to send up Star Trek in yet another Mel Brooks style spoof. Everybody in Hollywood seemed to think at one time or another they had to take a run at Mel, and Vinnie had been no exception. Thank God for the sex scenes with the zaftig three breasted Martian beauties or that one might not even have made it to Hong Kong.

I poured her an espresso, straight black the way tough-gal Julia liked it. I'd just about wiped out the chocolate chip cookies, but I had a few slightly hardened lemon wedges left over from last week's pre-production meeting on Carnage Days, which was due to "maybe start in another few weeks" after Vinnie hardened his verbal agreement with a restaurant chain owner who was interested in taking an unwise little walk on the financial wild side.

Other people's problems were everywhere; I couldn't save the world. But maybe this morning I could do a little good for Julia, something positive besides trying to figure out ways to get her pert and nubile frame under me in my king-sized bed of love.

I pointed to the chair on the other side of the granite tabletop. "Sit down and take the load off. Tell old Havoc what's on your mind."

She eyed me skeptically, but she sat down and dunked one of my last remaining chocolate chip cookies in her coffee.

"Hey, we've got lemon wedges," I offered.

"Lemon wedges suck," she mumbled around most of a chocolate chip cookie.

"Do not," I said.

"Do too, also. If they were any good you would have already eaten them, you idiot."

Bertrand's kin seemed just as argumentative as he was, but I didn't want to go tracking down that blind alley. She was right, the lemon wedges tasted like cardboard dipped in grapefruit juice.

"Alright, alright. Back to Bertrand of Nigeria."

"He's missing again."

"We left him next door not 12 hours ago."

"Matthew, I'm not going to argue about this. I was supposed to meet him here an hour ago. He asked me to take the day off, and so I shifted around my whole week for him. He said he needed me. And now he's not here."

I didn't know what to do, but she was looking at me with those trusting blue eyes, so I thought I'd better come up with a better plan than strip poker. But I didn't have to, because we were interrupted by a beep from my computer.

"Come on," I said, "And bring the few remaining good cookies which it is intended you should share, in spite of your selfish and greedy nature." She trailed after me into the study and slouched into the low green barrel chair I kept for guests.

"I told Halliburton Rooks about Bertrand's situation."

That won me a smile, "You got the National Security Agency of the United States of America involved in whether or not Old Grampers is losing his marbles?"

"More or less." I brought the message up and it was from Rooks. "These days they call it INSCOM."

GO TO YOUR ROOM was all the email said.

Dad's old army buddies ran a website at www.oldspooksandspies.org. It had hidden panels and secret rooms and you had to know how to tap into it to get past the open face. I had a little black box on my end and it was about as secure as anything you could do over commercial landlines. My "ROOM" was the same one dad had used, though the land lines had been replaced by the internet. Once we'd gotten to know each other, Rooks had left it active for me, and updated it as the electronics advanced. .

HAVOC ON, I typed.

As a young man, Rooks had done covert intercept, that is, he had intercepted messages from people in other countries who did not wish the U.S. well. Men with his skills were called *Dittyboppers*, and people like him could type like lightning, some of them incredibly fast using only two fingers. He was still a fast typist, and the words spilled out across my screen practically as fast as I could read them.

SHAMSEEN USUDMAN ACTUALLY WAS A DEPUTY GOVERNER IN THE NIGERIAN GOVERNMENT, AT LEAST UNTIL RECENTLY. HE IS A

> PROLIFIC AND INVENTIVE
> SCAMSTER WITH A KNOWN
> RECORD OF CORRUPTION.
> 2ND NAME ON FAX, GENERAL
> PATRICK UGBALLA IS MORE
> OBSCURE. GENERALS ARE AS
> COMMON OVER THERE AS
> STARBUCKS OUTLETS ON VENTURA
> BOULEVARD. THERE WAS A
> CAPTAIN PATRICK UGBALLA
> ACCUSED OF RAPE, MULTIPLE
> ASSASSINATIONS AND ORDERING
> MASS MURDER OF CIVILIANS TEN
> YEARS AGO, DISAPPEARED FROM
> VIEW.
> ANY QUESTIONS?

I suddenly felt I had a thousand questions, as well as an overall awareness of dread. I typed

> DO THESE PEOPLE OPERATE IN
THE U.S.?

After the briefest of pauses, he responded

> THEY HAVEN'T IN THE PAST, BUT IF
> YOU'VE GOT ENOUGH MONEY
> ANYTHING'S POSSIBLE.

Julia shook my shoulder, trying to get my attention. "Ask him if Bertrand is in danger."

I typed

> WHAT IS THE CHANCE THEY MIGHT
HARM SOMEONE IN THE U.S.?

The answer was quick and to the point.

ABOUT 100% IF THEY FELT THEY
COULD GET AWAY WITH IT.
THOUGH THE GENERAL IS A FREE
MAN IN NIGERIA, HE IS WANTED IN
ENGLAND FOR MURDER. HE IS A
KILLER WITH NO REMORSE, AND HE
HAS MEN WHO WOULD KILL FOR
HIM WITHOUT A SECOND THOUGHT.
SHAMSEEN USUDMAN IS MORE OF
A MYSTERY. BACK IN THE LATE
1980'S WHICH IS ANCIENT HISTORY
THERE WAS A SCANDAL IN THE
GOVERNMENT SO GREAT IT
COULDN'T BE HIDDEN EVEN IN THAT
CORRUPT COUNTRY AND HE
DROPPED OUT OF SIGHT. I WOULD
GUESS SHAMSEEN IS THE BRAINS
AND THE GENERAL SUPPLIES THE
MUSCLE. MORE QUESTIONS?
I thought for a moment and then typed
ANY SCAMS INVOLVING TRUCKS?
There was a longer pause, and then the brief
note
NOTHING IN THE DATA BASE,
RUNNING 'NIGERIA', 'SCAMS', AND
'TRUCKS'.
I gave Julia a quick glance. She
shrugged and shook her head. I knew Rooks
hated long transmissions and this one was a
bible compared to his usual cryptic notes. I
typed, OFF IN THE WEST.
After a moment Rooks signed off,
WATCH YOUR BACK. OFF IN THE EAST. I
could almost hear the sigh of relief that I had
broken the connection.

I gave Julia the faxes I'd sent Rooks and went to the kitchen for another home-made latte. But when I came back she was staring at the shelves packed with scripts and research books that made up one wall of my study.

"You don't think Bertrand's crazy, do you, idiot-boy..." It wasn't a question, and there was a hint of softness in her voice. "You wouldn't have called your father's old friend if you didn't think he was in trouble."

I ended up telling her nearly everything, starting with the two thugs who had attempted to murder me and ending with the threatening call I'd intercepted the previous night.

"You're taking this a lot better than I would have imagined."

"I don't do histrionics, yelling or blubbering for your sorry life, Matthew."

"Ouch. That's cold."

"You made your own stupid bed," she said. I knew she was talking about Peanuts. There was a calm, intelligent look and a firmness I'd never seen there before, or perhaps it was there all the time and I just hadn't noticed. *That's why I could love this girl*, the thought rose unbidden in my mind. *She's tough and she's smart and she cares for people.*

Well, I didn't really know how tough she was, but she *seemed* tough, or maybe that was those tricky pheromones talking. The idea of an emotional attachment, a real and serious relationship with this bright and bristly girl, had caught me by surprise, and I was still struggling to catch up, to figure out if it meant anything or not. I had to set it aside, at least for the moment. There was work to do, and I couldn't have impulsive old Hollywood Havoc getting in the way of real life.

"So what do we do now?" She asked.

"Doesn't he have a cell phone?"

"Yes, but he keeps it on mute and he never answers it. He thinks he's saving the batteries."

"You sure?" .

I tossed her my cell phone. She dialed his number, and Old Grampers answered on the first ring.

"Grandpa Bertrand? Where are you?" She listened for the briefest of moments and passed the phone across to me. Bertrand of Nigeria came across the line sounding winded and tired, like an 80-year-old man who'd just run the 100-yard dash.

"Matt. Don't talk. Listen. My place is being watched. I need my keys. I'll be at the fish place."

"Julia was going to drive you-"

"No time for that," he snapped impatiently.

"You've made Shamseen Usudman very unhappy," I said.

"What do you know about that?" His voice sounded wary.

"I know you're in what sounds like big trouble." I added, "Your pal Shamseen threatened to kill us all—Julia, you and me."

"Tell him we must go to the police!" Julia said, shaking my arm as she tried to get my attention. Bertrand heard her even though she didn't have the phone.

"No police!" He shouted from his end of the line. "You'll ruin me! Just bring my keys! Matthew, this isn't one of your silly movie adventures! You must do exactly as I say!" He clicked off and I was left staring at the cell phone. I wasn't used to people hanging up on me. People don't ordinarily hang up on movie producers, not even cheesy small fries like me.

"He called my movies silly," I said.

"Your movies are silly, idiot-boy. Where's Old Grampers and what does he want?"

Well, that yanked any tenderness out of the moment for. It was the same old Julia, and it was time to get on with real life.

We went next door to Bertrand's place to look for the keys. No problem, they were in plain sight on his desk where he'd left them, probably to make sure he didn't forget to take them in the first place. The big ring held as many keys as a janitor or a biker's chain, but Julia seemed to know her way through the maze.

"He has safe deposit boxes everywhere," she said. "Three different post office boxes. Here, two sets of the same car keys on the same ring."

"We'll take those," a smooth and deep voice said from behind me.

I recognized the voice. It was one of the black thugs who had tried to drown me. As I was turning towards him, I was already launching the deadly body kick with my left foot, the sure and certain death-move that Tran Lee's martial arts instructor had taught me.

Unfortunately, these guys must have seen Dragonfly Madness. The closer of the two of them grabbed my foot and in another second I found myself dizzily staring up at him from the ground.

"Ugballa's thugs," I said to nobody in particular. "I know that's who you are. You guys tell the General he's messing around in the wrong country."

He nodded once, not bothering to deny the connection. *Why should they?* In their minds, we were probably already dead. The snappily dressed black man ignored me while he adjusted his tie. "The keys, please," he said to Julia.

I was glad they were so fixated on the keys, and even more pleased that I had remembered Rook's suggestion to stuff the uncomfortable .45 pistol down the back of my pants before I left my own apartment, even though it felt like it had nearly broken a few of my vertebrae when I fell on it. But when I reached back it came easily enough to my hand.

There was a click as I jacked a round in the chamber. That got their attention. They jumped back in surprise and slowly raised their hands in the air.

"Americans are not allowed to carry concealed weapons!" The taller one said.

"How can it be concealed if I'm pointing it at you?"

I was again reminded that real life is nothing like the movies. *Now that the thugs were on the business end of my automatic, what was I to do with them?* They were dangerous guys and probably loaded with knives and maybe a hideout gun or two. They were too close, and there were two of them. The bad dudes in my movies always had plenty of tricks up their sleeves, and if I was looking for sinister I would have cast this pair in a minute. Should I tie them up with kitchen twine or belts? Lock them in the bathroom? Make them lie on their stomachs until the police came? Okay for a movie, but in real life none of that made sense. They meant us serious harm, and we were already late for a meeting with Bertrand at the fish place. I had to keep the action going.

"Move," I said. "Back up. That way."

I kept my pistol pointing in the general area of their stomachs while I marched them over to the patio. Once there, I had one of them open the sliding glass door. Bertrand's condo was on the second floor, with a view looking out across busy Jamboree Street to a large backwater bay in the near distance. The two of them went out on the patio reluctantly, fiddling with the cuffs of their expensive shirts.

"How rude, old man," the first one said.

"Say, now, where are you taking us? We are guests, you know. Mr. Bertrand Berke did ask us to drop by."

"And drop by you shall," I said. "Have you fellows seen the view?"

With Julia looking on in wide-eyed surprise, I gestured with the gun.

"Out," I said. Once they were on the patio I urged them back against the rail and said, "Up."

"This is wickedly not correct, old fellow!" one of them protested.

"I know, but I'm under pressure and I'm not really thinking very clearly. Now get on up there."

Against their protestations, I made them climb on the rail. There was a strong on-shore wind, and the only way they could keep their balance was by holding the frail aluminum tube that held up the canvas awning over the patio.

"Now, jump," I ordered.

"But no… we'll be falling to our own deaths."

"Maybe you die and maybe not, if you jump. Certainly you die, if you stay."

The closer of the two black men eyed me carefully. "I see," he said. "You are using one of the toy pistols from your little adventure movies."

"I warn you, it is really the wrong day to comment on my hopeless career, just when I'm thinking I'm trapped forever like some Jonah in the low-budget belly of Hollywood."

"I – I don't think we follow, old bean."

I'd had enough of their jovial banter. These were deadly killers, and I had Julia to look after. My first shot sounded like a small explosion in the confined space of the patio. The bullet tore a huge hole in the canvas fringe of Bertrand's expensive green-and-white striped Sunsetter patio shade and went whining out over the bay. I had to hand it to those thugs. They managed to contain their surprise pretty well for real life bad guys in a situation where they could actually get their brains blown out.

"Very good," the one closest to me said, looking down from his unsteady perch on the railing. "But how are you when it comes to actually shooting a real person?"

I couldn't be sure, but it looked like he might jump back down on the deck and try to take the automatic pistol away from me, and I wasn't in the mood to talk about it in the first place. I was still smarting from Bertrand calling my movies silly and Julia calling me *idiot-boy* and telling me to grow up, and now here were these thugs I hardly knew deprecating my cinematic achievements. I mean, maybe Berger Royal Pictures isn't Columbia or Universal, but do I have to eat crap from everybody who ever rented a video?

"Usually I'd want to talk it over," I said. "You just got me on a bad day."

The shot buckled his knee the wrong way and knocked him backwards off the deck. He turned over once, flying back through the air nearly as graceful as an Olympic diver until he landed with a grunt on the small of his back in some of the dense shrubbery that rimmed the outer edges of Sea Garden Cove. As the land down there sloped steeply away from the buildings, the low bushes weren't enough to stop his progress. He rolled downhill through the flowering ice plant like a sack of apples and finally came to rest in a wide concrete gutter rimming the private service road that ran alongside Jamboree Drive.

I waved my pistol at the second thug and gave him a little nod with my head.

He jumped without argument, but landed badly on a decorative boulder hidden in the low shrubbery. I saw his leg snap sideways like a dry twig, and he too went tumbling down to the service road.

"It just isn't the day for thuggery," I told Julia. "Come on."

Julia didn't move. She was staring at me, transfixed, as if she was seeing me for the first time.

"You...you *shot* him..." she said.

"This isn't a Stephen King movie—Julia, they were going to kill us, for real. The same guys that tried to drown me, remember?"

"But, you turned that man's knee into red pulp..."

"Hey, Julia," I said, "are you listening to me?"

She took an involuntary step backwards. I couldn't blame her. After all, there I was, waving a gun around and yelling at her. I don't know if it was exactly still smoking, but she'd seen what it could do.

"Another thing, sweetie-pie princess. I'm not an idiot and I am grown up. I'm just not exactly the person you wanted me to be." I took her arm. "Come on, let's get out of here before somebody calls my favorite police department."

"I didn't mean you were really an idiot. And don't you ever call me your sweetie-pie." She was startled and confused and pissed at me, but at least it snapped her out of her funk.

"Why not? That's what Bertrand calls you."

"What?"

"Yep. You're my sweetie-pie princess. Old Grampers said so."

Her face went beet red. She followed me back through Bertrand's condo without saying anything. She still had his keys, so we went directly to Bertrand's big grey Caddy.

But even then, we couldn't motor on directly over to the fish place. We had to stop at the guard gate to untie Dim Eddie.

"It was the same guys," he said, triumphantly gathering up his clipboard and shoving it in front of my face. "Different car, though."

"Better call the police and have them tow the car away."

"Why? What happened?"

"They left in a hurry and I don't think they'll be coming back to pick it up."

"That's an expensive car, man."

"Fine. Hot wire it, change the plates and sell it in Mexico. Take my word for it, Eddie, they're not coming back."

"Serious?"

"Serious as it gets."

As we drove out the gate, Eddie was still staring after us, brows knit together and mouth open like he was trolling for flies. He looked exactly like a man who was trying to remember if he knew anybody he could trust to unload some hot metal in Tijuana.

Chapter 10

I was feeling strong negative vibrations about meeting Bertrand at what was known in our little extended family circle as *the fish place*, otherwise known to the rest of Newport Beach as the Tutto Mare. The fact is, the Burke's had a somewhat notorious history there, so much so, that, whenever I was along with them, I suspected the kitchen people routinely spit in our food. I tried to fall behind as Julia marched us in the front door, but it didn't do any good. In fact, she came back and took me by the arm.

As I've suggested, the Tutto Mare Ristorante was a fixture in Burke family tradition, and in my younger days I'd been invited along for the lunch and dinner outings more often than I liked to remember. It was located in the heart of Fashion Island, which is not really an island but a shopping mall situated on one of the low, rolling California seaside bluffs overlooking the coastal areas of Newport Beach. Many's the time, I'd wished it were a real island, tropical and deserted...and quiet. Burke family outings had nothing about them resembling tranquility.

The Tutto Mare had high ceilings and dark walls hung with vintage art deco posters featuring European bicycle races, bored 20's Gatsby-like people dining on sun-washed patios that were perched on sea cliffs high above the Mediterranean or lounging on oceanic liner deck chairs, and stylized carafes of Chianti presented by stylized waiters in stylized tuxedos.

The actual Tutto Mare waiters were just as stylized as the posters. They were uniformly dark and handsome young men with strong chins and five o'clock shadows. They were imported from Rome for their combination of authentic flavor and cheap labor. They would do anything to be assigned a table other than ours. The Burke family conducted affairs over pasta, and with Bertrand at the helm it didn't take much to get the spaghetti flying.

Bertrand's twin sons Herbert and Philbert both announced their divorces from their wives and their subsequent engagements to Jimmy and Raymond over steaming plates of *Duetto Di Pesce Spada*, a delicious presentation of grilled Pacific swordfish, fresh water prawns and rosemary roasted potatoes in a lemon-caper butter sauce. Julia first revealed her plans to fly the coop and run away to Harvard grad school over a bowl of her favorite *Zuppa Di Pesce*, a hearty Italian style bouillabaisse with crab, jumbo prawns and assorted shellfish.

Angry bellows, profanity, flying bread sticks and an occasional overturned table followed news of this sort. But there were other times when Bertrand would greet unwelcome tidings in tight-lipped fury, and these moments could be even worse, as his rage leaked out in angry spurts like jets of volcanic steam. These were the times the waiters feared the most, for Bertrand would erupt at a misplaced knife or fork, a nearly finished plate removed too soon, an inaccurate reference to an item on the menu or even an offensive shuffling of the feet or innocent, distant laugh from the galley leading to the kitchen.

"Is the salmon fresh or frozen?" he would ask.

"Ahhh, fresh, sir," the waiter would reply, clearly guessing.

"Is it Atlantic or Pacific salmon?"

This was Bertrand's best and most nearly unfailing trap. Invariably, they answered Atlantic, and he had them over the barrel. Being in shipping for over 50 years, he knew even the vaunted men of FedEx wouldn't, wouldn't or at least didn't fly an unfrozen salmon west across the country.

"Hah! I've got you! You're a liar!" He would shout. "You're all liars!" And I would spend the rest of the meal scraping imaginary spittle from my *Linguini Alle Vongole Veraci*, linguini with Manila clams and garlic in an olive oil and white wine sauce. Yes, we had a history at the Tutto Mare.

"He's over there," the young man in the black coat pointed, gingerly handing me a menu as if he half-hoped I wouldn't take it.

"Thanks. We see him," I said.

How could we not have seen him? Bertrand has always been a great one for the semaphore arm pump. We made our way between the crowded tables to the favored round table in the corner.

And yet, my day was full of surprises. Bertrand wasn't alone; he was seated with my boss, Vinnie Berger! That was a scene I thought I'd never see in this life. The last time Vinnie had been to Sea Garden Cove a seagull had crapped all over the back seat of his Corvette, and he swore he'd never return.

"Vinnie..." I said, my enthusiasm trailing off as I realized this meant additional layers of complications. "This is Bertrand's granddaughter Julia."

Vinnie never was much for introductions, and he started right in. "Young lady, your grandpa here's just sitting on a huge pile of foreign investment money!" He shot me a suspicious glare, "About which said fortune my own most trusted lieutenant has never mentioned a single word!"

I threw up my hands in a gesture of innocence, even though I knew it would do no good. Vinnie had built his little pile of low-budget movies on the bones of investors like old Bertie Badtooth, and I'd kept them apart for good reason.

"Vinnie, Bertrand can not afford to lose his pension..."

"Not Bertrand's money," Vinnie said with an impatient shake of his head. "His Nigerian investor friends."

Bertrand spoke quickly, before I could get in a word of protest. "I think Matt's is trying to cut you out, Vinnie. I think he wants to do his own movies."

"What?!" I tried to protest. "I'll give you credit when it comes to lying, Bertrand, but this is too much!"

"I wouldn't doubt it," Vinnie said, pouting his fat lips and shaking his head as he gave me a long regretful stare. If this went any further, I could stop doing any prep work on Carnage Days. Chop of Death would be my last production ever for the King of Schlock.

"Vinnie, there is no investment money! There are no investors!"

"Ohh?" a deep bass voice at my shoulder said, "then who am I?"

Oh great, a bit player, right on cue from the Dark Continent. He was an older version of the two jet-black fellows I'd already met twice before. Close-cropped graying hair, broad shoulders in an expensive suit, dark eyes twinkling or snapping at me, depending on how you looked at it.

"I don't know," I said, "The guy who parks the car?"

"So, a black man is only fit to park a car?"

"Hey, calm down," Vinnie said, unexpectedly coming to my aid. "Havoc don't got a racist bone in his body."

The man huffed a little, but, apparently mollified by Vinnie's remarks, he gave me a brisk little snap of a bow.

"General Patrice Ugballa, at your service." It was the kind of bow that said he wasn't really bowing as generals didn't bow except as a worthless courtesy before they pulled out an antique Nazi pistol and killed you.

"I believe I've already met your two sons," I said.

His semblance of civility went away like a misfit tribal mask and he shook his head, "I don't know what you are talking about."

"Nephews, then. Or maybe just employees. The same two cheery fellows I caught breaking and entering Bertrand's condo. The guys who tried to drown me."

"I assure you," Ugballa said with a smooth rise to his eyebrows and a glance around the table, "I have no idea what this young fellow is blathering about. I assure you there will be nasty repercussions for your unwise remarks."

I looked around in turn and saw nothing but skepticism and doubt aimed at me. Nobody but Julia seemed to want to give me the benefit of a doubt. None of this made sense, but I naturally didn't believe the general. As Horace Keg might say, *Three men in a tub with exotic blue-black skin is not a coincidence.* And, after all, how could I expect this guy to admit his own involvement in attempted murder?

"Okay, come on, enough of this stuff. What's the deal?" Vinnie barked impatiently and looked at his watch, the important producer with things to do other than argue over murder and mayhem. .

"The Nigerians have all kinds of money," Bertrand started in.

"Oh yeah? Where'd they get it?" Vinnie liked to play the New Jersey skeptic, but he was the world's biggest fool when it came to money. If you wanted to hit him up for cash, you had to scratch his card when he was flush. His assortment of hangers-on, his kids by three marriages, his wife, his steady squeeze and his babes-of-the-moment would carefully watch and wait and pounce on his bank account in that brief but flush time after a picture was funded but before principal photography began. Since the funds on Chop of Death were nearly depleted and Carnage Days wasn't yet green-lighted, I figured we were fairly safe; but you never knew—where financing was concerned, Vinnie was as creative as they came.

"We have been blessed with plentiful fields of petroleum," the General said as he energetically waved one of the reluctant waiters over to our table. "But Nigeria does not have a stable government. The question for us is always how to keep the money we make. And that means getting our profits out of the country."

"What kind of money we talking about here?" Vinnie asked.

Leave it to Vinnie to cut to the chase. He leaned back and grinned at me. I could read him better now that the first moment had passed—he wasn't pissed at me about Bertrand. And with Vinnie's dim sense of morality, he'd never have come after my neighbor for financing—Bertrand must have sought him out. And, maybe, even at that, he was feeling a little guilty.

The General cleared his throat and accepted a menu from one of the lads from

Italy. "There is a sum of $35,500,000 that we are attempting to move at this time."

From my place across the table, I could see Vinnie's eyes widen. Those were the kind of numbers that got his attention. We'd been in bed with a German financier for two years and Vinnie had only blown half that much, not even $20 mill. And he'd done the same with some Indonesian investors before that. People loved to be involved in films, to invest in Hollywood. To me it didn't seem Vinnie was sufficiently surprised or suspicious, but then, he hadn't heard Halliburton Rooks warnings. To Vinnie it was just a new—albeit rather large— outpouring of the usual manna from heaven.

I ordered *Zuppa di Pesce* for Julia and angel hair pasta with the clams for myself. *If the Nigerians were going to take us to the cleaners, I might as well enjoy my last meal on Berger Royal.* I'd been with Vinnie to these meetings before. Slowing him down enough to talk common sense was a problem. Once he was on a roll, he couldn't sidetracked with the direct approach. Over the years, he'd presented so many financial lies (development packages) to so many suckers that when it came to any number with six, seven or eight zeroes attached to it he himself couldn't tell truth from fantasy. It's a retinal disease, a special blindness reserved for thieves and Hollywood producers. I was going to have to hide in the brush and roll a boulder on the tracks at the right time before the freight train of disaster showed up.

"You, of course, would be Executive Producer on every picture you financed,"

Vinnie assured the General. "I guarantee it, your name will be above the title." Vinnie sat back, a plump and cheery Hollywood god bestowing semi-worthless and yet universally coveted laurel wreaths.

The General beamed, "You must get it right, my name is spelled P-a-t-r-i-c-e, not Patrick."

"No problem. One thing we're really good at is spelling!" Vinnie laughed and the mandatory chuckles went around the table.

"What about me?" Bertrand demanded. *Oh boy.*

I couldn't believe it. Madness reigned. My straight-laced neighbor wanted his name up front and center on a Vinnie Berger Schlock-a-rama flick.

"You too," Vinnie said without a second thought. "Right up next to the General. Same size, guaranteed."

And, why not? Credits cost Vinnie nothing. But the words had barely vanished into the woodwork when a frown crept over my boss's pudgy face. I knew him after all these years I'd spent in Schlock-town; I could see he was thinking this was too easy, even for him.

"When can we get this financing?" he asked. "I've got a slate of six or seven pictures ready to roll."

That was news to me. There was Carnage Days waiting in the wings, and that was about it for the new slate at Berger's Royal Pictures. And we could do Carnage Days for under two million real dollars, not counting the million (also real dollars) that Vinnie would slide into his private accounts to accommodate his various vices.

Bertrand and the General exchanged a worried look.

"There has been a minor delay," the General sighed. "A detail. Nothing serious, and yet it holds us up. I have asked Bertrand here to handle this little problem, but he is unable to come up with a solution on his own. And this is why we have contacted you."

"Just remember," I said to Vinnie, "I didn't give him your phone number."

He waved me off with a generous toss of his hand. Vinnie wasn't in a small-minded mood; it was the good old forgiving Vinnie, and he wanted to get on with it.

"What's the hang-up to getting the money?" he asked Ugballa.

The black man huffed in outrage. "There is one obstreperous minor official in the Central Bank of Nigeria who has decided to hold up the funds. A very greedy and foolish little man. There is a TELEX key code to wire the sum into Bertrand's account here in the U.S., but only he knows it. We have promised to pay him for this vital scrap of information, but he insists on his money up front."

Vinnie, having tasted the heady sum of 35 million dollars, was full of easy solutions.

"So what? Pay the poor bastard off."

The General sighed and threw out the contrasting pink palms of his hands, "I have dedicated my life to the military service of my country. I find I am not myself in a position to pay even these trivial sums."

"And I've already kicked in over 50 thousand to get the deal to this point." Bertrand grumped. "Don't look at me. I can't afford any more."

At this Julia raised her eyebrows and gave me a dirty look, but things were moving fast and the best I could do was shrug my shoulders, silently proclaiming my innocence.

"How much are we talking about?" Vinnie asked.

"He must have his bribe in three days, or the money is subsumed back into the national treasury," Ugballa said. "That is according to our laws."

"How much does he want?" Vinnie insisted.

"Two hundred and ten thousand dollars," Bertrand said in a low voice.

"Two hundred and ten thou to open us up to 35 million," Vinnie said, talking to himself. He was quivering like a bowl of Jello, the perfect image of greed personified, I guess, if greed was Jello-like. "Matt, how much we got left in the Chop of Death account?"

"Uhh, Vinnie, that's not a good idea," I said

"Why not?"

"Well, there's still some production bills outstanding—over 40 grand to the post house—and you wanted to pay your—uhh, Gloria, you know, will be looking for her payment."

Vinnie didn't skip a beat. "Write a check to this man for the 210 thou. Gloria can wait." He saw my distressed look, "Don't worry, Matt, we'll be covered. We'll just take it out of the 35 mill. With interest." He glared at the General, daring him to say otherwise.

"Oh, yes, surely, of course," the General said, spreading his own arms wide.

Vinnie could see I wasn't pleased. Hell, the lurking waiters and even total strangers could see the depth of my displeasure. But my boss shrugged, looking around the table to his new friends for understanding. "Of all the production assistants around town, I have to get the honest one." I was thinking, *Demoted to production assistant with the twitch of the devil's tail.* And the way Vinnie said it, honesty wasn't a coveted virtue. "Christ, Matt," he added, "the Germans will never know."

He was right about that. The Germans had long since given up trying to unravel the impossibly knotted financial puzzles Vinnie presented their accountants. I knew for a fact they had written off Berger's Royal Pictures, which was why Vinnie's current smile was so large and honeyed.

On the other hand, you don't get to be a Hollywood producer, even one of moderate credits like me, without your own stockpile of guile. I tried my well-practiced look of humility followed by the shrug-of-defeat, "Okay, Vinnie, give me an address and I'll send it over."

Unfortunately, after all these years, Vinnie knew me too well to buy in on my surrender. I'd thrown in the white towel a little too quickly.

"No, Matt," he said. "The General needs the money now."

Ugballa nodded vigorously, showing his extreme gratitude. "A moment of hesitation, and all will be lost," he added quickly.

"But..." I stalled, trying desperately to figure some way to save the boss from himself.

"Use the extra check you always carry in your wallet," Vinnie said.

I sighed and took the Chop of Death Productions check from my wallet, wrote the numbers and handed it over to Vinnie for his counter-signature.

I got up to leave. I couldn't stand being there any more. We were sitting with the crook that had tried to have me killed not once but twice, and here's my boss ordering me to write him a big check.

"If that's all you wanted, I'm out of here," I said.

"But the food hasn't even come," Julia protested.

I shook my head and started for the door. Then I remembered this was the Tutto Mare and we had a tradition to uphold. The waiters, who saw it coming, cringed and began to scuttle away, headed for the kitchen.

"I just want you to know," I yelled back to Vinnie, "This is nothing more than a scam; you're going to get your ass scalded and I don't want to be a part of it!"

The General jerked to his feet as if someone had shoved a hot poker up his butt. "No one insults me that way!"

Vinnie grabbed his arm, "Ahh, sit down, General. He's just trying to look out for the store."

"I do not trust this man!" the General cried. "He should not leave! He should stay here with us!"

"Sorry, General," I replied. "This isn't your little flea-flick of a dictatorship country."

Vinnie couldn't help but chuckle. That was one of his favorite lines from Keg's War. Actually it was his personal line. He'd rewritten Keg's, just as he did all the scripts. *Punching them up*, he called it.

There was a distracting flurry of activity as the waiters brought the main dishes and I made my escape without any further complications. I could see Ugballa still didn't want me to go. He looked around as if help was going to appear from off-camera left or right, but I knew if the General was counting on his employees to harass and detain me, he was going to be disappointed. They were probably nursing their leg injuries in adjoining rooms over at Hoag Hospital.   I hoped for their sake the scamming business paid for major medical; getting hurt in America was an expensive proposition.

Chapter 11

I used the parking ticket to retrieve Bertrand's Cadillac. I was handing money to the valet parking guy when Julia came boiling out of the front door. She was carrying two heavy packages which I assumed contained our meals, hastily wrapped to go. She jumped in Bertrand's Caddy, set the packages on the floor in front of her and started fisting my shoulder.

"Hey," I protested, "I have to drive, here."

"Matthew Havoc!" She yelled. "You idiot! You were just going to leave me!"

"No I wasn't," I said guiltily. She was right, but confession isn't my strong suit. I figured it would be a good thing to change the subject fast.

"How did Old Grampers get messed up in this thing, anyway?" I asked. She flipped down the mirror and adjusted her hair.

"It's your fault, Matt. You live right next door, and that fat Vinnie is your boss!"

"Well, thanks for doggie-bagging our dinners."

"My dinner. Yours is sitting back on the counter."

"That's pretty selfish," I said. "You're not working very hard on our relationship."

"We don't have a relationship! And you don't have a guilty bone in your body! He spent $50,000 of his own money on a scam—and it's your fault, and all you can do is joke about you and me!"

There wasn't anything constructive I could think of to reply to that. She continued glaring at me as we pulled out of Fashion Island.

"You know business hasn't been too good for him since Grandma died," she said, the accusing tone clear in her voice..

"Stop accusing me!" I yelled back at her. "Vinnie met him that time he came over to my condo for the wrap party to Klish Clash and Bertrand schmoozed right in and started eating—hell, you all horned in!"

She gave me a suspicious look. "You crap-head! You swear you didn't set any of this up?"

"Christ, Julia—I swear on my last pair of underwear!"

"Oh, gross," she said, but I could see she believed me. *Strike while the iron is hot*, Horace Keg always says, so I did.

"I think Old Grampers went looking for that one last big score, got burned a little, kept coming back for more. And I'll bet he called Vinnie. He knows the number, he's always calling me to pick up his Orange County Register when he's out of town.

"He can't afford to lose $50,000, Matthew."

"I promise, Julia, if there's anything I can do, I'll get it back." But, even as I said it, I was hearing the lingering echo of Halliburton Rook's warning, *Money goes into Nigerian pockets—it never comes out.* Maybe that was the updated version, the modern curse of the Bight of Benin.

Julia finally sighed, breaking the silence that had developed between us.

"And where are we going, idiot-boy?" she asked.

"To the bank, dear-heart." I grinned at her. "I've got about fifteen minutes to stop a check, close down an account and open a new one."

"You can do that without your bosses okay?"

"Sure. Vinnie hasn't signed a check in years. That display back at the fish place was just to show everybody that he's the boss."

"I don't think you have a plan, here. Won't he be mad when he finds out you screwed up his $35 million dollar deal?"

"I can handle Vinnie. All I have to do is tell Gloria that her lord and master thinks he can outwit a handful of Nigerian scam artists."

"Gloria's his wife?"

"Of course not. She's his steady West Coast lay. Gloria has a serious personal interest in where his money's going. And stop calling me idiot-boy."

"You are an idiot-boy. You actually like this Gloria person?"

"Why not? She's a survivor, she only takes what she thinks is her due, and she's got a sense of humor. In a way she's the best thing that ever happened to Vinnie."

"Is she pretty?"

"You kidding? Ugly as a brick." I thought it over, not liking what I'd said, "That's a little harsh. I take it back. She's strong featured. Gloria is a woman of character."

"What about his wife?"

"Yeah, she's pretty."

"Boy, are you screwed up. No, I mean about protecting Vinnie's interests."

"Doesn't have a clue. About money, that is."

"Bet she'd be furious if she knew her hubby was playing around."

I shook my head, "Don't be silly. She knows all about Gloria. This is show biz. How could she not?"

"She does? What does she think about that?" Julia said, skeptically eyeing this brave new world of show biz relationships.

I shrugged. "It keeps Vinnie out of the house. Makes him less grumpy, too. When Vinnie gets in a mood he can be a handful."

"Idiot-boy, if you and I were a number, I'd make you pay for that attitude."

I grinned at her, "I know you would, you sweet little porkchop, you. But we're not."

Julia waited in the car and fed the short-term parking meter while I ran into the bank. I stopped the check and closed down the Chop of Death account. We had about a half million left, but I knew there were bills due and payable in the next thirty days and most of that money would be gone. Believe me, what the postproduction house didn't get, Gloria, Vinnie's wife and his assorted other vices would.

I got back behind the steering wheel. We drove along without saying anything for quite a while.

"What do you think Bertrand should do?" Julia asked. At least she was talking to me without all the name-calling. My spirits rose a little.

"Old Grampers should probably get his butt out of town, and fast." I replied. "Hide in the mountains. Rent a beach shack down in Baja."

"That's what you'd do, right Mister Show Business Wonder?"

"You bet. These people are playing for keeps."

"But he can't."

"No," I corrected her, "he won't." Bertrand doesn't think he's in any danger. His problem is, he's been in international business his whole life. He's passed along a kickback or two, I'm sure. But he's never dealt with people like this."

"It's just the General..." She said uncertainly.

"Julia, I'm not so sure of that any more. There's a lot of loose ends, and nothing fits."

My thoughts buzzed like flies around the mess we were in. General Patrice Ugballa wasn't a stupid or foolish man. He was about to find I'd whisked away 200 plus G's right from under his nose. And that, as the heavies in the old detective flicks used to say, could get me seriously dead.

Still, I could practically smell that something else wasn't quite right about the setup. If I were writing a screenplay about all of this, the story would be full of holes. In the first place, Nigerian scam artists did their schemes long distance from Africa, from the swampy coastal city of Lagos or nearby Port Harcourt. They were safe there, protected by a government that encouraged their wily tricks and participated in the graft. And where did Shamseen Usudman fit in? And what about the mysterious and somehow important truck he'd mentioned?

"It would take something special to lure these guys to come to the U.S. and risk the F.B.I," I said, thinking out loud.

"Maybe there really is $35,500,000."

"Maybe. But if there is, Bertrand will never get a dime of it. These guys are great at what they do. Money flows into their pockets, never out. The U.S. Embassy says that, even with the full force and might of the U.S. government, they have never gotten any money back from scam artists. Not once, not ever"

Julia was the first to break the silence. "Thank you for trying to help us. I'm sorry I always think of you as Dick-for-brains. It just comes out automatically."

"Well, I'm motivated on my own. Don't forget those bastards did try to drown me. As for your garbage mouth, I guess I just have to love you as you are."

Even nearsighted as I was, I could sense that she was looking at me.

"We do have kind-of a brutal history of kicking each other around. I guess I've been thinking you were still a dipstick little producer of crap movies," she said. "I'm sorry."

"You've said a lot of evil things, but I always thought somewhere inside you respected what I did for a living. I know it's a crappy job, but it's all I've got."

"Matt, I said I was sorry. Don't get all crazy-serious on me. I don't think I could take it right now."

But, being Hollywood Havoc, I blundered on, running straight ahead.

"Once, I remember you said you were waiting for me to grow up. Ironic, because I'm older." That didn't make her any happier. I realized, a beat too late, that I shouldn't have said anything. Sometimes when a woman gets something on her mind, there just isn't any right answer.

"Yeah. Like you didn't do for me," she said.

That took me by surprise. And I was more than a little irritated. Maybe it was the pressure of the moment. Who knows why we blow our chances in real life?

"Me? What, Miss Fancy Pants? When did I ever do you wrong?"

"Idiot-boy, how old were you when you married the Ice Princess?" she asked, the remark flying out of nowhere to hit the bull's eye of my largely ignored conscience.

Don't ask me how women's minds work. They seem to take great circular sweeps in unexpected directions and then zoom in on your weak spots like birds of prey. Consider the legend of the harpies. First the sweet singing, then the claws. She was talking about Peanuts. *The question.* I tried to concentrate on her question. *When had I married Peanuts?*

"Twenty-one," I said. I tried to make light of it. "I was almost twenty-two years of age when I took the most stupid and fatal plunge of my life."

"And how old was I?"

"I don't know…fourteen?"

"I was eighteen, Matthew." She was looking like she expected me to say something, but I knew there was a chain saw somewhere around, and I wasn't going to risk my tongue. But I didn't have to open my mouth; she was on a roll.

"And what did you tell me at the country club dance on my 12th birthday?" she asked.

My mind rattled around like loose film cans in an empty van. We were talking Neanderthal times and primal days back before men knew the earth was round.

"That you would live a happy life?" That was pure guessing, I know, but I had to think of something. After all, I wasn't going to admit I didn't remember. I'm slow about personal relationships, but I'm not suicidal.

Her lips were thin and she stared straight ahead, seeing nothing. "No, not exactly. I'll give you a clue—that was right after daddy announced his new lifestyle."

I remembered. She was in braids and wearing her best school clothes, an ugly

Scotch plaid jumper. Julia at twelve: She was an awkward pre-teen in braces, and she was almost too embarrassed to show her face anywhere in public as the various parts of her struggled on their unequal way to maturity. Julia at twelve: Terminally shy, frightened of the changes in her life brought on by the breakup in her family, and utterly miserable at the sight of herself in the mirror. At her grandfather's urging, I had convinced her to show up at the country club for a small dinner in her honor. She had clung to me like a small, pathetic octopus, and at one point I had found myself on the dance floor with her. I never had a kid sister, but for me it was exactly what dancing with a kid sister must be like. She had said something about being born too late, and I had said in a joking way that it didn't matter, I would wait for her.

Of course, that is just something you say to a miserable little girl you didn't want to make any sadder than she already was, and in real life I hadn't waited for a heartbeat. A few years later I'd been on location in Ixtapa and had run off to Mexico City and gotten married to the Ice Queen, she who was soon to be immortalized as America's favorite set of boobs.

I glanced across the seat. Julia had that inward stare, thinking back on that same moment on the dance floor at the Newport Country Club. That night they'd had a real live old fart's band and they were playing The Tennessee Waltz and little Julia was standing on my shoes and hugging me like she knew I would some day run away from her like everybody else in her life that she had ever cared for.

Too late, I thought to myself. Julia was right; I was growing up ten years too late. We didn't talk much after that. I pulled Bertrand's big luxury liner back into his garage and she got out and headed for her yellow Thunderbird roadster.

"Want a nightcap?" I called after her retreating back.

She just shook her head, not even bothering to turn around. Her way of saying I was right. It really was too late.

Chapter 12

The calls started at three in the morning. Rooks had explained to me that it was a common scam artist's trick, wear down the lonely old victims with a flurry of non-stop calls in the middle of the night. Get them to write checks when they are particularly vulnerable, lonely and confused. Only on this evening they were getting in touch with the wrong guy. I didn't worry about picking up the phone because Bertrand hadn't come home. I knew that for sure. I'm a light sleeper and I would have heard him shuffling past my condo, muttering to himself as he fished for his keys in the darkness. And beyond that, I'd also had my telephone repairman friend Ken rig a beam outside his front door. Bertrand was away, leaving me free to answer his phone and say whatever I wanted.

In the scant space of an hour I had a call from a Nigerian congressman, two Nigerian doctors (doctors *of what*, I wasn't sure), a Nigerian ex-Vice President (very close ties to the present administration, he assured me), and an actual real life Prince of the Dark Continent (or at least a very good imitation) who said, speaking in an impeccable upper-class English accent, that he had fallen on hard times and had accepted a position of great responsibility with the Nigerian Central Bank, a post of authority that we might use to our mutual advantage.

I spoke in a low voice and acted sleepy, sloppy-headed and full of confused bewilderment. It was the Berger Royal school of acting at its finest; all of the callers thought I was Bertrand.

It took a while to begin to sort out at least this bit of my wily old neighbor's affairs, but after listening to the mad rambling of a dozen fakes and cheats, I thought I was getting an insight. It seemed that his crazy game was a disorganized attempt to scam whatever scam artists he ran across.

Those of you who remember the complicated mischief achieved by Paul Newman and Robert Redford in The Sting will realize the long-shot nature of Bertrand's efforts. Julia's grandfather was an old man with plenty of time on his hands. He was lonely, his legitimate business was evaporating, and his income flow was probably close to bone dry. What's more, he'd spent a lifetime doing business with all sorts of people from every continent on the globe. His recent outlay of $50,000 notwithstanding, maybe he would be okay; he certainly knew enough to get his payments verified and in his own bank account before he released any goods.

Bertrand might open an escrow account with twenty dollars in it, but I didn't think he was going to give away any personal bank account numbers. In short, even if his game might be a waste of time to others, it was keeping him occupied.

And yet, what an exceptional string of phone calls! In the time it would take you to watch a 90-minute movie, I was courted, cajoled, lied to, persuaded and finally threatened. The prince ranted the $20,000 check that apparently I (Bertrand) had said was in the mail hadn't showed up. The ex-Vice President pushed me to meet him in Budapest (yes, Budapest) where I could sign in person the government papers giving me access to the first installment payment on $15,000,000. One of the doctors angrily wanted to know why he hadn't received the ten X-ray units he'd ordered; the other doctor had ordered fifteen, and he hadn't gotten his, either. The Nigerian congressman assured me that, although his country was plagued—nay, riddled—with untrustworthy rascals, my (that is, Bertrand's) claims against the government for fees already spent were being processed; my company was to be paid along with a dozen other companies, including Ford Motor Company, Bendix and General Electric, and would be paid as soon as I wired the seventeen thousand dollars necessary to bribe the one very wicked man standing in our way.

After the first half-dozen calls, I started rooting for Bertrand the way you cheer a hopeless loser who's spent his inheritance on 200,000 lottery tickets, or some fool-for-Vegas hooked on high stakes blackjack, or a poor farmer who mortgages the farm on the absolute falling-down long shot destined to run dead last in the Kentucky Derby.

It was clear my old neighbor had gotten his name on a very special but not very exclusive list, and that he was a prime target and was saying yes to everybody. Beyond this, in the past, Bertrand had apparently paid some fees, not once but twice. Having been stung several times, the good news seemed to be that he was no longer pouring good money after bad. But the scam artists didn't seem to have gotten the message.

The phone was silent for all of three minutes when came a plaintive request from the Reverend Sir George Magumbo for any sum at all to help construct a chapel to bring the One True God to the miserable savages of the jungle. I politely told him I was tapped out, having given in the collection basket at St. Raymond's last Sunday. I was about pull the plug and go silent until dawn's early light when the call I'd been hoping for came through.

"Hello, Bertrand," the coldly whispering voice said.

"Hello, Shamseen," I answered, shaping my voice to echo his tone, which was one of menacing creepiness.

I had guessed the scoundrel's name, and he didn't even miss a beat. I was starting to see why *Few came out while many went in.*

"You have been busy, Matthew," the voice said. "Now get Bertrand and get off the phone."

"Not likely, my friend. I'm representing Bertrand's interests with regard to the truck and the various bidders who you would be wise to consider your serious rivals."

"Put Bertrand on the phone—now!"

"As you say, you are a long distance away to be giving orders…from your swampy jungle wilderness or whatever you called it."

There was a pause, and when he spoke again it was through clenched teeth. "What—other—bidders?"

"General Ugballa, I think, is currently the front-runner. He's offering $35,500,000. Are you prepared to top that?"

"Patrice Ugballa is not a general," Shamseen said bitingly. "He was thrown out of the military. And he doesn't even have one million dollars."

"Perhaps the people he represents do," I suggested. "I met with him earlier today, and he seemed pretty confident."

"Ugballa would never come to the United States."

"*Au contraire, mon frere.* A very black man; short, powerful stocky build, late 50's I'd say. Shiny bald spot on the back of his head."

This time the pause was almost as long as a television commercial. "What do you want?" he finally asked.

"Release the money like you said you would. Here's a new bank account number." I took a crumpled scrap of paper from my wallet and read him the numbers from the new Keg's War account.

"I will release half this morning," he promised. "But if you do not deliver Fat Boy you will not be alive to enjoy your precious money."

A truck named Fat Boy! It was enough to make me giddy. *I was living one of my own stupid movies!*

"Just fax me where and when you want your truck with the idiot name," I said. "I'll drive the damn thing myself."

"You can drive a cement truck."

"You send the money. I'll drive the Fat Boy to hell and back, if I have to."

There was a long pause while he considered his options. "No fax," he finally said. "Call me when you and Bertrand reveal the location of the truck. I will give you instructions from there."

"Right. Goodbye, Shamseen."

I'd never driven a cement truck before, but I didn't figure I would have to. After all, Harrison Rooks had set my mind at ease on this one—scam artists never sent money, they only took it in.

The true joy of being single—and between pictures—is that your time truly is your own. I turned off the phones and slept well, dreaming no dark dreams of careening cement trucks or cajoling scam artists. Dawn paraded across the gently west-sloping hills of Newport, the FedEx man dumped a load of scripts at my door, the illegal-alien gardeners that upset Bertrand's delicately balanced sense of *America The Beautiful* showed up with their howling accompaniment of blowers and trimmers, and I slept the sleep of the nearly-just and almost-innocent through it all.

Toward noon I woke and had a stretch and a yawn. My recorder showed I had 34 new calls, but I ignored them for the moment. I padded into the kitchen wearing my soft Minnetonka moccasins and nothing else and ground a cupful of French roast coffee beans and threw them into my coffeemaker. I used Kirkland House Blend, which the label on the plastic 2 pound bag assured me were exclusively roasted by Starbucks for Costco.

"I'll come in if you put on some clothes," a female voice said from outside the window.

"That figures," I replied, "you just like to peep."

"Mattie, I have to talk to you."

Everything was happening at once. It was my ex-wife, Joy Benefeté, otherwise known to me as *Peanuts*, to Vinnie as *the cunt that screwed me*, to Julia as *The Ice Princess*, and to the lowbrows in the biz as *America's favorite set of tits*. I hadn't seen her in over a year, not since I'd come to her agent's office to finally sign the long-overdue divorce papers.

I set down the bag of coffee beans that I'd been using as a strategic decoy and retreated into the bedroom. I pulled on a pair of cotton Sponge Bob Squarepants shorts with Sponge Bob on the front and his sidekick Patrick on the butt, and one of the ever-present Keg's War T-shirts. By the time I made it back out to the kitchen, Peanuts had let herself in the front door and was looking around, waiting for me to make her some coffee.

I don't know how I felt—mostly, I think, annoyance that she could waltz back into my life whenever she wanted. I took some low-fat milk from the refrigerator and steamed a cup of milk for my café au lait.

"That looks good," she said. As a general rule, my ex-wife wanted whatever I had. I gave it to her and started to make one for myself. I had actually figured she would do that, so I'd used my not-most-favorite cup.

"To what do I owe the pleasure?" I asked.

"Oh, Matthew, don't be such a dunk-head."

We weren't really on bad terms. She hadn't done me right, as the old song says, and she knew it, but that was a while ago, ages in the past by Hollywood standards.

"I'm not, Madge. Just a hangover. Sorry."

Tinsel town is a place of brief bitter moments followed by mass forgiveness, the cycle generally running the duration of time it takes to get on to the next picture. For a while Joy—formerly, Madge—had walked around me on tiptoe, waiting for the loose cannon to blow. But I never had and she'd gradually relaxed, started to take me for granted like she had in the old days. *Familiarity breeds an old shoe*, or so Vinnie says. Maybe people do grow, but you have to be interested enough to see it. And, obviously, she wasn't.

"Matt, I've been nominated for a Golden Globe for my part in Intimate Remembrances."

"I know," I said. "I read about it in *The Reporter.*"

Intimate Remembrances was one of those complicated pieces of Tinseltown business, a pile of mistakes that somehow coagulated into a decent movie. It had a great part for a female lead, but it was a role for a real actress, the sort of part that had avoided Joy like the plague. The great Bill Godaby, back from a devastating stroke, announced he wanted to direct Intimate Remembrances as his farewell swan song to the grand art of directing. Joy heard that and signed without reading the script. The male lead was outraged, the weather in Montreal was cold and rainy, the project turned sour, the shoot dragged on and on while Joy and the male lead dueled over dialogue sequences…and somehow, improbably and unpredictably, Bill Godaby flourished in his Indian summer, lasting through the editing and music scoring before his fatal heart attack, and the end result was glorious, an absolutely marvelous film. Joy had with this one picture been able to shuck aside some major part of the tits & ass reputation she had first earned with Berger Royal, and that she had embellished after leaving Royal Pictures. And why not? Even Jane Fonda grew past Barbarella to become…well, whatever she became that was different.

I'd thought my ex would never have the courage to take a chance and find out if she was a real actress, but I was wrong; with Intimate Remembrances she had started to live up to her potential. I was glad for her—proud, actually.

"Think you'll get the gold?" I asked.

"Well, I don't know," she said. She set her cup down and did this fussing thing with her hands. It was one of those old familiar gestures. She was upset and at a loss for words.

"Well, then...?"

"Matt, this could be a big moment for me, but something's come up." She paused, looking down at her hands. "There may be a blemish on my career, and—and it involves you."

"Me? How could that be?"

"Well, I'm not sure." The frustration was evident in her voice.

"Madge—Joy...this is a very strange conversation." I was determined to be as patient as I could, but she wasn't making any sense.

"Just hear me out, Matt. I need your help. You have always been a strong person, and you've always had your own ambitions. It's just that our paths seem to cross sometimes, and what's good for you isn't good for me."

I didn't say anything. It seemed to me she was going over old ground, the reasons why she'd left me. She saw the look in my eyes and put one hand over mine.

"No, not that, Matt. Look, that's the past, okay? You made some mistakes, I made some mistakes, but we can never go back there."

The one big mistake I could remember was marrying her in the first place, but I wasn't going to say that.

"What is it?" I asked

"You're involved in some serious negotiations right now. I know you are. Horny got a call this morning, and it involved you."

She was talking about Harry "Horny" Hiatt, her agent, the guy who had persuaded her to say *adios* to Vinnie Berger's Royal Pictures, and probably to me, as well.

"What kind of call?" I asked.

"Serious..." She hesitated, "And threatening."

"Why didn't Horny call me himself?" I asked.

"I begged him not to. Matt, I wanted to talk to you personally. You've got to help me. You have to understand how much this means to me."

"How much *what* means to you? Joy, I'm not trying to be purposefully obstructionist, but you're not making any sense."

" 'Purposefully obstructionist...' Only you could say something like that at a time like this." She thought of me as a literary type, and, compared to the junkyard people she'd grown up with, I guess I was. She sighed and took a deep breath. "Well, okay. Here goes: Matt, listen up. Back before I met you I did a lot of bit parts, anything to get some time in front of the camera."

"Okay...sure you did. I knew that."

It came out in a rush, "But you don't know that I starred in a picture called "Anastasia in the Barnyard" and it's got some pretty embarrassing stuff in it..."

"How embarrassing?"

"They gave me some dope so it's all a little fuzzy, but I think there was a goat and a huge pink pig and—"

"Never mind," I said, waving her to silence and trying to get the images out of my mind. *Peanuts with a pig.* I felt like heading for the shower.

I shook my head, trying to scatter the unbidden thoughts to the wind. She had come to me for help. She deserved better than I was giving her.

"I know," she said, reading the look on my face. "I was young and stupid."

"But…okay, you made a mistake early in your career. So what?"

"Well, Horny got a call this morning. Somebody out there just bought the rights to "Anastasia", and they say they're going to re-release that awful footage on the porn circuit."

"Can they do that?"

"Maybe not legally, but by the time we stop them it will be all over the country."

"And there goes your chance for the Golden Globe."

She nodded, and looked at me.

"Unless you give them Fat Boy," she said.

I felt like a lightning bolt had struck me. I don't know if I was more stunned that Shamseen had gotten to Joy, or at the speed with which he'd done it. He knew all about my life and me. And it seems he was already in position to squeeze America's favorite set the moment he needed something from me. Because I, you see, was his squeeze on Bertrand and his precious but mysterious truck.

"What do you know about Fat Boy?" I asked.

She gave me a look of alarm.

"N-nothing. Don't be mad, Matt. To tell the truth, Horny tried, but we couldn't really trace it. We thought it was some screenplay you dug up, or probably the rights to an unpublished book. All I know is, this man called Horny's office and said you had to give Fat Boy to him or my career was in the crapper."

I nodded, saying nothing.

"You will give it to him, won't you, Mattie?" A note of panic was creeping into her voice. I was once again Mattie, the name she'd called me in that brief six-week period when life was but a dream, sweetheart. Madge Sacknall was back, she was America's favorite, she was calling me Mattie again... she was playing me like a piano. Of course I would be putty in her arms, just like I'd always been... hah, not really. I wasn't interested any more, not that way, and it wasn't just her barnyard friends. Still, we had a history. When it came right down to it, I was in her court and I felt I had to do something.

"Of course I'll help, Peanuts," I said. "Fat Boy is a very special Harley-Davidson motorcycle. Tell Horny the script is pure box office gold."

I may not have risen to her heights, but as I've said before, you don't get to be a successful Hollywood producer, even of schlock sex, horror & sock films, without some knowledge of guile and deceit.

"But..." I could see the doubt flutter up in her eyes. That old Hollywood Havoc problem: I had given her what she wanted, but too quickly.

"Not to worry, Peanuts. Vinnie was about to sell it, anyway. He was just trying to jack the price. They get Fat Boy, you get Anastasia back, Vinnie gets even richer."

"That Vinnie!" She broke into the gigantic radiant smile that had, apparently, brought many a dog into heat. A quick peck on my cheek and she bounded for the door. I watched her through the slats in the blinds. She got in a big Mercedes coupe, nodded happily to the driver, and Horny Hiatt drove her away.

Chapter 13

It took so little to keep Peanuts happy. It made you wonder why I'd never been able to do it. But she drove on down our little hill, and before I could fully ponder the sucking realities of my life on the lowest rungs of Hollywood's food chain, Julia banged her way in through the still-open front door.

"Was that the Ice Princess I saw being driven away from here in a big, fat car?" She shouted.

"Yes," I admitted, "Peanuts herself." No use denying it. I had been caught with the goods.

"What was she doing over here, *merde*-for-brains?"

"Come on, Julia, we used to be married. And don't get all French on me."

"You were just talking over old times?! Idiot-boy, that is so lame!"

"I didn't think you cared, my sweet hug-a-boo."

"I-I don't, you stupid—I mean, not in that way. But you and I have had serious discussions about that woman and she's no good for you!"

I couldn't remember more than passing comments between Julia and myself regarding the amazing Joy Benefeté, but selective memory isn't an entirely bad thing in a hectic lifestyle. At least, it fits well with a light conscience.

"Julia, I can't tell her when to show up. She hasn't been here in years, my little goldfish. Hell, why am I explaining any of this to you, of all people?"

She looked extremely fetching in an angry, disheveled sort of way. Not the absolute sex rocket that was Peanuts, but I thought she held her own in comparison. With Julia there was no complicated fuss, no acting. What you saw was what you got, garbage mouth and all.

"What are you doing here, anyway?" I said, reaching for my neglected coffee cup. Even its vaunted thermal properties had been overtaxed, and the remains within were tepid. I put it in the micro and gave it a warm up zap.

"Old Grampers is missing again," she said, slumping into one of my kitchen chairs, the wind out of her sails.

I shook my head in bemused dismay. Bertrand lost again. Of late, that guy had the flight path of a butterfly.

"How do you know, my butterfly chicken-wing?"

"Stop calling me silly names! I made him promise he would phone in every night until whatever his problems are would blow over."

I saw by the blinking red light that my own phone was ringing again. The readout said I now had 53 unreturned calls, undoubtedly many of them from Julia. It didn't seem like the right time to confess I was intercepting her grandfather's calls. Even without my wiretapping, I could be pretty sure Bertrand really was among the missing; if he'd showed up last night, I would have known.

The light on my phone continued to blink. Somebody really wanted to talk to me. Persistence pays, I thought. I held up a hand to slow down Julia and picked up the receiver. It was Andy Thulis, my personal banker, personal thanks to the volume business we did through Berger Royal Pics.

"Matt, my boy, I've been trying to get you since 9:05 this morning." His voice sounded enthusiastic and oily. That meant something was wrong.

"What, did I bounce some more checks? Andy, doesn't the Automatic Overdraft feature automatically kick in when I run out of funds?

"Funny boy," Andy said. "I thought Keg's War was in video cassette."

"Keg's War did okay," I said defensively.

"Matt, listen to me. Did you or did you not release Keg's War to video?"

"Yes, we did. But it made back its nut in domestic distribution alone, and foreign piled on plenty more. That picture was way in the black." Videocassette release is the last gasp of distribution. After that, a picture figuratively becomes a member of the old motion picture home.

"Matt, I don't care about that. What I want to know is How come you got $5 mil U.S.

dumped in the Keg's War account this morning?"

I was speechless. Looking back, I think that's the precise moment when I realized the deep shit I was in. Not Bertrand's continuing disappearances. Not the grand appearance of the Ice Princess at my door, begging for a favor. The sudden appearance of $5,000,000 dollars in the bank account of my choice, money from people who never, ever paid out a dime, actual money from warped and greedy scam artists so twisted and rotten they made us Hollywood rascals look like blessed saints. This was big trouble. I knew then that Bertrand was on to something monumental, and monumentally dangerous, as well. This deal had to be huge; whatever it was, they could use $5 million as bait.

"You sure it's real money, Andy? No tie-ups, no strings, no the check's in the mail, baby?"

"No, it's a solid deposit." His suspicion welled in a mille-second. "Why, what's wrong?"

"Nothing's wrong, Andy." I thought fast. "It's just that I was expecting it the day before."

"Oh," he said. "Well, you know the banking system." In another second he would be whining about uncertain electronic transfers and computer crashes, all things I didn't want to hear about. Meanwhile, Julia was looking like a little lost kitten.

"Be right back with you in a minute, Andy," I said, setting the phone down on the granite sink top.

There was $5 million in the Keg's War account. My hands were shaking as I selected one of my favored cups from the kitchen cabinet. I picked the one from Seek Out & Destroy with the picture of noble but tragically flawed Captain Royce Garrison of the USAF stenciled on the side. I handed the priceless trophy to Julia and urged her to pour her own mug of java. All the time I was thinking furiously. This was slick money, and money that showed up this fast could vanish as readily as the legendary leprechaun's pot 'o gold, if it hadn't done so already. I had to move it, and I had to do it right now.

Lucky for me, Vinnie had taught me financial shenanigans to apply to nearly every shady circumstance people like us might think of. The art of successful filmmaking, at least done the Berger Royal Pictures way, was about snatching funds from the wary and hiding them from the greedy under the walnut shell of the righteous. I reached in my wallet and withdrew the same crumpled piece of paper I'd used the night before. It had the numbers of every one of Vinnie's accounts, and two of my own.

"Andy," I said into the phone. "I've got some numbers for you." I gave him my Belize account number. I would have given him Vinnie's but I wasn't sure how deeply Mister Cheapo Hollywood was in cahoots with the missing Bertrand of Nigeria. Vinnie thought he was very tough about the bucks, but I'd seen him do some kooky things.

Low budget Hollywood loves the breezy business attitude in Central America, but Andy didn't like my instructions all that much when I redirected the big lump to an account in a shady banana republic. *He'd thought he was doing me a big favor by calling me, and I repay him by whisking millions out of his bank.*

"How about giving me a couple of days?" he grumbled.

"Andy—now!" I barked into the phone. Julia was staring at me in wide-eyed amazement, seeing another side to the apple-cheeked kid who had helped her with her algebra. First I shoot off somebody's kneecap and then I fly money around like it's paper airplanes.

I clicked off with Andy and turned my attention back to Julia. Regardless of what she or Andy thought, if I'd acted in time the funny money would be on its merry way south of the border. I didn't know what to make of it, but I wasn't worried. That kind of bucks always showed up with strings carefully attached so the scoundrels could yank it back once the hook was in. Still, there was a chance…just maybe I'd whisked it away in time.

I wasn't going to let myself get overly excited. In Vinnie's world, the world that had become mine through association, big piles of dough came and went. He was a money-magnet. We spent a chunk on whatever picture we had going, Vinnie siphoned off for his lifestyle and the rest seemed to vanish into some mysterious ether. How could this be any different? I was sure everything would sort itself out. And that shows you how little I knew about the mess I was slipping into.

I did know Andy would get over his current sour mood. He was more disappointed than surprised; he was used to huge deposits moving through the Vinnie Berger accounts, but he liked to hang on to the money a little longer than a few hours. With big chunks of change like that, you could make a decent living in short-term parking. I had put up with the cajoling, but had stood firm that the money had to be sent to Belize right away, explaining that it was part of a much bigger financial package. Andy grumped, but for now he was going to have to make do with my promise that further huge sums would be coming under his watchful eye at The Union Bank of Beverly Hills.

Now all I had to do was figure out why Shamseen Usudman would pay ageing (and missing) export-import maven Bertrand Burke big bucks for a cement truck named after a motorbike. And I figured I'd have very little time to unravel the secret before Shamseen sent some very unpleasant people after me to either pick up his truck or collect his money's worth.

I made a mental note to call Belize in a few hours and split the money and send it on to the Bahamas and The Isle of Mann. Five million dollars is a lot of money. Just because there were some gnarly strings attached didn't mean I shouldn't try to hang on to it as long as possible. As Keg always told the virginal Tui, *Let us now together bow to the twin gods of fate and good timing.*

Chapter 14

A few hours later, at about the same time I was talking to Andy about shifting my ill-gotten gains to other parts of the world, the Santa Ana police arrested General Patrice Ugballa. Alerted that there were some strange goings-on in an alley behind a Best Buy, a squad car arrived on the scene about five minutes before the General's thugs, both limping painfully in leg casts, were able to beat a U.S. citizen named Bertrand Berke to death. It didn't look like they really wanted to kill him, at least not quickly. They wanted information. But I could have told them that task would be more difficult than it might seem on the surface. Old Bertrand may look like a quirky old push-over, but he had stormed the beach at Okinawa and wasn't about to turn into a jellyfish for some slick, dark-suited gangsters from the Bight of Benin.

Still, it was a close thing, and he wasn't in any shape to talk when Julia and I arrived at Hoag Hospital. There wasn't much to see, just an unconscious man wrapped in gauze bandages to where he was unrecognizable. I left him with Julia and went over to the police station.

The two black thugs were in the general holding pound, but Ugballa had his own cell. The police weren't exactly eager to let me talk to him, but since the General had spent his call on the Nigerian Embassy in New York, their phones had been hot and the cops figured he would be out on bail in a matter of hours. A high-price lawyer was on a fast East-to-West charter jet and unless Bertrand woke up in the immediate future there would be no witnesses to what actually happened, and that meant Ugballa was going to flap the coop, as Vinnie might say.

Various members of the police in Orange County were a major resource for Berger Royal Pictures, and I personally knew my share of them. Thanks to show biz and the promise of a *really good* bit part in our upcoming sure hit movie, Carnage Days, I was able to convince the detective in charge to give me ten minutes alone with the General.

Once the Ugballa and I were alone, I slumped into a chair and waited.

"Your friend Vinnie's check bounced," he said, giving me a glum and sullen look.

"General..." I shook my head sadly, saying nothing.

"What?" he finally asked.

"You know you can't go back to Nigeria."

"What are you talking about? It is my home. I should have never come here."

"True enough," I agreed. "But now you can't go back. Your life is no longer worth a penny back there."

"What are you talking about?" He looked angry enough to strangle me.

"Shamseen Usudman is very upset with you."

Since the look on the General's face was one of sudden terror, I thought I'd push the truth a little. "He tells me to pass on the word to you that you are a dead man. I don't see how you can want to go back to your homeland."

"But—I have done nothing to Usudman!"

"Nothing except interfere with and totally screw up Shamseen's deal with Bertrand Burke of Uni-Amer Industries."

He was shaking his head helplessly, mouth open to this new and unexpected disaster. They say scammers are always the easiest to scam. I think it's probably true, because their perception of the world is that lying is so complicated and difficult that everybody else must be telling the truth.

"General Ugballa," I said. "I've got very little time to straighten this mess out. You can help if you want."

"But we—I had nothing to do with Shamseen Usudman."

"I can't believe that."

"But it's true!" he pleaded.

I shook my head. "No, not entirely. Here's what I think: You, Usudman, and various other pranksters started hammering Bertrand, calling him day and night and showering him with tasty offers."

The General shrugged. That much was common knowledge, not worth protesting to someone who didn't matter, anyway.

I continued, "The problem is, Usudman had his own private scam going with Bertrand, something nobody—not even you—knew about, something worth ten, twenty, a hundred times whatever you could hope to squeeze out of Bertrand."

"What could it have been?" He looked at me with wide, believing eyes. Crooked generals and low budget film producers, it seems, are among the first to buy in on the untrustworthiness of their confederates. Actually, I had no real idea, but the little I knew was vaguely like the complicated plot in To Crush A Thief, one of Vinnie's early film epics back when he still thought of himself as a serious filmmaker.

"I don't know," I said. "But I do know this; he is very, very pissed at you. You can't go back to Lagos and expect to live more than a day."

"But he's arranging the best lawyers to get me out of here."

"Exactly," I said.

He slumped on the hard wooden chair, thinking it through.

"Why are you telling me this?" he finally asked.

"You've got money outside the country," I said. "You don't have to go back there. Anywhere in Europe. Costa Rica, maybe, might be safe for you."

He didn't say anything.

"Money in secret accounts, in other parts of the world," I prompted. "Everybody has a retirement plan."

"Yes," he agreed. "But not enough. I thought Bertrand could be my last big score. I should be furious at you."

"No," I said. "Not me. Vinnie sets things up that way. We've done that a dozen times. There was no money in that account."

"Tricked by a trickster," he said, shaking his head sadly.

"Not really. I'm here now, and I can help you."

"Help me!" He laughed, making me feel like the ant-eater that would do a good deed for the whale, another Vinnie one-liner.

"Yes. I can have $500,000 United States dollars, untraceable, tax-free, in the account of your choice in twenty minutes. But you have to do something in return."

He gave me the wide-eyed stare that all scamps use, the one I'd long ago learned not to trust. "What?" he asked.

"Talk to me on the way to the airport." He threw his arms out in a gesture of helplessness. "But I don't know anything about Shamseen's plans."

"You may know more than you think. It's worth a half million U.S. dollars to me to find out."

Was he tempted? Was he acting? Did he just need a bit of pushing over the edge? I had nothing to lose by trying.

"Look," I urged, "your lawyer will be here in a few minutes, and he will have made arrangements to get you out of the country. Take the tickets he gives you and somehow make sure he does not get in the limo with us."

"How can I do that?"

"Your nephews will be getting out of jail, as well. Perhaps you can arrange for them to delay the lawyer."

It sounded like a good plan. I thought it had a chance. I didn't know what the General could tell me, but he probably knew more than I did.

We were interrupted by a well-manicured voice from the door.

"I'm afraid you'll have to leave my client now," the lawyer said.

He introduced himself as Peter Manning, esq. I was surprised he was so young looking. He said he had recently graduated from Harvard and represented Highboy, Lightner and Slather, one of the most prestigious and respected law firms on the East Coast. The only reason I knew that was because that's what he told me as he handed me his card, effectively abbreviating my conversation with the General. I would have cast somebody older, more distinguished, with white hair at his ears, for the part, but that shows you what I know.

"I'd rather stay," I protested. "I have unfinished business with General Ugballa."

"Your business is finished as of now," he said firmly. There was no room in his tone for debate.

He held open the door, and I had no choice but to exit. And he was right about myself and the General. We had, indeed, finished our conversation. In fact, I never spoke with Patrice Ugballa again. For barely five minutes after I left the room, while I restlessly waited in a nearby lobby, the

General suffered the symptoms of a massive heart attack. He never recovered. He was rushed to the same hospital where Bertrand lay unconscious and General Patrice Ugballa was announced dead on arrival.

Directly after this unfortunate incident, Ugballa's young Eastern lawyer disappeared. Worse luck, but no surprise, the card he'd given me proved a fake; I called the several numbers on it and they were totally fictitious. Although the area code was for Boston, my calls netted a pizza parlor and an irate and somewhat confused elderly lady who said I was a 'peeping Tom,' doing it over the telephone. And the long distance operator confirmed there was no law firm in or near Boston named Highboy, Lightner and Slather.

Chapter 15

Billy "Horse" Proximo was a big dick in more ways than one. He had arrived on the Hollywood hardcore scene in the sexually go-go 1980's, fresh from Eastern Tennessee and sporting an appendage that would make the entire stud stable stamp about in envy. Not close to being a generous, or even what you might call a *nice* man, it was reported that he still had the first wages of sin he'd ever collected, safe and earning interest in a bank somewhere out of the country. They called him 'horse' because of his size and his legendary staying power under the hot studio lights. And maybe because, with his long, narrow face, unruly forelock of brown hair and big sorrowful chestnut eyes, he looked a bit like everybody's favorite pony.

Billy Proximo's company, Horseflesh Pix, was located in the heart of the porn business in the San Fernando Valley, housed in a bustling three-story brick office building near the Van Nuys airport. It was your average indy flick house except that the young hustle was a little more hard-edged, a bit more knowing and cynical. The porn business grows you up fast, like maryjane under the hothouse lights.

The police had found Billy's phone number in General Ugballa's pocket, but as the General was already dead, they didn't think it had any significance.

They had already decided the General's death was untimely but accidental, and as he had a criminal record that spanned three continents, few if any police resources were going to be expended on trying to clarify the reasons for his passing. That meant they weren't considering Billy The Horse a clue or anything that they needed to follow up on. I disagreed with them on that decision, but, of course, I didn't say anything.

"Horse," I said, breezing in past the secretary. I had status at Horseflesh, Berger Royal Pix being the next step up and out of the filmic gutter. Horse was doing very well where he was, but he liked the fact that I'd come to see him.

"Hollywood Havoc, himself. Slumming, I see." he said, waving to one of the leather director's chairs scattered around his large office. "How they hanging, bro?"

"Finished Chop of Death, waiting for a go on Carnage Days."

"To what do I owe the honor?" Even with those big, soft brown eyes, Horse managed to look world-weary and skeptical. Maybe it was the bags under his eyes that looked big as food pouches.

I sat forward on my chair, feeling a little too up-in-the air for comfort. That's the thing about director's chairs—like directing itself, you can't ever relax, not for a minute. Too much crap flying, too many loose ends, too many problems. But a lot of producers decked out their offices like that, with the canvas back panels saying things like "STAR", "SUPER STAR" or "MEGA-STAR". Billy's chairs said, "Property of Horseflesh Pix."

I teetered on my chair while Billy's slack-jawed secretary got us cool bottles of Starbucks Frappuccino. I gazed around at the giant color portraits on the wall. They were all of the Horse with his leading ladies. He'd had romantic shots pulled from the dailies and had them blown up and then painted on canvas. There was nothing XXX or even single-X. There was Billy the Horse as a cowboy, as a disco dancer, as a champion surfer, as a fighter pilot, as a James Bond type spy. It was like looking at forty giant pictures of Elvis in costume, with a different lady draped in surrendering adoration in each scene. I shook my head, trying to clear my brain from too much horsing around.

"Billy, my ex came to me with the craziest story. She says, back in her childhood she starred in a barnyard flick, and you're going to re-release it."

Billy sat behind his massive oak desk, giving me a heavy-lidded stare over the mounds of scripts waiting his attention.

"Yeah. All true. So what?"

"Well, the question comes to mind, *Why would you do that?*"

"Simple. No secret to it. Good old boy, Horny, asked me to."

"Horny Hiatt, her agent?"

"The same."

"Billy, that doesn't make any sense. She's up for a globe for Intimate Remembrances. She'll never get it if-"

"—if that artsy-fartsy crowd finds out about a mule going down on her." He eyed me for a moment. "No offense meant."

"None taken."

"Right. I don't know what Horny's got on his mind. He's one greedy bastard."

"But it doesn't make any sense," I protested.

Horse shrugged his wide shoulders in a gesture of indifference, "Maybe he thinks she's not going to win unless he does something."

"So he does what? Convinces her to commit career suicide?"

"Maybe…" Billy was rolling his own cigarette, his own personal blend of tobacco with a little green marijuana mixed in. He snapped his fingers as if he'd solved it, with the effect that his homemade flew all over the desk. He ignored the little mess, excitedly getting to his feet and pacing back and forth.

You see, everybody in the biz loves a plot. Nothing's real, and everything's a movie. And nothing gets you jazzed like figuring out motivation. I could see The Horse had a little story buzz on and it wasn't chemically induced.

"Look, Havoc, everybody uses everybody, right? It's true on the screen, it's true in my life, it's true in your life. That's why you're here, after I don't see you for over six months, right? So maybe what Horny does, he sees Peanuts isn't going to pick the golden apple unless he figures an angle. He gets me to release the barnyard flick, Joy comes across as the pure and abused female being fingered for something she did in her innocent youth, she engineers some great sobbing penitent clips on Extra, Extra—that's acting, baby—maybe she walks with the gold after all."

"I don't know, Billy. That's a big stretch. For one thing, right now she's the front-runner. Why would Horny take a chance on anything that might screw it up?"

"She's really got a shot at it?" Billy gave me a skeptical look.

"I think she does," I nodded. "She's come a long way since Berger Royal."

"Okay...so what do you want from me?"

"I'd like to buy all rights to Anastasia in the Barnyard."

"Forget it, pal. That would cost you a million bucks."

"I figure more like a hundred thousand. It's a cassette re-release, for pity's sake."

"Starring the one and only Joy Benefeté, Golden Globe nominee who definitely knows her way around the hayloft with a Great Dane named Freddie. And Horny's offering me a clean half mil to release it."

He had me, and he knew it. We settled for $650,000 of Shamseen's money.

The Horse, having many times observed for himself the unbelievable speed at which a glorious Hollywood flower—or a verbal promise, for that matter—can wilt, allowed it would be a fine idea if I phoned Belize directly from his office and had the money sent to a set of numbers he had tattooed on the inside of his left bicep. That was okay with me. I smiled at the thought of Shamseen Usudman screaming in hopeless rage from the balcony of his condo in Lagos...if they had condos in the Bight of Benin. We have to ask ourselves, *What is a scam artist's money for, if not to set things right?*

Chapter 16

Back at Sea Garden Cove, Bertrand's favorite scapegoats, the Up-From-The-South people he referred to behind their backs as *rotten, crooked wetbacks*, were busily transplanting clumps of yellow and white chrysanthemums that already looked the worst for wear. Too bad Bertrand himself wasn't around to give the hard-planting border runners a piece of his mind.

Halliburton Rooks, however, had emailed me a piece of his:

SHAMSEEN
USUDMAN NOT IN
LAGOS. HASTY EXIT
TWO REGIMES AGO,
REPORTEDLY SKIPPED
WITH HUGE SUMS OF
CASH. LAST SEEN IN
LONDON,
FREQUENTING
CASINOS, HIGH STAKES
BACARRAT PLAYER.
LEFT ENGLAND FOR
MOROCCO AS MUCH AS

SIX MONTHS AGO.
LANDLADY ANGRY
OVER UNPAID RENT.
UNCONFIRMED
MEETING IN
MARRAKECH WITH
UNSAVORY RUSSIAN
DISSIDENTS. WATCH
YOUR BACK. ROOKS.

So my mysterious contact had not called me from Lagos or from the deepest interior of Nigeria, as he'd said. He had been in London and then Morocco. That meant he could be anywhere. I was scrambling some eggs and John Morrell Smoked Sausages in my own special mix of Dragon Brand garlic soy and Hurricane Jenny hot sauce when Julia showed up from the hospital.

"Grandpa is still unconscious," she said before I could ask. She took a forkful of eggs and chewed thoughtfully for a moment before spitting them out in the sink.

"You could have warned me, idiot-boy!" was all she managed to say.
Her eyes were watering and she drank a half glass of water..

"Why? You never listen, anyway, peg-o-my-heart" I said. "By the way, did you know you can whistle any three notes and I can name the song?"

"Grampers put you through that, too, huh?" She riffled around in the refrigerator and settled on a Dannon yogurt with blueberries at the bottom.

"It's better when they pre-mix the fruit," she complained. "Don't you buy anything right?"

She took a bite and spat that out as well.

"Don't you ever look at the dates on these things?"

"Don't *you?*"

I figured the tears in her eyes didn't have much to do with the hot sauce or the curdled yogurt.

"Come on, Julia," I said. "Everything's going to be alright."

I took her in my arms, and she sobbed against my shoulder. The old Matt Havoc would have figured that was a great time to hustle her off to my bedroom, but too much was happening at once. And I'd been doing some thinking lately. I'd always known actions had consequences, but I was finally realizing I had some feelings for Bad-mouth Julia that went at least a little bit beyond simple lust.

It was complicated; of course I wanted to get involved in all that steamy, hot sex, but I didn't want Young Miss Hotpants to get hurt, and girls who hung around Matt Havoc seemed to be in it for the short haul and *Via con Dios, mister.* She had enough going on in her life right now. There was crazy old Bertrand of Nigeria, lying in an expensive ocean-facing room at Hoag Hospital. And, face it, she had fancy Robert the highbrow literary type to take up the passion-slack once she recovered from her current setbacks. She didn't need a wandering troubadour low-budget flick-maker to complicate her life.

Still, the flesh is weak, and I don't really know what would have happened if Peanuts hadn't called from her hilltop condo retreat in Santa Barbara.

"Mattie," she gushed, "I am so overjoyed, overwhelmed, eternally grateful, everlastingly in your service."

"Billy the Horse called you?" I asked, shrugging at Julia across the room.

No sense denying it. Sweet Julia knew instantly, with the special radar that all women are born with, that I was talking to my ex, and our moment together, if that's what it was going to be, was now lost in time beyond recall, as the romance writers like to say.

"Yes, yes, YES!" Joy emoted into the phone. Meg Ryan's over-the-top restaurant sex scene from When Harry Met Sally has gone a long way to ruin intelligent conversation between the sexes, if there ever was any such thing.

"Did Billy say how he got wise to the barnyard project in the first place?"

"No," she said. "But that doesn't matter, now. I'm going to be eternally grateful to you and Vinnie."

She was assuming that Vinnie was picking up the tab.

Glib as ever, Hollywood Havoc rolled with the direction. "BR Pix takes care of its own," I said. "You know Vinnie would never let you down, Madge." Hell, I figured, let him have the glory. *Better than some crack-headed scammer from the Dark Continent defiling America's Favorite Set.*

By the time I clicked off and tossed the phone on the kitchen table, Julia had composed herself.

"I'd better be getting back to the hospital," she said.

"If you'd like, you can tag along with me, my little waif," I offered, "I have to go see a man about a dog…and a pig and a goat."

"Does it have anything to do with Grandpa?"

"In a strange way, it does."

I never in a million years thought she'd say yes, but a few minutes later I found her sitting on the passenger seat at my side. We puttered North in my battered and dusty Rover, heading once again toward the false glitter and dusty broken promises of Tinseltown. I figured we could get to the Horny Hiatt Agency at about 3 p.m., just about the time the great man got back from his lengthy lunch which, if the rumors were true, included a few martinis and a full body massage at the Purple Princess Palace, a wonky little storefront on La Cienega Boulevard.

Traffic on the 405 was heavy passing LAX, and the 10 intersection wasn't much better. Sweet Julia seemed sunken in her thoughts, and talk radio wasn't offering much. We got off at Sunset and headed east past the Bel Air gates, ultra-posh Holmby Hills and the UCLA campus, but it was closer to 4 by the time we arrived at the 9100 Sunset building. Eastbound traffic was crawling all the way from the Beverly Hills Hotel, and we didn't find out why until we arrived at our destination. The underground parking garage to 9100 was closed and I had to park illegally on a nearby side street.   Two things were certain; I would get a parking ticket and Vinnie's slush fund would pay it.

A third thing was even more for sure—there was a dead body under the tarp on the sidewalk in front of 9100 Sunset. I had a quick, queer, crawly sensation and the suspicion it was the guy I'd come to see—as Keg told the river pirate before he revealed his cleverly concealed trunk of priceless, glittering rubies, *No coincidences, my dear fellow.* My best guess was, Horny had taken an unfortunate winger out of the 23rd floor, the floor where his office was located, and wouldn't be answering any questions today.

"Who is he?" I asked the nearest cop. Best to play dumb in moments like this.

"Don't know yet," he grunted. "Didn't have any I.D. You better move along, pal."

But I knew better than he did. That was Horny's unique blimp shape under the tarp, and those were his smashed owl-thick horn-rim glasses lying on the cement beside him.

"Who is it?" Julia asked.

"Joy's agent."

"But…"

"Come on, sugar-buns." I hustled her inside the building and walked across the shiny pink granite lobby.

The elevators were running, and no one stopped us so we went up to Horny's office. The door wasn't locked and the police hadn't been there so I used a Kleenex tissue from the bathroom down the hall and let us in.

"Don't touch anything," I warned Julia.

She rolled her eyes. "I do watch television, idiot-boy."

Horny's offices were low-rent, with no big plate glass windows. There was just a deserted reception room and his main office. It featured the usual claustrophobic dark wood paneled walls crammed with pictures of Horny hugging, shaking hands, smiling broadly, and generally palling around with three generations of Tinsel town celebrities. By contrast, his desk was neat and clean. His notepad, open to the day's date, said only SU, $5 mil. If I read the tea leaves correctly, Shamseen really got around. And all this just to pressure me into pressuring crazy old Bertrand into handing over a truck the old fart had presumably stolen from a Nigerian scam artist. It didn't add up.

We backed carefully out of Horny's office and retreated down the elevator without any problems. The Channel 7 Eyewitness News helicopter was clattering overhead, several news crews were jostling with the police for sidewalk space, and Horny's demise was largely ignored for the moment, put aside by the arrival of his superstar client, the distraught Joy Benefeté who had heard of his untimely leap while driving back from Santa Barbara to her Beverly Hills pad.

I thought Julia and I might disappear through the gathering crush of onlookers, but it wasn't my lucky day. Peanuts was facing my way and rushed over to clutch my arm.

"Matthew, Matthew! What a tragedy! What a horrible thing to happen!" The video camera lights swung around to light the scene, already in shadows as the sun set behind the hills of Beverly Hills. I knew enough to stay out of the direct line between her and the cameras.

You could hear the rustle through the news crews as the lenses poked their black circles in our direction. *Matthew? Matthew who?*

Peanuts sucked up publicity like a hungry black hole. Her voice rose another octave and she waxed eloquently, "Why now, Matthew? Why now, just as we are about to enjoy the crowning achievement of his, of our careers—his greatest client receiving the greatest filmic award, that is, greatest next to the Oscar, that an actress can achieve!"

That Peanuts, already working on her Oscar nomination! I was witnessing true Tinsel town grit. Horny would have been proud. Before I could begin to frame an appropriate and totally unnecessary reply (she didn't need anything from me and my bit part would end up on the newsroom floor, anyway), the male lead from Intimate Remembrances leapt out of a red Ferrari convertible to be at her side.

Gaudy and show biz it was, but that was the sort of distraction I'd been hoping for. Peanuts dropped me like the cold fish I was in her life, and I managed to grab Julia's hand and pull her away through the crowd.

By the time I picked up my Rover and my parking ticket and we retreated west on Sunset back to the freeway it was already after five, and it was close to eight before we got back to Hoag Hospital. I don't think Julia said two words to me all the way. At the hospital, Bertrand was on an even keel, except that now he was drooling. The nurse told us that was a good sign, without bothering to explain how that could be.

I drove Julia back Sea Garden Cove to gather up her Thunderbird. She stood there, arms on her hips, as I lingered on the curb, fussing through several day's worth of junk mail.

"Sooo, idiot-boy...you drive me on a totally useless trip to see your ex-wife's agent who turns out to be dead and now you're just going to leave me?" she said.

"Julia, why are you always so miffed at me? What did I ever do to you?"

"Too much and too little," she said. "Matthew, I haven't eaten all day."

"Come on, babes, you gobbled my yogurt just a few hours ago. My favorite, too. Blueberries on the bottom."

I could see by the set of her jaw and the tap of her foot that I wasn't going to get off so easily.

"What is it, really, poopsie?" I asked. I loved it. *Poopsie.* I don't know where I come up with these things on the spur of the moment, but I guess that's just show business.

"What it is, really," she said through clenched teeth, "is that you treat me like a baby—or worse, like a stupid, ignorant kid sister."

"My God, woman! What are you blathering about now?!"
I had to admit, sometimes she drove me crazy.

"For one thing, grandpa is in a lot of trouble and you know a lot more about it than you're saying!"

"Julia, I hardly know any more than you do," I said.

She came close and poked a finger in my chest. God, I wish people would quit doing that. "No, idiot-person. You know more. But you just don't trust me. You don't trust any woman since that—that Peanut ruined you forever!"

I could feel the heat in my face and knew I was getting red. "Nobody ruined me! I'm a grown man!"

"Oh, great! You ruined yourself!"

"Nobody got ruined! I wasn't ruined! I'm not ruined!"

"How do you know? Ruined people never know they are ruined! That's why they are so—so useless!"

"Not only ruined, but now I'm useless! I've got no use for this!"

I caught myself, shook my head and took a deep Zen breath the way Horace Keg always did to collect himself. *Air's cheap*, he always said. *Take in a little, while you still can.*

"Julia, we're standing out here in public shouting at each other at the top of our lungs!"

"So what?! What are you afraid of, Ruined Boy!?"

"The neighbors will call the police." I sighed, "Come on in, sweet-cakes, I'll cook you dinner."

"What took you so long?" she asked, brushing past me and marching towards my front door. "If I was your precious Peanut, you'd already have her blouse off, and probably that push-up bra, too."

"Joy doesn't wear a push-up bra."

"Well then she's had a boob job—those twin peaks of hers are stiff as bricks. America's favorite set, my ass..."

I shook my head, silently following her in through the front door. With Julia steaming like a volcano, there was no way I was going to defend another woman's shape, size or surgical implants, even if she was my ex.

Julia marched into my study and plopped herself in the Harvey Miller chair in front of my computer.

"So?" she said with a wicked grin. "When do we eat, Ruined-boy?"

I guess it was better than no smile at all. I had one of those gourmet cheese baskets left over from the Chop of Death wrap party, and four opened half-bottles of red from Vinnie's cellar which actually was a short tunnel some wealthy idiot had dug into the Bel Air hillside behind the big Tudor style house before Vinnie bought it.

By the time I came back with a glass of wine and a plate of cheese wedges, Julia was reading my novel manuscript.

"Why don't you go on the internet," I suggested.

"Matt, I don't want to have to get pissed at you all over again. Go cook dinner."

I still had some jumbo shrimp and a few lobster tails I'd bought from Trader Joe's for last New Year's dinner when I'd had my plans changed and ended up going out with a gang from Vinnie's not-very-exclusive inner circle. I made a garlic butter sauce, adding three tablespoons of lemon juice and one of teriyaki sauce. While that was simmering, I chopped the tails into inch squares and de-veined the shrimp. I threw some Huxtable's mashed potatoes in the oven. They were pre-made, but they would have to do. I found some Brussels sprouts and put them on to boil and cracked open a can of Pillsbury Grand biscuits and popped them in the oven, just like the Doughboy instructs.

When I refilled Julia's glass, she didn't say anything, which I took for a big improvement. I went back to the kitchen and set my small table. I bypassed the obvious convenience of paper plates and even lit a fat candle I'd ignored for several years. It said *Waxing it,* on the side, a one-liner for our dog surfing movie of the same name.

The food seemed to mellow Julia out, and of course there was the wine.

"Now, the secrets," she said, talking with a mouth full of shrimp and lobster. "This is delicious, Matt. No, really. Go, Ruined-boy. Secrets, secrets." She waved her fork in my face.

I figured, What the hell. Julia was a smart person and considerably tougher than when I'd known her as a little girl. Maybe she could think of something I'd missed. Two heads were better than one and all that Horace Keg wisdom. My head was spinning from the verbal battering and maybe the wine. She looked pretty in the candlelight. *Concentrate, Matthew Havoc, concentrate.* I started at the beginning and narrated my adventures right from discovering Bertrand's front door broken in and being thrown in the salty brine through Billy the Horse, and finished with Horny Hiatt's long step into eternity. About all I left out was the $5 million, the rest of which I was hoping I might hold onto for emergencies or old age, whichever came first.

"And this is all about a truck named Big Boy?" she said incredulously.

"Fat Boy, sweet cheeks," I corrected her. "Big Boy's a hamburger."

"So he is," she nodded in agreement.

By this time, we'd worked our way through all four half-bottles of red, and were busy with brandy snifters and a box of Sea's chocolates, walnuts double-dipped in dark chocolate. The mood had lightened and love, I fervently hoped, was in the air. Her blue eyes were mysterious and full of promise, and any possible dangers from the outside world of scamps and knaves had retreated to the furthest corners of the room.

We left the table with the vague mutual intention of meeting in the bedroom. I remember she took a brief detour to powder her nose, and I woke to brilliant sunlight with the shrill telephone driving spikes through my temples. I was lying in bed next to Julia and sometimes life just wasn't fair.

"Get the phone, Robert," she muttered, turning away from me and putting the pillow over her head without realizing what she'd said. Now there's a stunning mood shifter for you.

I remembered dumbly that the mute feature on my phone reverted to ring after 100 calls. I looked at the readout and yes, we were at 101. The scam artists must have had a busy night, burning the lines between here and

Nigeria. I wondered how many of the calls were from my friend Shamseen. I picked up the phone but it wasn't any of the Nigerians, it was the hospital. Bertrand had come around and was demanding to know why his loved ones weren't there at his side.

I shook Julia awake and retreated from the room before she could do me any physical or mental damage. I went to the kitchen and stuck my head under the cold tap water. There was yesterday's coffee in the warmer, so I slopped in half again of milk and zapped a cup for Julia and another for myself. My head ached, my mouth felt stuffed with cotton and about the only positive I could find about the entire night's misadventures was that I could still truthfully tell Bertrand I hadn't gotten to first base with his granddaughter. Well, technically, second base.

Chapter 17

When we walked into his room, Bertrand looked like he should be keeping his heavy wrapping of facial bandages on for another three or four weeks. But, from the angry and disgusted look the nurse gave me when I entered, I realized he'd probably given his case personal attention and taken them off, himself. On seeing us, he allowed a few seconds for Julia's tearful hugs and kisses before fixing me with his baleful stare.

"Where's the General?," he asked.

"In heaven, Bertrand. Or hell. One way or another, he's left this earthly realm, as the ministers say in those stories about truth and redemption."

"Why…?" he replied, giving me a wide-eyed stare.

"Your loving granddaughter and I thought maybe you'd tell us before you get us all killed."

"I don't know," he said, wincing as he threw his bruised arms wide.

"You better know something, Bertrand," I warned, "or we're all going to be dead."

"That's ridiculous, Matt," he scoffed. "These people are scamming artisans, not killers."

"That's why the General's dead and you're in here with all these cuts, bruises and broken bones, right?"

He blew out a deep breath and gave me a long, silent look. I could see he was mulling over his options.

"Old Grampers is collecting his wits," I said to Julia. "Get ready for the next big whopper."

"I know what I'm doing," he said petulantly.

"Tell us more," I urged. "Give us the faintest clue about what's going on."

"The General and I had a deal to shift some money from Nigeria into U.S. accounts," he said in a low voice.

"Forget the General," I said. "Patrice Ugballa had a heart attack. I suspect it was drug induced."

"Why?" he wailed.

"Stop asking me stupid questions. I think you know why," I replied. "I suspect it was because he was getting in the way of a deal you were in with Shamseen Usudman."

"Ridiculous," he scoffed, but his face clouded like he'd sniffed a skunk.

"Tell us about it," I said. "The deal."

He glanced from Julia to me and back again.

"Don't worry," she said, "You couldn't possibly look any more foolish to me than you do right now."

"Very well," he replied stiffly. "But I did not get taken for a big score."

"Go ahead," I said.

"It was an oil deal," he answered reluctantly. "I contracted with some friends of mine who lease cargo ships and tankers."

"You contracted with them?" Julia asked, the alarm creeping into her voice.

"Well, they actually took the risk…most of it, anyhow. It went sour. They're not really my friends any more."

"What happened?" I asked.

"Well, the Olaga Supreme showed up off the coast at Long Beach."

"Empty, I'll bet," I said.

"No, but there was no oil, either."

"What, then?"

"That goddamn tanker came half way around the world carrying a worthless cargo of common seawater."

It seemed like there had to be more to the story. I could see why Bertrand would be reluctant to admit to falling prey to a primitive oil scam, but I was sure there was something he wasn't telling us.

"Okay," I said, trying to follow the trail of logic and mull it through the way my hero Horace Keg would, "so a load of water shows up instead of oil and your friends are out a bundle—"

"And I had to pay $50,000 in fees," he scowled.

"Okay," I continued, trying not to let his genuine ire distract me. "So Shamseen double-crossed you and you ended up with a boatload of water…and then you stole something of his, didn't you?"

Bertrand clamped his jaw shut, glaring at me. "Too damn smart for your own good, that's what you are, Matthew Havoc. Just like your old man."

I thought I'd take a wild shot in the dark, "Since you can't carry a truck in the hold of an oil tanker, I'm guessing they had it lashed to the deck. Am I right?"

Bertrand looked like I'd stung him in the butt with a hot poker.

"Where is it?" I continued. "Where is the cement truck called Fat Boy?"

"It's just business. For God's sake, I can get nearly $70,000 for that truck, Matthew, it's brand new, never been driven more than a few miles. That represents my stake in the venture, plus a decent profit."

"Well, they want it back, and they're willing to do almost anything to get it."

"I doubt that. It's just a lousy truck."

"I'll give you a hundred thou for it, no questions asked."

"You're not in our league. You don't have a hundred thousand dollars, Matthew Havoc. Don't even try."

Julia waved around the room, "Look at yourself, grandpa! It's not worth getting killed over!"

"Calm your sweetie-pie princess down, boy," he said.

"I'm not his sweetie-pie princess!" Julia shouted. "Why do both keep calling me ridiculous names like that!?"

"Glad to hear it," he said gently, patting her wrist. The look he gave me said I may be good enough to answer his fax machine, but I was still a no-good show biz runt, certainly not acceptable as a real member of the family.

"Where is the truck now, Bertrand?" I asked.

"Like I would tell you," he scoffed. "I'm going to sell it to the highest bidder."

"How much do you want?"

"You haven't got that kind of money…"

I unfolded another of Vinnie's checks from my wallet.

"Forget it," he said. "Ugballa told me your last check bounced."

"This one won't."

He shook his head. I could tell I wasn't going to change his mind. He pinched his lips in a thin line and stared out the window. Time was wasting. I had to find a cement truck somewhere in Southern California before the mysterious Shamseen Usudman decided to take the matter into his own hands.

Julia drove me back to Sea Garden Cove. On the way we tried to figure out what our next move might be.

"You worked for Old Grampers part-time when you were a kid, didn't you?" I asked.

"Sure, in high school. I was his little messenger girl."

"Well, you must know something about importing things…" She didn't deny it, so I continued. "Wouldn't there be some sort of a paper trail? I mean, you can't just bring a truck into the country, can you?"

Her eyes went wide as she thought about it, "Maybe that's what Ugballa's thugs were looking for, some clues about that truck."

It took us most of the rest of the day, but we finally found the shipping papers in Bertrand's garage, in the thin black brief case I'd taken from the green Mercedes in Bel Air before I pushed it off the hill.

There were some details, but I wasn't sure we had anything important. Mack built the elusive Fat Boy. It was a new model called The Granite that had been shipped over to Saudi Arabia and somehow ended up on an oil tanker out of Nigeria. There was no way of knowing how it had come to be there, but we had the shipping papers that brought it into the U.S.

Julia decided to tag along with me and we went next door to my place. She hung out while I faxed the papers we'd found to Halliburton Rooks, just to keep him in the loop. Then she called the hospital and Bertrand was enough of his familiar crusty self to assure her he wouldn't be needing her services until tomorrow.

It was getting on towards evening, so I called the California Pizza Kitchen. Julia ordered the barbequed chicken and I had the six-cheese, though frankly, I've never been able to distinguish any more than two or three of the cheeses. We had red wine and pizza in my study. I sipped at a 1997 California Medoc while Julia went back to reading my novel manuscript. Amberhill, from Raymond Vineyards, reduced from 11.99 to 10.99, *valu priced* at Vons. I can't say whether it was a great California red or merely a good one, or even if it was better than Gallo Hearty Burgundy, the swill of choice at Berger Royal wrap parties. But I liked the name, there's this great golden hill of amber somewhere, pleasure beyond anything known to man.

"It bugs me," I said to Julia, "that you ignore the three screenplays I wrote for Berger Royal Pictures."

"Trash, Matthew Havoc, trash," she said without looking up from the page she was reading.

"Keg's War wasn't trash."

"No. It was derivative crap."

"Jesus, you're harsh. Do you know there are 10,000 screenplays written every year, and only about 300 of them become movies?"

She eyed me over the rim of her wineglass, "And how many of them are crap? About 290."

"It's a business, my sweetie-pie princess."

"Right. The crap business. This, on the other hand," she said, waving the page from my loose manuscript, "may even be literature." She gave me a wicked grin, "From whence did you copy it?"

"Real people don't use words like 'whence' any more, and I wrote it myself," I said with more heat than I actually intended. The silence that followed was awkward, so I kept on talking. "The nights were long after Peanuts ran off with Horny Hyatt and her Italian frog-prince."

I had written one long howl against the inhuman war men and women seemed to engage in. It wasn't pretty and it had a sad ending, but I guess you could call it a modern romance where cruel life wins but at least the hero and his woman leave their footprints in the sand before the next wave comes crashing in. I figured if anybody ever published it, Loose Days in La La Land would sell about three copies, all to compulsive readers or literary masochists. Since Julia was already reading it, all I had to find was another two.

"I'd like to give it to Robert," she said.

"Robert!?" I howled. "That manicured ballet dancer!? Never!"

"Don't be silly. Robert is a literary agent," she said.

"An oxymoron if I ever heard one..." I grumbled.

"He is, Matthew," she insisted. "And I think he could sell this."

"I thought he was your boss," I mumbled. "Anyway, I don't like him."

"Why not?" she asked, coming over and sitting on the love seat next to me.

"You know." I glared at her.

"Robert and I are just friends, Matthew."

"It didn't look like that the last time you were over here."

"I think you're jealous."

"Am not."

"You think your sweetie-pie princess was kissy-face with Robbie."

"Damn it, Julia—"

She leaned over and kissed me on the lips.

"Robbie and I tried it for a month and it didn't work," she said. "I mean, it was awkward, it was silly, it was a dismal failure and we were both terribly embarrassed. Has that ever happened to you?" Her grin widened, "No, I see it hasn't. 'Hi, I'm Matt Havoc; love is about humping, and I can love anybody, any time, any where. Let's go hump. We could use the damp beach, or that rock over there. You on the bottom, of course.' What, cat got your tongue, Ruined-boy?"

That was the thing about Julia. One moment she had that wicked mouth of hers going, and the next she was the sweet little girl next door I'd known practically forever. At least I'd progressed from idiot-boy to Ruined-boy. She leaned close to me and put her cheek on my arm.

"You willing to risk it, Mr. Big Time Hollywood Romance?"

"Risk what?" I croaked, starting to feel excited and plenty worried at the same time.

"To risk it with me, you sho-biz idiot.

"W-well, I—"

"We have half a lifetime invested in each other, sort of. If it came down to it right now, do you think you could possibly live up to the legend of Mr. Hotpants Hollywood Havoc?" She said it like I was being intro-ed on the old Johnny Carson show.

There it was, the dare to be great. Impossible as it seemed, after all the dumb stunts I'd pulled, Julia was going to give me a shot. I felt light-hearted, like I was swimming, no, *flying in air.* If I was sure of anything in my life it was that this was the real thing, the one true thing that, if I passed it up, I would regret for the rest of my life.

"I don't know," I said, taking her hand and presenting her with a gentlemanly kiss (Not unlike Keg had done to his lady's soft hand in that brief interlude when they were floating down the Mekong on the stolen pirate's boat. It may have been derivative crap, but it was *effective*.). In for a dime, in for a dollar, I thought as I continued, "But I certainly would like the opportunity to improve upon the legend."

She was close and we were looking into each others eyes and, if there were scary problems in our lives, they had backed off for the moment, and I was thinking that was the wonderful thing about love, it could make the world go round if you just accepted what was offered and did your best to loop along in the same orbit.

"You've dreamed of me from the depths of your ruined-ness?" she whispered.

"Yes, I have, my sweetie-pie princess. More than you'll ever know."

"And you're not afraid?"

"Only that this is a dream."

I stood up and turned off the computer, the fax and the beam beeper on Bertrand's front door. I figured I might as well call it a night. Rooks wasn't going to get back to me right away, and there were only 42 messages on the answering machine, so we had nearly 60 to go before the override kicked in.

I'd been looking for something extraordinary in my life. And now finally, after all my wrong moves, including the foolish leap with Peanuts, I believed I was back on the right track, back where I belonged.

Unbelievably, Julia brought the pages she'd been reading to bed with us. There I was, thinking heavenly thoughts and she still had her nose buried in Loose Days In La La Land. I turned on Extra! Extra! and tried to practice Far Eastern meditation. I'm here to tell you there are certain moments in life when all those monkish lessons in oriental self-discipline don't work very well.

"That must be a hell of a writer," I said, a glum attempt at humor.

"Oh, yes," she said, grinning at me over the rim of the page. "Very stimulating."

"I've got something else that's stimulating."

"Let's see it," she grinned, lifting the bed sheet. "Oh my, yes, that is a truly large and splendid development. I seem to be losing my concentration entirely. I I don't think I can finish this chapter right now.." She carefully placed the pages Of my manuscript on the bedside table and reached for the light switch, hesitating before turning it out.

"I don't know…are you sure it operates in the dark?" she asked.

"Yes, it glows in the dark, actually."

"Glows! This I've got to see!" Her merry laughter sounded in the room as she turned out the light.

And in point of fact, the object of attraction may or may not have actually lit up the warm and comfortable nest under the sheets, but there can be no denying that we both glowed, over and over and over again.

Chapter 18

The gentle rheostat of the dawn dialed up soft light from the hills to the East out over the shore of the Pacific and that light spilled in my kitchen window. Bertrand had a view of an inlet bay, but from my window all I could see was that Sea Garden Cove was shrouded in a blanket of the ocean's foggy finest. Julia was still sleeping so I left her side for the pounding embrace of my Ondine shower system. After that, feeling refreshed and somehow ten years younger, I laced a hot milk with coffee and wandered into my study.

Rooks had been trying to contact me. I clicked on the black box and went to my room, typing GOOD MORNING. HAVOC HERE.

GOOD NOON, his reply spilled across my screen in big block letters. WHAT WAS THE TRUCK CARRYING?

What was the truck carrying? Why would Rooks, on the East Coast, be interested in that?

DON'T KNOW. HAVEN'T SEEN TRUCK. IT'S A CEMENT TRUCK.

CEMENT, MAYBE? WHY DO YOU
ASK?
Again, Rooks lightning typing filled the screen.

COMPARED BERTRAND'S SHIPPING
PAPERS TO MANUFACTURER'S
SPEC SHEETS. FAT BOY IS 10,000
POUNDS OVERWEIGHT. HAVE
ALERTED VARIOUS DIGNITARIES.
WATCH YOUR BACK.

I couldn't help but wonder who the
dignitaries were. Rooks moved in a world of
heavy hitters, quiet amorality, swift deeds and
secrets left untold. My father had known that
world, but the little I myself knew was just
enough to send the alarm bells ringing in
remote corners of my memory.

WHAT DO YOU SUSPECT? I typed.

CAN'T SAY. WATCH YOUR BACK.
ROOKS OFF IN THE EAST.

I hesitated for a moment, then reluctantly typed
the familiar goodbye,

HAVOC OFF IN THE WEST.

I sat in my Harvey Miller chair,
appropriated from the props we'd used on Klish
Clash, staring at the blank computer screen.
What was Fat Boy carrying? The first thing
that came to mind was gold. I clicked the
computer through the math; At current prices,
10,000 pounds of gold would be worth millions.

. But how would you hide it? You couldn't fabricate sheets of gold to replace any metal parts; gold was soft and wouldn't bear any stress without bending.

I tried to put myself in a scam artist's fancy Italian shoes; I had value I wanted to get out of Africa. I could invest in gold, and maybe melt it and pour it in the hollow cement container while it was rotating. It could dry as a thick coating on the inside of the container! Then, after it cooled off and dried, I might just spray it with gray paint, and who could tell the difference?!

I guessed that would work—if it was gold. But that was a lot of metal. I imagined the process, a forge somewhere melting a big pot or big pots of gold, stifling heat, acrid fumes, powerful black men with their shirts off sweating in the inferno, carting the molten gold in heavy crucibles, spilling it into the open mouth of the rotating cement truck. It seemed improbable. For one thing, that process would take a big crew, and you couldn't count on all those men to keep their mouths shut. Rumors would have leaked out about the cement truck with the golden heart.

But then...it didn't have to be gold. It could be platinum, or maybe diamonds or other precious stones. I had read stories in the papers about terrorist groups funding their activities with diamonds and other precious gems smuggled out of South African countries. Purple tanzanite came to mind. Nigeria was a little north, and they weren't known for diamonds, but still...You could even hide bags of precious stones in the gas tank, or maybe weld them to the underside of the frame. But if it was diamonds, they would be too light, even if they were only rough-cut. A few bags of semi-cut diamonds wouldn't weigh more than a couple hundred pounds and certainly not a ton... unless maybe the stones were welded inside very heavy metal containers. But I had read somewhere that diamonds were brittle, and worse, it seemed like a complicated way to do a simple thing. For instance, you could tie a big canvas bag of diamonds on a fishing line and submerge it in the hold of the Olaga Supreme, the same oil tanker that carried Fat Boy over to the states.

I gave up on diamonds; it seemed they would have a better way if they were actually smuggling precious gems. Like Horace Keg said when facing a river that branched off four ways, *The messy guess is never best.*

After a moment I brought up Netscape Navigator and went to Yahoo Search. You may laugh, but when I've got writer's block or am just in need of an idea, I'll go to a search engine and putter around. The computer has a different way of thinking; it's like presenting your problems to a sentient alien, a life force that can strip away the rubbish and leave you with the good stuff. In reality, the good stuff often turned out to be more pure gibberish, but it was an old habit and I did it anyway.

When the Yahoo page came up, I typed in FAT BOY and hit search. Incredibly, there were 598,000 references, many linked to the model Harley-Davidson motorbike of the same name. But as I scrolled down through the bike shops I started to see other connections. Fat

Boy's Bar-B-Q in Titusville, Florida, had a dining room overlooking the space shuttle site. Fat Boy's Early Iron Glass in Visalia, California, provided glass for antique American made motor vehicles. There was a Fat Boy's Beauty Salon, also in Florida. An organization called Fat Boys International claimed dedication to the pleasures of beer swilling and gorging. The Fat Boy Climbing Club advised web visitors to *"Aim Low and Overachieve!"* There was a Fat Boy Web Design and a Fat Boy Scuba, and somebody named Fat Boy Slim, whose real name was either Norman or Quentin Cook.

Because the computer will come up with cross-references picking the words FAT and BOY from different parts of any site, after a few pages the entries began to stray. There was a site for Fat Lace, the magazine for ageing b-boys (web under construction). Little Miss Muffin, a Chicago based wholesale bakery, specialized in reduced FAT muffins and donuts at Http://www.donutboy.com.

Urban Legends (snopes.com) discussed the validity of the rumor that Harley-Davidson's Fat Boy motorcycle was designed to represent the dropping of atomic bombs on Japan. That was a crazy reference, and I'd actually clicked on past when something stopped me in my tracks. I took a second look, and it said that the name Fat Boy was supposedly created from a combination of the nicknames Fat Man and Little Boy, the designations given the two atomic bombs dropped on Japan. According to the site, the naming of Fat Boy was symbolic revenge on the Japanese motorcycle companies who had eroded the sales of American made motorbikes during the 1970s and 1980s. It wasn't true, Snopes.com advised. Just another urban legend laid to rest.

An odd and far-out connection, I know, but it was enough to make rusty tumblers begin to move in the remote corners of my brain. There was a movie produced sometime in the 1980s starring Paul Newman...
I went back to the Yahoo main page and typed in the words FAT MAN & LITTLE BOY. And that is how I got to the website with the pages about the Birth of the Atomic Bomb Gallery located at the American Airpower Heritage Museum website. The museum itself was in Midland, Texas. They featured life-sized models of both Fat Man and Little Boy. I didn't figure on going there, but I didn't have to; the website had pictures of the bombs.

Fat Man gave me the shivers, I guess because it was painted bright yellow and actually had a shape that reminded me of the round fat barrel that made up the cement container on the back of a cement truck. The original Fat Man was 12 feet long and weighed 10,000 pounds.

I wasn't sure which amazed me more, the amount of detailed information available on the atomic bomb to anyone who wanted to look at it, or how simple they actually were. I felt oddly out of place, like a man having an out-of-body experience. I could hear Julia singing an old Harry Bellefonte love song from the shower. I could go put the coffee on, start a latte and maybe all this would vanish like a bad dream. But I knew it wouldn't. I scrolled down, reading about bombs that could vaporize entire cities.

Little Boy was a conventional looking bomb, shaped like you would expect, a long metal cylinder with a blunt nose on one end and fins on the other. It fit this classic bomb shape well because of the way it worked internally. A chunk of uranium of a sub-critical mass at one end was fired the interior length of the bomb to add itself to a larger chunk on the other end. By themselves, each chunk was sub-critical, but when combined, they started the fission chain reaction and the bomb exploded.

Fat Man was different in a scary way; the device itself was a plutonium bomb rather than uranium. It had small charges arranged like spokes around the hub of a wheel. These charges, when ignited together, applied pressure to the plutonium in the center, imploding or crushing it to attain critical mass. Even though it weighed 5 tons, the only reason it looked like a bomb at all was that it had been encased in an egg-shaped aerodynamic shell and given fins so that it could be reliably dropped from an airplane at high altitude. Five tons, five tons, five tons. How much weight was that?

Now my brain was going a mile a minute. No longer a messy theory, I could see it clearly, I could actually visualize the wheel of an implosion-type bomb built into a space no wider than a few feet at the front end of the rotating cement barrel.

I signed back on the black box, and furiously typed Rooks,

HALLIBURTON, I THINK IT'S A NUCLEAR DEVICE.
But he already knew. His reply spilled onto the screen like acid.

HAVOC, STAY OUT OF IT!!

YOU KNEW BUT YOU DIDN'T TELL ME?!

MATT. PLEASE. NO MORE. WE'LL TAKE IT FROM HERE.

ROOKS, EVERYBODY'S SEEN THIS IN THE MOVIES. GOVERNMENT AGENTS ALWAYS SCREW UP THE BIG BREAK.

IT IS NOT A BIG BREAK. IT IS A THEORY. WE ARE MOVING WITH ALL DISPATCH. LET US DO OUR JOB.

BUT I CAN HELP.

THAT'S WHAT YOUR FATHER SAID. IT DID HIM NO GOOD.

MY FATHER DIED IN A FISHING BOAT ACCIDENT.

There was a slight electronic flinch to the letters. Rooks had cut the connection without signing off, the first time ever.   It didn't matter; my brain was spinning so furiously I was sure I'd explode. In the years I'd known him, Rooks had never even implied there was anything about my father's death that was more than accidental. Was he so upset with me now that he'd revealed something he hadn't intended?

My secure little life, the one that consisted of helping spin Vinnie's filmic tales of sex candy and social violence suddenly seemed far away, replaced with the horror that my neighbor Bertrand had probably unwittingly smuggled an atomic bomb into Los Angeles Harbor. And at the same time, I had reason to suspect there may have been more to my father's death than I knew.

Yes, I think like a Tinseltown writer. I look for angles, dig for motivations, mull over every bit of dialog that comes my way. But Rooks and I had established a pattern of communication over the years. In a moment of overload, he'd acted in a way that I thought was unusual and maybe even suspect. As Horace Keg always muttered under his breath to Bucky, *Trust No one.* I'd seen Rooks in person at my father's funeral, and a few summers after that, but I hadn't seen him for over a decade. I don't know that I would recognize him except for the faded Ektachrome prints of him with Jack Havoc, comrades in arms stationed at Tan Son Nhut airbase, young men waving from a table at a bar with pretty Saigon hostesses at their side.

Julia came into the room, dressed in one of my XXL Keg's War T-shirts.

"Matt, what's wrong? You're face is white as a ghost..."

I don't know if I would have clicked the screen off, but she scanned it before the thought entered my mind.

She stared at me in open-mouthed wonder, "What do we do?"

"We've got to find that truck. Quick. Today. Right now!"

I had to hand it to her, she didn't stop to ask questions, and we were out the door in minutes.

Chapter 19

"You jerk-head! You are going to tell me what this is about, aren't you?" Julia yelled at me as we ran for her Thunderbird. So much for tender relationships, but with the world about to blow up, I didn't think it was time to make a fuss.

"I think Fat Boy has a bomb in it. In fact, I think Fat Boy *is* a bomb. Rooks as much as confirmed it."

Crazy as it sounded, I tried to explain while we made our way down the hill to the front gates, which stood open against the rigidly enforced laws and covenants of Sea Garden Cove. Something I'd seen bothered me, and I was suddenly on my guard. We'd passed a big black Ford Expedition with dark tinted windows going up the hill as we were coming down. And if I needed validation of my worst fears, a red smear and a bullet hole starring the glass in the designer-cute guard shack told me more than I wanted to know about Dim Eddie's end.

I saw in the rear view that the black truck had made a U-turn and was following us out of the complex.

"Be careful, Julia," I warned. "That SUV is following us."

"Huh," she said. "As if they could." She accelerated into the flow of cars and started weaving her way like a mad woman late for the Macy's 24-hour sale.

Brave words, but the heavy crush on Jamboree wasn't going to let us get away from these goons. We were headed toward the freeway, but the commuter traffic hadn't yet died down and the black Expedition was able to pull along side Julia's T-bird. They crowded in on us, honking their horn and trying to force Julia to pull off the road. I saw it was at least two men, young white guys in suits. The one on the passenger side wound down his window and tried to wave us over.

"Hey, back off!" Julia shouted angrily, holding her ground.

But they didn't, and in another moment they bumped her, grinding fender to fender.

"God damn bug-humping fart lickers!" she shouted.

I would have thought their truck was much heavier and could easily push us over, and it would have, but the owner intended to tap us first, as some sort of a warning that he meant business. That was his mistake. I don't know what I would have done, but Julia didn't waste a second. She turned the steering wheel slightly to the left, ramming into the black truck with far more than a little tap. She jammed the accelerator to the floorboards, but just for a split second. Then she hit the brakes and, as soon as her now-seriously-crumpled yellow fender separated from the black one, she spun the wheel hard to the right and we did an instant, wheel scorching 180 degree spin and started back in the same lane, heading the way we'd come.

For a moment it looked like we were fishtailing out of control. The noise was deafening and the smoke from the tires added to the thinning fog. We must have been a sight, the yellow Thunderbird from hell driving wrong-way down crowded Jamboree Drive with cars scattering out of our way like frightened sparrows.

The Expedition tried the same maneuver, but the opportunity closed in before they could take advantage of it. The truck was far less nimble than our little T-bird, and, as it tried to swing around three or four cars, a white Roto-Rooter van plowed into it, rolling it on its side and bringing it to a steaming halt in the ditch near where Ugballa's two bad boys had rolled down the hill from Bertrand's condo a few days before.

Julia darted her car this way and that, narrowly missing a Mercedes and a BMW convertible before she jumped the center curb with a scraping noise and got us back on the right side of the road.

As soon as I caught my breath, I asked, "Where did you learn to drive like that?"

Julia grinned, "Hey, idiot-boy—what a rush! I bought a Kellogg's Rice Krispies Bar and filled out the entry form on the back."

"Oh, that explains it!"

"No, it does! I won four days at a driving school in Arizona. Race car driving, tricks and get-aways!"

"Well, you can drive stunt in any movie I ever do!"

"Right. If the world of Oriental Art goes down the toilet, I'll take you up on that." She was thinking about the goons, "Did you see who those people in the black SUV were?"

"I'm not sure…"

"What do you mean, Matthew? You saw them or you didn't."

"I mean, I expected more African dudes. These guys were clean-cut college graduates, looked like they should have been maybe working for National Car Rental."

Julia swerved sharply across four lanes and made a left turn, and then sped another a few blocks and we were headed for the freeway.

"My poor baby." She was talking about her Thunderbird. "You better have good insurance."

"Vinnie will cover it. I'll say we were out location scouting."

We shot onto the freeway and exceeded the speed limit the entire way to the Harbor Freeway. I got out Bertrand's shipping papers and a Thomas Guide and directed Julia to the Evergreen Shipping Company.

Evergreen was a huge series of blank warehouses, any of which could have held a hundred cement trucks. Dozens of clerks milled about, hovering over computers and tracking merchandise. We waited in the customer line until it was our turn.

The Customer Service Rep was bald and overweight. "Huh," he said, "must be some hot truck."

"What are you talking about?"

"I remember it. I've got a good memory for detail. You're the third party's been in here today, inquiring after the same damn cement truck. Hard copy paperwork's still in the bin." He lifted a clipped folder from a wire basket on a ledge that ran behind the row of clerk desks.

"Well, do you still have the truck?"

"Nope. Signed for last week by somebody else. Driven away three or four days ago."

Julia pushed closer to the desk, leaning over so only a blind man could see she wasn't wearing a bra under her T-shirt. She had exchanged the oversized Keg's War shirt for a skimpy California Climax number and was wearing it to great effect. She pouted, "You said two other parties were here. Can you describe them to us?"

The bald man blinked twice, collecting his thoughts. "Uhh, yeah," he said. "The last ones were two government employees. Young guys. Arrogant punks."

"How did you know they worked for the government?"

"Because they waved their badges and cut in line. Nobody was happy."

Julia nodded, flashing me a glance, and turned back to the clerk. "You said there were two parties."

The bald man nodded, thinking back, "It was a guy, here when we opened."

"What was he like?" I asked.

"Not much to look at. A small, thin man. Well dressed. Wearing a big gold Rolex." He grinned, remembering, "My first thought was it was a fake, but he carried it off somehow. There was something about him, and I ended up thinking it was a Rolex."

"What about him?"

"I'm not exactly sure. He spoke real good English, too good, almost. A touch of an accent, like maybe some French movie star. And he was quiet...good manners, you know?"

I nodded, encouraging him to say more.

"Well, he was dark complexion, maybe a Greek, a Turk or even an Egyptian. He had a light accent, we get a lot of foreigners in here, but I couldn't really place it."

Another tumbler seemed to click in place in that shabby computer I call my brain. I had the sudden notion he was describing Shamseen Usudman. If the mysterious and threatening voice from Nigeria was actually in the U.S., we would have to be more careful than ever.

"Who signed for the truck?" I asked. "You know, last week when it was picked up?"

He hesitated, "I'm not supposed to show anybody."

"But you did show someone." His face flushed red and he didn't deny it. "You showed the gentleman with the gold watch."

I extracted one of the hundreds that just seemed to fall from my wallet when stealing location shots.

"The folder could just fall open to the right page," I suggested.

"Yeah, it could," he agreed, snatching the green *hundie* and opening the folder with a practiced quick flip of his wrist.

It wasn't Bertrand Burke who signed the receipt for docking fees and import duty, as I would have expected. The name was scribbled in a familiar lazy hand I knew like my own...a looping signature that scrawled out the name Vincent Berger.

Vinnie and Bertrand, the dynamic duo, still out to scam the scam artists of the world. The unknowns compounded themselves, but one thing was clear—with the rash and impulsive king of Berger Royal Pictures making off with a truck named Fat Boy, anything was possible.

I began leafing through the file.

"You can't look through that," the clerk snapped.

"I'm going to drop another hundred over the edge of the desk," I said. "Take your time picking it up."

"You're not going to take my file."

"No, I just need to look through it."

That seemed satisfactory, so I said goodbye to another of Vinnie's production bribes.

It was worth the money. Justifiably upset at having been swindled out of a shipment of oil that turned miraculously into salt water on it's trip from Africa, Bertrand's Uni-Amer Industries had sought legal restitution and had been awarded any and all 'removable goods' that were not part of the vessel itself. Chief among these had been the cement truck that had been lashed to the hull, a small ship-to-shore helicopter, and three or four cargo containers filled with primitive hardwood carvings and bolts of cotton cloth in colorful designs.

"They took the ship's helicopter?" I asked.

The clerk shrugged, "It was quite a commotion around here. That old guy from Uni-Amer would have taken the anchor and the engines if they weren't bolted down."

"How do you know?"

"Everybody here has met Wild Bertrand. He used to come in here all the time and badger us until he got his court order."

"Bertrand went to court?" Julia asked.

"Yep. Actually, he claimed the whole tanker, but it was owned by a third-party shipping company, and they swore they were just a carrier, they didn't guarantee contents. The judge let them sail away. Wooly Old Bertrand was furious."

"So, if somebody wanted to ship a load of salt water, it was their business and completely legal," Julia said.

"Actually, that happens a lot. You don't ride a tanker empty, it would sit too high in the water. So you do oil one way and water the other." The clerk reached to take the folder from my hands.

"Let me invest another hundred for another minute," I said, pushing two fifties off the end of the desk.

While he bent over to retrieve the bills, I pulled a handful of pages from the folder and stuffed them down the back of my pants. I don't know why I did it, we already knew the unlikely partners, Bertrand and Vinnie, had taken the truck

Julia's eyes widened as I lifted the papers, but she didn't say anything. It had barely been a few hours but I believe she was getting used to having a scuff-law for a boyfriend.

By the time the clerk came up from his dive for the money, the folder was closed on his desk and Julia and I were already edging through the crowded room towards the door. "Thank you," I said over my shoulder, fervently hoping the papers I'd filched wouldn't fall out of my pants.

I scanned what I'd stolen as Julia rocketed us back towards Newport. It was her idea to drop me off at my condo and go alone to talk to Bertrand.

"Julia, do you honestly think he'll tell you where it is? He's a greedy old man, but he's also paranoid."

"I've always been his favorite," she said. "He'll tell me, if he knows."

"I don't think we have much time."

I had visions of the panic that news of an atomic bomb set to go off in L.A. would cause. Jammed freeways, end-of-the-world chaos and looting everywhere. It would make the Watts Riots look like kindergarten stuff.

I must have looked impatient as we came to an off ramp and a stop sign. Julia leaned over and kissed me on the nose, "I'm paddling as fast as I can."

The police had come and gone to Sea Cove Garden, and Dim Eddie was just a memory and a red smear on the side of the guardhouse. The gates stood eerily wide open.

I got out of the Thunderbird and watched her drive away, wondering if it was the last time I'd see her. You think about everything differently when faced with a danger so chilling as to be almost unimaginable. I jogged to my front door, believing I would call around to see if anybody in town knew where Vinnie had hidden a giant cement truck, and Julia would be back inside an hour.

That's how I would have written it in Havoc's Horror, a movie about how I saved Los Angeles. But again, the movies aren't anything like real life.

I was reaching out to put the key in the door when it opened from inside. Peanuts was there, her face strained from grief and fright. And there was someone else—a small, well-knit man with olive skin wearing an expensive dark suit and a large gold watch. *Shamseen Usudman, in my house?!* He gave me a little shrug and his eyes moved slightly in a telltale flick. I had a brief moment to realize it there was someone behind me. Of course, it was too late to try any of the moves I'd learned in Dragonfly Madness, as something heavy came crashing down on my head.

Chapter 20

When I woke, I saw I was attached to my own Nolan Miller chair with thick, heavy duct tape. My upper arms were taped to my chest, and my body was in turn taped to the chair.

This left my lower arms and hands free, presumably to find Big Boy on the computer.

"I'm sorry, Mattie," Joy apologized. She was holding the dripping remainder of a jug of cold water she'd poured over my head. "He made me do it."

Shamseen nodded once, a brief acknowledgment. "Introductions are not necessary, I presume?" he said. He had olive skin, dark eyes, a thin, hawk-like nose and a forehead wrinkled from years of concentration.

"Right," I gritted in agreement. "The Butt of Benin, himself. Would you tell your people to stop knocking me on the head?"

"Those others were General Ugballa's men," he said. "And mocking insults are beneath you."

"The General worked for you."

"No. Never. That idiot tried to blackmail me. My own fault; I accept responsibility for the mistake. Never send an officer to do an assassin's job."

"Blackmail you? How?"

"He claimed he would drive Fat Boy somewhere out on the desert, where it would do little harm...unless I paid him some hundreds of millions of dollars."

I could see Joy's famous oval mouth forming the silent words, "...hundreds of millions..." I wasn't surprised she didn't follow the logic past the money to the present danger. Peanuts thought of everything in terms of herself and her career. She was thinking a person could make a lot of pictures for a hundred million.

"Yes, famous sexy lady," Shamseen said, "my little project is worth more than the gross national income of many third world nations."

"What now?" a cold voice behind me asked. I strained my neck to see who had spoken and it turned out to be one of the two men who had tried to run Julia off the road earlier. He was just another clean-cut white guy in a suit, except he was probably a cold-blooded killer, as well.

"Now Mr. Havoc here finds Fat Boy for us," Shamseen said.

"Why not just dump him? We know his boss signed for it, so it's somewhere in L.A."

Shamseen lifted one shoulder and an eyebrow, cocking his head in my direction, "Yes, but where? It's not at Bel Air. It's not at his offices at Raleigh Studios. It wouldn't do if Fat Boy was off somewhere in the Santa

Monica Mountains, Ridley. Our plan is to take out the city, not shave a few mountaintops."

"And what makes you think I'm going to help you and Ridley, here?"

His cell phone rang, and he listened for a moment with no emotion.

"Ah," he said to me. "The answer to your question. We have your pumpkin sweetie pie Julia and Bertrand in our custody."

Peanuts raised one eyebrow when she heard what Shamseen called Julia, and it started me thinking as well. Joy dumped her men, but she never completely let go. But that wasn't what alarmed me. *How did Shamseen know about 'pumpkin sweetie pie'? He must have my place bugged!*

But Shamseen went on as if he'd not been interrupted. " Now it's your choice, *Mister Hollywood Havoc*.. You help us and we let you all live to take your chances with the bomb. Or you resist and we kill you all now...starting with your dear little Peanuts, here."

As if on cue, his young accomplice pulled a Glock from his shoulder holster and pointed it at Joy, who winced and held her eyes tightly shut, just like I remembered she had in a scene from California Climax. But Joy no longer did Berger Royal pictures, and this was no scene from a hits-and-tits movie.

"Wait," I said. "Okay. Give me a chance. I'll find the damn truck."

Shamseen gave me a cold look while his man held a steady bead on Joy's forehead.

"Are you just saying you'll help or do you have a real idea?"

I did have a real idea. But it didn't have anything about it that would help Usudman.

"My first inclination—like yours—would be that Vinnie would park something as big as a cement truck at the studio. You know, hide it in plain sight. But the truth is, he's way too cheap for that. The studios marks everything up 50% automatically, so it's an outrage—"

"Yes, yes, film problems, get on with it, Havoc."

"Well, I'm going to have to make a few calls...and if that doesn't work, activate my computer and do a little fishing around."

"Tell us what you are thinking," Shamseen said, the distrust evident in his voice.

"Off the top of my aching head...there are three or four places around town he might have parked it."

"Where around town?" Ridley cut in.

"Don't be so impatient, Ridley. What, you didn't get to shoot anybody yet today?"

Ridley raised his gun hand to take a swipe at my head, but Shamseen stopped him with a brief shake of his head.

"You're not making any friends, pal." Ridley said.

"You could also say, '*You're not making any pals, friend.*' Work on your dialogue. Less stet that way."

"Where, Havoc?" Shamseen cut in.

I figured it was getting too obvious I was stalling, so I gave him a bit of the flavor of my thinking. "Old Hollywood, below Sunset...West L.A...or one place in the valley."

Shamseen frowned, clearly unhappy with me.

"What specifically are these possibilities?"

"Rentals. One place you can rent a tank, a semi-truck or anything like that. Another place mostly makes up stuff to order…maybe a futuristic all-terrain vehicle or a dune buggy mounted with machineguns. Third place…well, they do mostly big sets, but they do have the space."

"Call them," Shamseen ordered. "I will dial the numbers for you."

I wheeled my chair closer to my desk and managed to activate the phone system by pushing one button on my computer keyboard.

"Voice recognition," I said to Shamseen. "Picture Vehicles Unlimited," I said. The woman on the other end of the line said, "Picture Vehicles Unlimited."

"Hi. Matt Havoc, here. Did Vinnie Berger leave a cement truck with you?

"A *cement truck?!*" She put her hand over the phone but I could hear her muffled voice in the background, saying *cement truck* like it was a bad word. She came back on the line. "He *tried to,* but we didn't have the space." Her voice assumed a tone of arch superiority, "Picture Vehicles Unlimited rents motorcars. We don't store vehicles for others. If Mr. Berger wanted storage, he should have called Bekins or L.A. impound.".

I disconnected and made more calls. Timeless Motor Cars in Sherman Oaks and Rick's Stunt Car Service in Canoga Park had the same response as Picture Vehicles

Unlimited, while Five-Star Military Vehicles said they had no cement trucks, but they could let me have a clean looking dump truck for a reduced rate if that would fit my needs. The last place I could think of, Classic Car suppliers, was really a long shot, but the owner was an old friend of Vinnie's, so I thought it was worth a try.

"Havoc, you dog!" the voice boomed over my speaker. "When are you going to give me some business."

"Clarence! We're going into pre-production in a week or two."

"Yeah? What's the pic?"

"Carnage Days. It has so many crashes you're going to get rich!" You may think it was hard to put on a happy face when I was all tied up, but working for Berger Royal, that's the way I felt most of the time.

"Hooray for me!" Clarence said. "When do we start?"

"Not for a week or so yet. Listen, Clarence, did Vinnie park a cement truck on your lot?"

"Well, he tried to. I had to tell him no. We don't have the space, *kapish*?"

"I understand."
I was about to disconnect, when he volunteered. "I think he took it to the ranch."

"His ranchette?"

"Yeah. He was bitching the thing was murder on wheels, all them gears, eight forward, you know."

"He was driving it himself?"

"How you think Vinnie started in the business, kid?" Clarence answered his own question, "Thirty years ago, driving for me."

As Clarence hung up I swiveled my chair around to face Shamseen, "Vinnie owns 19 acres in the Malibu mountains."

"Where is it?" He seemed agitated, which I took as a good sign. Horace Keg always said *The first step to victory is a fly in the eye of the enemy.*

"Inland a mile or so, off one of the canyon roads." I thought I'd see if I could increase his concern, "It's a natural little bowl surrounded by steep mountains on all sides, lots of oak trees and horses, small ranchettes, the rich getting back to nature."

"You must take us there at once!"

"I've been there once or twice, but we should get a map." I nodded to my computer.

"Alright," he agreed.

Taped as they were to the chair, my hands barely reached the keyboards, but I was able to jump on the internet and used Yahoo to give me Mapquest. I typed in Jamboree Boulevard, Newport Beach as our current address, and Springwater Canyon Lane as our destination.

"I don't know the exact address," I explained. "But I've been there. I can find it."

While that was printing, I managed to brush against the Rooks link, activating the connection.

The screen went blank, and suddenly filled with

ROOKS IN THE EAST.

"What is happening?" Shamseen said. For the first time I detected a note of urgency in his voice.

"Instant message," I said.

"Tell him to ignore it," the young accomplice advised Shamseen.

"What will happen if you ignore it?" Shamseen asked.

I shrugged. "Everybody with instant messenger knows I'm online. That's the way it works."

"And who is this Rooks?"

"Just a pen pal."

"Get rid of him," Shamseen advised. I typed,

NOTHING HAPPENING. GO AWAY.

After a brief pause, the screen again filled with Halliburton Rook's high speed typing.

WELL, YOU COULD HAVE FOOLED ME, PAL.

I looked at Shamseen, and he nodded, "Get rid of him." I typed,

CAN'T TALK NOW. TOO BUSY WITH PRESSING MATTERS. YOU KNOW SHOW BUSINESS.

The reply came

OH WHAT A WEB IT IS WE WEAVE WHEN FIRST WE SET OUT TO DECEIVE.

"What does that mean?" Shamseen cried, standing and pointing his finger at the screen.

"Rooks is a poet," I said. "It doesn't mean anything. Or rather, it means he is accusing me of being a thieving filmmaker, which I am."

I turned the computer off without my customary signoff, knowing Jack Havoc's old partner would be on the next plane heading west.

"Cut me out of here and let's go find Fat Boy," I said, happy to change the subject.

"We don't need him any more," the accomplice said, waving his automatic in the air for emphasis.

"No," Shamseen said. "Not yet. You are too quick with that gun. This man will work for us. Matthew Havoc will do anything for his sweetie pie princess...won't you, Matthew?"

He saw the look of awareness spread over my face. "Yes," he said. "You are not the only one clever enough to bug a telephone."

"Telephone," the accomplice said scornfully, "look at this." And he walked around my study, flipping over books and garbage cans to reveal electronic listening devices.

I may have mentioned I don't get around to housecleaning nearly enough. I was discovering one of the less obvious drawbacks to my slovenly behavior.

I looked at Shamseen and nodded my head in the direction of his young gunman. "What's Ridley's problem?"

"You are my problem," the young gunman replied scornfully, "And the solution is simple!" He waved his gun in my face.

"Lord, who writes your dialogue?" I asked. "Ridley-Didley!"

"One more bad joke, you're dead.".

I grinned at him. "That's what they say at the Comedy Store."

He shook his head, trying to puzzle it out, but he couldn't. It was something straight out of Keg's book: *Always stay buddy-buddy with the guy who plans to kill you.*

Shamseen stood, clearly irritated, "Enough fool's talk. Do you know how to get to this exact place in the Malibu mountains?"

"Yes, I do," I said, smiling as the accomplice reluctantly put his gun away.

Shamseen didn't have a ride. I suspected he'd arrived in the black Ford Explorer that had tried to run Julia's Thunderbird off the road, but I didn't say anything. He got in the passenger seat of the Rover and Ridley climbed in back with America's Favorite Set. I backed my trusty Rover out of the garage and we headed north toward Malibu. I figured I needed about five hours until Rooks arrived with reinforcements.

There was a car fire on the 405 that had things crawling for 45 minutes. Traffic was thickening into the usual afternoon sludge, and we came to a near stop at LAX.
Things weren't getting any better as we approached Westwood, so I took the Santa Monica Freeway west and started the stop-and-go trudge north along the Pacific Coast Highway.

I could see Peanuts in the rear view. She was in the eye-batting first stages of her virtuous-virgin-in-peril routine. Peanuts was tough, and she was a star. She had no intention of ending up on the cutting room floor in the sixth reel of somebody else's movie. I knew at least that I wasn't going to have a gun pointed at the back of my head when I made my move, if I could only figure out a move to make that didn't get us both instantly killed. .

We were driving north along the Pacific Coast Highway. The surf was up, the aqua waves cresting in white foam tops before they crashed into the rocks on our left. The sky was crystal clear blue and there were wind-surfers off Pacific Palisades. It was just another sunny afternoon in Southern California, without a care in the world except for a nuclear device named Fat Boy that Old Bertrand and my boss Vinnie had tucked away, thinking they might net a few grand on the used truck market.

Since Shamseen and his grim accomplice didn't know the area, I breezed through Malibu flats, caught the green light past Las Virgenes Road and kept on going north. We were half way to Santa Barbara when Shamseen, who had been frowning over a map he'd taken from my glove compartment, yelled, "Turn around!"

"What?" I said.

"You are too far north. Here, it is here, back there!" He was pointing the way we'd come.

"I told you, you should have let me pop him!" Ridley yelled, his voice loud in disgust.

"Silence!" Shamseen said, his voice rising to a near shriek. "Turn the car around!"

"Okay," I said, starting to make a U-turn. We were at a picturesque, curving bay near Oxnard where the highway cut along the edge of the surf. As I swung my Rover around in a crisp turn, I leaned over and unsnapped Shamseen's seat belt. And then I hit the gas and let the wheel straighten.

The Rover leapt forward, but as I was only half way through my turn, our path cut directly between several wildly honking cars in the oncoming traffic lane. We hit the gutter on the sea side and jounced heavily, the hood flying up to obstruct my view. I jammed the gas pedal to the floor and the Rover took a clumsy last leap. All desire and very little natural leaping ability, like a snapping turtle possessed to attempt the Olympic long jump, old Rover lunged cleanly off a 20 foot cliff into the waiting arms of the deep blue sea.

At least, we started a clean leap. For a moment, to me all seemed frozen in time, and then gravity took its natural course and the nose tipped and the hood came banging down as the Rover reversed course and went into a short, ugly plunge.

Somewhere in the middle of the madness a gun went off and the bullet missed me, thanks to Peanuts who was struggling frantically with Ridley in the seat behind us.

My trusty Rover's ambitious flying leap came up a few feet short of the water. We landed nose down and hard on a small spit of gravel and then rolled over into chest-high surf. We were upside down, the tide was in, and icy water was everywhere. As to the matter of air bags, my old Rover didn't have any. I don't know what happened to Shamseen, but his accomplice flew past me from the seat behind us. I saw Ridley's head punch through the glass windshield, followed by the upper half of his body. And that was the last I saw of anybody as the compartment went dark with seawater and debris from the interior of the Rover.

Chapter 21

Odd as it may seem, this situation was more familiar to me than to even the most intrepid of movie goers. How many big screen releases have you seen where the hero is trapped underwater in a car, helpless and hopeless as he or she tries to smash the difficult way out of a jammed door or a window that won't break? In this case, however, the advantage was mine. I'd not only had my share of nightmares about this very thing, I'd choreographed two or three similar scenes, including Horace Keg's hellish underwater exit from a Huey 1b helicopter that had gone down in the Mekong.

So, while the compartment of the upside-down Rover filled with water, I floundered around with purpose, looking for Peanuts and coming up to breath in a shrinking pocket of air around the gas pedal. When that was all but gone, I submerged and rolled down the window. It opened easily and at the same time I got lucky, bumping into one of Peanut's gorgeous, albeit limp and lifeless, legs.

The Hollywood Havoc luck held, and I was able to slip through the window, and then pull her out after me. Hugging onto Peanuts, I surfaced with my lungs feeling ready to burst. *Just another underwater adventure, courtesy of the Bight of Benin*, I thought foolishly as I struggled to keep my ex-wife's limp head above water. I half-staggered in through the surf, towing the unconscious Joy after me.

Unfortunately, Shamseen had gotten there before me. He was sitting on one of the tumbled rocks that made up the breakwater under the brow of the highway. He held a gun firmly in his left hand. He pointed it directly at me, and I had no doubt he was a far better marksman than had been General Ugballa's thugs.

He motioned for me to make my way to shore, and as there was less than ten yards separating us and I had to get help for Peanuts, I thought that was as good a plan as any.

"So," he said as my feet caught on the gravel and I limped in to shore, "You prove to be more of a problem than I calculated."

"I lost control," I pushed him out of the way, lifting Peanut's limp form over my shoulder. "Yes, I did lose my way, but I'm not used to all the shouting and gun pointing."

"I'm not going to punish you just yet. I will now put this powerful little handgun in my pocket, with my finger on the trigger. You are going to move ahead of me up this little cliff."

"Right," I agreed, delighted he had decided not to shoot me once. I know he needed me to find Vinnie's place, but if the situation had been reversed I don't think I would have been able to dredge up his restraint.

A crowd was gathering, and all I could think of was getting the water out of Joy's lungs.

"Don't even think it," Shamseen said, misreading my intentions. "I would shoot you without hesitation. Gut-shoot, rub my ass and smear the wound, so you die painfully, slowly, but absolutely."

I had to hand it to him; that was pretty fresh stuff. In my old world at BR Pix, I would have hired him in a flash to help Vinnie *punch up the dialogue.*

By then we had scrambled up to the road elevation, no thanks to Shamseen, who was having trouble hiding his gun in his soaked suit jacket and still keeping it pointed in my general direction.

Two tan surfers gathered Joy from my arms, spread her generous body on the roadside gravel and started artificial respiration. It took a few moments, but there was no way Peanuts was ready for her final curtain call. She gave a few sputters and wheezes, and then sat bolt upright. In no time at all she was getting her hair in place. She had things to do to prepare for her next scene in life, and she certainly couldn't have her fans see her looking like a common, ordinary rescued nobody.

In fifteen hectic minutes, by the time the police arrived, she was in top form and moving toward overdrive. She wrapped herself in a protective blanket of surfers and beach fishermen. She gave me a little shrug, and I lifted one shoulder in return, silently agreeing with her. *No sense all of us getting killed over a silly little misunderstanding.*

The cops made busy-work, taking statements from witnesses who had watched, wide-eyed, as my Rover went over the side. The tow truck came and they began backing it in to get a line on my soggy Rover and winch it from the water. One of the witnesses, a guy running a little mobile hot-dog stand that was parked on a small roadside pullout, said he'd seen everything close up—I'd nearly taken out his business—and once he pointed me out, Shamseen and I found ourselves in the back seat of a squad car, huddled in blankets.

"We'll get around to you guys in a few minutes," one of the cops said with a friendly smile.

Shamseen watched him walk out back to the tow truck.

"There are only four of them," he hissed at me. "I'll kill them all if I have to.

"You don't have to," I assured him. "I'll think of something."

I held back, waiting for my moment. I wasn't sure what kind of moment. I had vague thoughts of holding Shamseen's gun arm and screaming, "*He's got a pistol!*"

But the truth is, the cops were a slow, humorous foursome of beach patrolers, and I couldn't envision them getting their heads turned around in time, much less whipping their guns out before Shamseen turned them into dead meat on the highway. They left us alone while they threw flares, slowed traffic and directed the tow truck, and that's when I got the bright idea to steal the squad car.

I don't know what it is about California cops. You'd think one of the first things they'd teach you in Cop Class 1A is to turn the engine off and take the keys with you. I decided to clear my plan with the man with the gun.

`   "Let's take this car," I said.

"Steal a policeman's vehicle?"

"Technically, we're only borrowing it. And really, Mr. Bight, what other choice is there?"

He remained suspicious, but he said okay.

"It's a good time. Look—they're distracted."

There wouldn't be a better moment. Joy had revealed who she was and all eyes were focused on America's Favorite Set, standing up tall and bra-less with the nipples revealed like delicious little pearls under her wet silk blouse.

"Come on, let's do this," I urged.

Shamseen and I stepped casually out of the back seat and slid into the front seat of the cop car. I put it in drive and we slowly slipped out of the scene. After about a hundred feet, I smoothly accelerated and found myself in the traffic flow, headed back south toward Malibu.

The radio was on, so we heard when they finally realized we'd taken their car. But by that time we were so far down the road there wasn't much they could do about it except radio on ahead. Shamseen couldn't resist the radio. He reached for the speaker and fingered the talk button.

"Do not attempt to follow us. I repeat, do not attempt to follow us. I have a captive, and, with no regret, I will shoot him in the head."

"That's cold, Shamseen," I said. "After all our pleasant banter about the weather in Nigeria."

"I never was in Nigeria when I called you, Matthew."

"I know, Mr. Benin."

"Stop calling me that!!"

My eyes widened. I guessed I'd pushed a no-no button on his psyche.

"Hmmmm, touchy."

"Just drive the automobile."

I figured I had nothing to lose, so I kept on talking.

"You're going to kill me anyway, so I'd like to ask you a few things." He gave me a dark look, but he didn't say anything so I went on talking. "Why did you pick on Batty Old Bertie in the first place?"

"We didn't, Matthew. We came after Jackal 6…your father."

"My father quit being a spy years ago."

"Your father personally destroyed an operation…before you were born."

"What operation?"

"Something in Egypt." He shook his head impatiently, "We don't have the time, nor the patience. The sad reality is, in our business you never retire and your enemies never forget."

"But how did you know it was him?"

"We'd paid off everybody else. But then, years later when we came for him, he was already dead. Somebody got to him first."

"It wasn't a fishing accident...?"

"No." He shook his head once, a silent, lethal missionary of death at my side.

"Who, then...?"

He shrugged, "Your parents were gone, and you were too young to know anything. But you were living next door to a very nosey and greedy man who did import-export for a living. That was an opportunity we couldn't pass by." I was ready with the next of a dozen questions that sprang to mind, but he waved me silent. "Enough. Take me to Fat Boy."

There was no hope that we would be intercepted by another squad car before we reached Las Virgenes Road, so I drove on in silence. We reached Pepperdine College and turned left. Still no police helicopters. I was hoping the Lo-Jac commercials were more than just blather, *So good the police use them on their own squad cars!*

Shamseen gave me an impatient shove.

"How far is it?" he asked.

"Jesus, don't push! I've got to keep the shiny side up."

"How far?" he repeated.

"We're almost there. Another two miles, give or take.". I took a right off Las Virgenes and we were on a small paved road that made its lazy way between ancient oaks, pastures with rustic fences, and low-slung stucco homes with red-orange tile roofs. Vinnie's place was on the far side of a stout little one-way wooden bridge he'd had one of his crews build over a narrow creek that ran in dark thin braids between large boulders.

As we made our own way over the bridge, I felt sure the cement truck was close, because something too large had crossed recently, knocking down the ornamental wooden railings on one side of the bridge.

We were surrounded by the fairly high hills of the Coastal Range, and darkness was settling fast in there under the spreading oaks.

I could see Shamseen was unhappy.

"Unlucky for you, I guess," I said. "I'm sure Vinnie didn't know what he was doing, but he's picked a place where Fat Boy's likely to do very little damage."

"You know what's in that truck?" He gave me a sharp jab in the ribs with his pistol. I was sure that, if we'd already found the truck, he would be pulling the trigger.

"A natural little bowl surrounded by hills. And did you notice the off-shore breeze?"

"Meaning what?"

"The mushroom's going to blow out to sea. People will die, but only thousands instead of the millions you want," I said. "Not exactly the statement you were looking for."

I drove the black-and-white squad car slowly across the bridge, trying to avoid the splintered edges where several planks had given way in addition to the railing. The bridge creaked under the weight of the car, but we made it across. I drove up an incline to a large cement apron between the side of the house and the creek.

I stopped for a moment, stalling for time.

"See over there? Vinnie got the crew from Seek Out & Destroy to dam the creek."

"That is against the law, of course."

"Coming from you, I should be amused…but you're right, it is against the law. He used a few sticks of dynamite and created a small natural pool, and he keeps it stocked with trout."

"Move on, Matthew Havoc. This fails to interest me."

I slipped the squad car into drive, "It was the only wrap party I've ever attended where they had a backhoe and a bulldozer as the featured entertainment.

"Who is that?" Shamseen shouted, slapping my shoulder with the pistol.

I looked toward the house to see Gloria coming out the side door to greet us. A ruddy-complexioned, fifty-ish lady with auburn hair and a burnt orange silk caftan to match, she was carrying a chubby orange-and-white striped Cheshire cat in one arm and a tumbler of bourbon over ice in the other.

"Shamseen, take it easy, you don't have to yell, I'm right here! That's Gloria, She lives here."

"Vinnie's wife has blond hair. I have met her."

It was hard to arrive at Vinnie's place without attracting a reception. Dogs were barking from a small barn, and a horse looked up from a small corral.

"Who is it?" Shamseen repeated, his voice tight with anxiety.

"Relax, I already told you. It's Vinnie's main squeeze. Gloria, his girlfriend. You'll find her socially drunk and harmless."

He nodded once.

"I'll handle it," I said, trying to reassure him. "Just follow my lead."

"Nice car, Kid," Gloria said, nodding to the police wheels.

"Taking it back to the prop house," I said. "Where's Vinnie?"

"He went to get a tow truck." Gloria grinned and shook her head at the same time, a girl with a secret.

Shamseen jabbed me in the ribs with the muzzle of the pistol. "Ask her, where is the cement truck."

Gloria, no dummy, saw what was going on, but I put on a happy face, actually little more than a grimace. I nodded my head toward the back side of the property, "Uh, Gloria, did Vinnie park a big cement truck somewhere around here?"

Gloria's grin widened. "Yeah, he did. Got it stuck in the pasture out back."

"We would like very much to see it," Shamseen said, the urgency evident in his voice.

Gloria looked him over with sharpening amusement. "Who's this guy?" she asked me, as if he was one of our drivers or maybe some insignificant stunt man.

"Big Egyptian movie star. Shamseen Usudman."

"Never heard of him. Come on, this way." She started walking us around the side of the house. We stayed in the car and I drove slowly along with her walking at my side. As we moved along, I hung one hand out of the car and quietly motioned that she was to hang back.

"Vinnie's thinking of using him in his next big production," I said.

Gloria shrugged and gave me the measured look that said she knew pure bullshit when she heard it.

"That Vinnie…what's he going to call it, Mideastern Madness?" she asked. But by then Shamseen's attention was on what was ahead, and she started dropping back even further.

We had rounded the back corner of the horse barn and there it was—the elusive and deadly cement truck of my nightmares. Fat Boy was looking anything but monstrous. The yellow-orange paint job assumed a rosy hue in the fading light of day, and the truck looked almost beautiful. Unfortunately for any plans Shamseen may have had to simply drive it away, the back wheels had sunken deeply into the pasture.

"What happened?" I asked.

By now, Gloria was standing back by the barn, and she had to practically yell. "Vinnie forgot that, since he dynamited the creek the pasture floods when it rains. It takes six weeks or more to dry out."

"He makes some country gentleman, doesn't he?"

"Alright," Shamseen said. "Enough of this. We must get this truck out of here and into the heart of Los Angeles by tomorrow morning."

"Vinnie should be back any minute now," Gloria said, eyeing him carefully. "Meanwhile, would you heroes of the cinema industry care for a drink?"

"I think we will wait for him here," Shamseen said.

Gloria started back for the house, and Shamseen took the pistol from his pocket. "No, all of us will wait for him here," he yelled at her.

Gloria laughed out loud over her shoulder and kept on walking. "Matthew, tell your friend to put the damn movie prop away."

Shamseen raised the pistol at her retreating back.

"Let her go, Shamseen. Can't you see she's harmless?"

"She could call someone."

"Who is she going to call? We're two business associates waiting for Vinnie."

By then she had disappeared around the corner of the barn. Shamseen jumped from the car and ran after her. I got out on my side and quickly followed. We could see to the house, but there was no sign of Gloria.

"I'll kill her," he said, starting for the house. But he stopped in his tracks as a huge tow truck made its way over Vinnie's rustic bridge. It was Vinnie, himself, driving one of his SUVs and returning with a man behind the wheel of a huge tow truck ordinarily used for hauling semi-rigs.

The truck shuddered to a halt next to us. Vinnie hopped out of his SUV and waved and pointed like a little kid with mud on his boots,

"Matt! Did you see what I did with that frickin' cement truck?"

"Vinnie, we've got a little problem…" Even as I said those words, the understatement was enough to make me wince. I indicated Shamseen, "This gentleman owns the cement truck you and Bertrand made off with."

"Well, we'll see about that," Vinnie said. But in the next second he took in the pistol in Shamseen's hand. "Wooh, mister—it's just a frickin' toy. You can have the goddamn thing."

That's the thing about Vinnie. You could never say he allowed his ego or his wallet to get in the way of an untenable position.

Chapter 22

The tow truck was idling. The driver looked down at Vinnie, waiting for his instructions. When he saw Shamseen wave his pistol in their general direction, he slammed his truck in reverse. That was a mistake with huge personal consequences. Shamseen took steady aim and shot the driver through the window. The innocent but foolish man slumped forward over the wheel and his foot slid off the gas pedal. The truck lurched a few feet and the engine stalled.

"You see clearly now, I am not doing the kidding around," Shamseen said. He waved at me with the gun, "Havoc. Drag that man out of the tow truck. He pointed at Vinnie, "I know you drive trucks. You will use this tow truck to free my truck that you have foolishly stuck in the mud."

"You shot a man for a used cement truck?" Vinnie asked. He raised his hands half way in the air and looked uncertainly at me. "Low mileage, but still..."

"Better do it, Vinnie." I advised.

We had trouble with the towing cable and it took some time to figure out how to use the winch, but Fat Boy finally stood once again on solid ground.

"We will go now," Shamseen said. He pointed to Vinnie with his pistol. "You will drive."

And then the pistol moved in my direction. "It has been a pleasurable experience meeting you, Matthew Havoc. I no longer have need of your services."

"Hey, Egypt-boy," a voice from the house said, "put down that pistol or I'll blow your ass off. You'll have a hell of a time playing the lead with no butt."

It was Gloria, right on cue. Her words were no idle threat, for she was pointing the police riot gun she'd taken from our stolen squad car.

"No! You shoot me, I shoot them," Shamseen said, looking and sounding like he was losing his cool manner.

The thundering rattle of a low flying police helicopter interrupted our Mexican standoff. It swooped in low and, spotting the squad car, banked to come around for another pass.

"Wait!" I shouted. "I can drive the truck!"

I know a lot about Mexican standoffs, it's one of the staples of Berger Royal Pictures. It seemed to me that at this point everybody needed a little urging, and the first person who takes action can sometime nudge things the right way. I had nothing to lose since he was going to shoot me anyway, so I yelled at Shamseen, "Let Vinnie go. Vinnie, go over by Gloria. Gloria, lower the shotgun down a little."

"You can drive this?" Shamseen yelled at me. He was pointing the pistol at me, but I saw his hand was shaking. I pulled the dead driver from the cab; he sighed as he tumbled in the mud, and I figured he might have a chance yet...if any of us did.

"Of course, I can," I yelled back. "Come on, you idiot!" That's another thing about Keg's book of war: *Never miss a chance to rattle the enemy. Call them chicken-shits, call them rat-bastards, but keep them off their happy hour!*

I'd already climbed up on the driver's side of the truck. I squirmed my butt around, settling in the big seat. The big engine, still warm, turned over on the first try. On the outside, I suppose I looked like I knew what I was doing, but I actually wasn't all that sure. I'd driven pickup trucks and even a dump truck, but Fat Boy was *huge.* Well, I told myself as the engine roared to life, I'd just have to be a fast learner. *Instant* learner, was more like it. Shamseen clambered up beside me in the passenger seat and I jammed the short, fat stainless steel stick in what I figured was the lowest gear. There was a reluctant grinding and Fat Boy lurched forward.

We rumbled around the side of the barn, headed for the little bridge.

"That bridge won't hold our weight!" Shamseen warned.

I kept going, the engine growling in whatever low gear I'd found.

"There's no other way out!" I replied. Actually, there was another way, a gravel fire trail that looped off the back end of Vinnie's ten acres, but I didn't think Shamseen knew that.

"Stop!"

Shamseen poked me in the ribs again. I could see in the wide rear view mirror on my side that the helicopter had landed and men in flak jackets were jumping out and running toward us.

"Will you stop jabbing me with that goddamn pistol! If you're going to shoot me, just get it over with!"

"I'm sorry," he said politely.

Unbelievable! We were making a getaway in a big truck wired with a nuclear device and he apologizes for scratching me with his pistol! "I have no good choices," he complained.

"Well, that's not my fault! Do you want to drive?"

"No, you drive, Matthew Havoc."

"And you agree, this is the only way we can possibly go?"

"Yes, go. Go forward across the little bridge."

We actually made it half way, more or less to the center of Vinnie's wooden bridge before it sagged and began to come apart under the tremendous weight of the truck. There was a splintering sound as the support beams gave way underneath. The structure yawed to the left, and I thought we would simply slide over on our side, but then the supports on the other side snapped and we swung back to center. The front end of the truck drifted down with a groaning wail as bolts popped and nails gave way.

And there we hung, the entire truck leaning forward, unsteadily balanced with the cab wheels hanging over the sandy trickle of water at the bottom. We were downstream from Vinnie's makeshift dam, and so at least we weren't going underwater. Twice in one day would be a little much, even for a Berger Royal adventure flick, much less real life.

"You did that on purpose," Shamseen cried out in frustration, waving his pistol in my face.

"Nonsense, that's crazy! I asked you and you said 'Go ahead'! The damn bridge just gave away!"

Fat Boy was swaying like a hippo on a high wire. Still using Keg's theory that *the man who makes the most noise in a crisis is listened to*, I yelled, "Come on, we've got to get out of here!"

I jumped out of my side, and Shamseen went out on his. By now the sun had long set over the rim of the hills, and it was darkening in the shady cut of the creek. I hit hard on the rocky far slope and rolled back down into the streambed. Somewhere in all that hasty attempt to flee from Shamseen and his pistol, I felt a sharp pain in my right ankle. Amateur heroes like me don't operate at their best in times like that. I was trying to figure out if I'd broken my ankle and to hide in the little trickle of waters hulking down behind the nearest rocks in case Shamseen decided he wanted to shoot me after all when another helicopter came in and hovered over Fat Boy. The roar from the chopper blades and the flaring blue-white beam from a searchlight made for a scene of absolute chaos. .

I kept my head down, and the roar from the whirling blades must have convinced

Shamseen the jig was up, because by the time Vinnie moved the tow truck from the cement pad so the third helicopter was able to land, the mysterious man who wanted to destroy Los Angeles had disappeared into the gathering gloom of night.

"Hey, Havoc, you down there?" It was Vinnie, calling from the edge of his bridge that still held up the back of the truck. "Havoc, come on out of there!"

I tried to stand, but instantly found I couldn't. In fact, I couldn't move. In my haste to get away from Shamseen's bullets, I hadn't stopped to think I was hiding under the huge bulk of the unsteady cement truck. While I was cringing with my nose to the damp, sandy creek bed, one of Fat Boy's front tires had settled on my back and was now pushing me ever deeper into the muddy gravel of the streambed.

Fat Boy took a little lurch and settled even more and I had to strain to pull air into my lungs and crane my neck to clear my nostrils out of the small trickle of water that seemed to be deepening as my body lay across the little streambed, blocking the small but steady flow. I, Matt Havoc, who had survived two brushes with death in the deep sea, was about to be drowned in two inches of water.

You might think drowning in a teacup is better than being vaporized by Fat Boy. But in fact, while the body can intellectually comprehend and even dread instant incineration, drowning is a far more immediate physical fear. I knew the heavy weight of the nuclear device pinning me down in the same sense that a miner knows he is deep underground. Being deep underground can kill you. But a lack of oxygen absolutely will kill you. In other words, I struggled and craned my neck and fought for each breath and didn't have the energy or imagination for anything more.

And life, being what it is, chose that moment to add trouble to my trouble. Someone on the bank of the creek spotted me lying below, being slowly squashed by Fat Boy's huge left front tire.

"Down there!" People yelled and pointed, and there was a commotion as flashlights flared and men ran to find pry bars or blankets or whatever they could think of. But the first person down wasn't a husky fireman with a shovel who could dig me out. It was Joy Benefeté, America's favorite set, followed closely by an amateur cameraman who'd been filming sunsets when the Rover went over the side and was now riding his lucky streak to big payouts from Extra Extra and the National Inquirer.

Joy moved in, close to me as she could get, which made for a very tight squeeze, the only available space that allowed for a camera angle being in front of and slightly on top of my head. Of course, pro that she was, she automatically figured out the shot, got the right angle, and assumed her position. Although she was nearly breaking my neck, and actually pushing me deeper into the wet sand, in the shots on the evening news it would look like she was cuddling my head to her generous bosom. One of my last dying thoughts, I had to agree with my sweetie pie princess about Peanuts' augmentation, it did feel a bit like she was resting a couple of firm outcrops on my muddy forehead.

It looked like we were finished with the shots, but just then a news crew showed up with a video camera and somebody pointed a really bright light down the slope in my face. And, of course, we had to do it all over again.

"Here he is, my husband and my savior!" Joy emoted in the precise direction of the lens. I told you she was good.

"Ex-husband," I managed to grunt.

"Yes," she continued as if someone had asked her a question, "Matthew and I are getting back together! I know the Golden Globe is something, but true love is everything!"

"Peanuts…"

I was having trouble getting my breath, much less trying to argue with her, "We are not—getting back together…"

"Oh, Matt," she gushed, realizing that my protests had been too faint to be picked up on mike, and with the shadows and the bad angle you couldn't see my face anyway. She smiled radiantly and gushed on, "When my agent was so tragically murdered, I saw the light, and, in that grim moment of truth, I realized how fleeting life is for us all. 'Go for what makes you happy' I said to myself. And now, Mattie, I realize that person is you!"

The light flickered and faded and I could almost hear a director somewhere on the bank say "Cut!"

She gave my neck a bad little tweak and hissed in my ear, "Matthew, don't ever call me Peanuts. Not in public. I mean, I like it, but some things are not meant to be shared."

"Joy—try to keep—my nose out of the water."

Maybe she meant to help, but she was careless and supremely self-centered. I was sure she was going to break my neck or drown me in show biz kindness, but then at the last possible second a burly guy finally did show up with a shovel. It took a half hour, but there was just barely enough gravel underneath my body so they were able to scoop under and then drag me to freedom. Assisted by several firemen, I was pulled and carried up the short slope to Vinnie's driveway.

Chapter 23

Peanuts was the star of the evening news, and the wet-blouse footage that was too revealing for family viewing ended up as a series of shorts on YouTube. My favorite was one set to the theme song music from The Bugs Bunny/Road Runner Show and inter-cut with Bugs, the Runner, and all their cartoon friends. I couldn't have directed any of it any better myself. The title "Actress Proves Self As Real-Life Heroine!" comes zooming out of a cartoon background. The song bubbles along, "Here we go/With fun in tow"

There's a shot of me trying to squeeze out from under Joy's famous set, luminous and daring in the thin silk blouse. "It's the Bugs Bunny/Road Runner Show" Here Bugs winks at us and the Runner winds up his fast feet and zips off camera. Back to me, with what looks like a drunken smile, just a lucky fellow in nipple heaven.

But I was out from under the crushing pressure of Fat Boy and alive, at least for the moment. Gloria found me a set of her old sweats, and, though I had a bad crick in my neck, I felt better than I should have, all things considered. Vinnie shoved a home-made latte in my hand.

"From one of the neighbors," he explained.

In the half hour I'd been pinned down, the area had taken on a whole new look. Several truckloads of marines had moved in and the troopers had established a rough perimeter around Vinnie's compound. Curious neighbors were straying by, and they were being routinely ordered off by a brisk young Captain who wasn't giving any reasons.

This being California, and a neighborhood populated by the wealthy and successful, the authoritarian bluster wasn't going over too well. I watched as the Captain changed tactics, confiding to the gathering crowd that there was a deadly viral infection and everyone should go home and slip on their gas masks. This had the desired effect, and the nosy neighbors scattered like the wind.

A man stood there, looking intently at me. He was lean and wizened with a head shaved bald and a huge bushy black moustache.

"Havoc in the West," he said, smiling and nodding in my direction.

"Rooks from the East," I replied. "You got here fast."

He nodded. "I was already on a plane, somewhere over Kansas, when my laptop got your last messages.

"Shamseen was there, holding a gun on me." My eyes flicked down the winding gully of the creek and took in the surrounding gentlemen's estates.

"I gathered as much," he replied. "And where is he now?"

"He was here," I said. I shook my head. "Too many trees, too much vegetation. He's got some men holding Bertrand and Julia. I'm not sure where."

"They're not at Bertrand's condo," Rooks said. "We'll find them."

He jerked his head in the direction of the truck. "You think he might try to sneak back and detonate it?"

"No...he's the kind of guy who gets others to do his dirty work."

"That's what we think."

"But, you know...from the way he was acting, I think it's already wired to blow."

Rooks eyebrows raised. "How so?"

"I had the impression there was a deadline. Now, if he was a villain in one of our movies, he'd want maximum destruction..."

"Maximum Destruction...good title."

"Yeah, we'll give you credit for it. No, listen, seriously...Shamseen talked about tomorrow morning. I'm sure he felt he had time to retrieve Fat Boy and drive it back into a populated area. And that means he probably had time to park it somewhere and make an escape out of the state."

A man in a rumpled suit interrupted us, "We're going to need you now, Mr. Rooks."

"I'm bringing him," Halliburton said, indicating me.

"I'm afraid...no clearance," the man shook his head.

"I'm afraid, yes," Rooks replied. "Matthew Havoc is Jack Havoc's son. He probably knows more about Usudman than any of us." He made the sign of the cross over my head, "I curse you TOP SECRET CODEWORD. May the devil be with you." With a brief nod of his head he indicated I was to follow him.

We gathered in a makeshift War Room in Vinnie's high ceiling entertainment and dining room. We had a panoramic view. Through the floor-to-ceiling plate glass windows, we could clearly make out the hulking orange threat that was Fat Boy, still tilted forward in the little creek bed.

"Where's Joy?" I asked.

Rooks grinned, "Your ex left with the Action News Crew. Something about making sure they got the right slant on the news. That's some broad—she had five minutes in one of Vinnie Berger's bathrooms, and came out looking ready for the cover of Cosmopolitan."

"Yeah, Joy is like that. How are you explaining Fat Boy?"

"So far we're going with the virus story. I'm not wanting to start a panic evacuation out of Southern California."

"Chips, anyone?" Gloria said, as she brought out a spread left over from the Chop of Death wrap party. It was a surreal moment. I looked past her to the kitchen where my boss was pacing impatiently.

"You better bring Vinnie in here," I said. "Before he has his fourth heart attack."

"That a good idea?"

"I think so. Vinnie is a problem solver. He gets things done."

The man in the rumpled suit shook his head and frowned, but once again Rooks trumped him. Vinnie came in looking suspicious and guilty at the same time, like the kid who got caught stealing the cookie jar and wasn't sure just who ratted on him.

"Sit down, Vinnie," Rooks invited him.

"Right. Thanks. I get to sit on my own couch in my own living room"

He glared at me, not liking to be in the dark about what was going on. It seemed silly, but nobody had thought to explain to him about Fat Boy. Still, Vinnie was no dummy. Whatever was happening, the heavy military presence that had invaded his property, the helicopters intruding from the sky and the heavily armed perimeter around his cement truck—this dramatic new reality was enough to keep him quiet, at least until he could figure out a bit more about what was happening.

There were about twenty of us, half military and half civilian. We were an odd mix, men with long faces sitting around in Vinnie's big living room, sipping Carta Blanca from brown bottles and silently calculating the odds of instant incineration.   The soldiers were a mix of men in fatigues and in dress uniforms, and the civilians were an even stranger brew. There was a fellow in a flowery Hawaiian shirt who looked like he'd been plucked from the 14th hole on some golf course, a short little man with a Romanesque hook nose and a grim downturn to his lips who seemed to have slept for three days in the same suit, and a lanky dude wearing sweats and running shoes and smoking a pipe.

"Matt," Rooks looked at me, "Do you think it's set to go off? Did he say anything about when it might blow?"

"Blow…?" Vinnie mouthed silently, his eyes widening in my direction.

"Well…" I hesitated, knowing Shamseen was a professional liar. "He said he intended to get it to downtown L.A. tonight. Important that it was there before tomorrow morning."

The man in the rumpled suit frowned, "Did he say exactly that's when it would detonate?"

Again, Vinnie looked at me. *Detonate.* The kind of words we used in Keg's War.

"No, he didn't," I replied. "That was the implication I took from him. He was upset Vinnie had moved his cement truck to Malibu."

"Balls," Vinnie grumped resentfully, "It's my cement truck."

"Your atomic bomb," I corrected him.

"My what?" Vinnie gaped, his eyes widening as his gaze slid to the truck visible out the window.

"Might as well tell him, " Rooks shrugged. "After all, it *is* his property."

The man in the rumpled suit pushed his wire rim glasses, which had been slipping down his rather large nose, "Somebody hired by a man named Shamseen Usudman wired a nuclear device of the implosion type into a cement truck that they shipped over on the deck of an oil tanker, the Olaga Supreme, if memory serves me." Here he referred to his notes. "Your, hem—partner, one Bertrand

Berke, engaged that ship. When he proved victim of a scam, he sued for all properties on the ship, in an attempt to recoup his investment. The papers were in order and U.S. authorities were supposed to believe the truck was an afterthought—they did believe it was, and the truck was released to the first persons who showed up and those happened to be you and Bertrand Burke."

Vinnie got up and stared right and left, looking as if he might want to head for the hills if he could only figure out which hills were safe. "But—but—but…What if it goes off?"

"What if, indeed," Rooks said. "That is what we are trying to prevent."

"But you want to move it to Nevada, don't you?" I prompted, hoping to stave off Vinnie's oncoming medical disaster. "Some atomic testing site way out there, far from here?"

Several of the men in uniform exchanged glances. Rooks calmed them with a wave of his hand. "Havoc's father was in the agency with me. Havoc here had access to his father's papers. He probably knows more about us than any of us."

The Captain shrugged, "Okay…Here's where we're at. We're dismantling the tub part from the cab of the cement truck. Then we could get it on a flat-bed truck."

"Balls," Vinnie said, "You need a crane helicopter."

"There aren't any crane helicopters any more," the Captain said.

"You don't know nothing," Vinnie cut back sharply.

"Pu-lease!" The man in the rumpled suit said, clearly annoyed that amateurs were disrupting his thought process.

"Crap," Vinnie said, not about to be intimidated by anyone. "We used one on Keg's War."

"Well, technically speaking," the Captain said, "the military phased them out in the 1980s."

Rooks eyes flicked from Vinnie to me, "How much weight can an air crane lift?"

"Erickson's S-64 E or F model Aircrane in the Construction Configuration can lift 25,000 pounds," I said, ticking the statistics off from memory. The chopper shots had been critical to Keg's War, so I wasn't about to forget the details.

"We know this stuff," Vinnie nodded happily.

"Who's Erickson?" the Captain asked.

"Erickson bought the rights to the S-64 from Sikorsky," I said. "They're still used for firefighting and lifting oil pipe lines."

"It was great in the movie," Vinnie added approvingly. "This big spider comes down out of the sky with hooks on it and snags a sampan right out of the river!"

"Is there one close?" the Captain asked.

"Call the fire department," I suggested.

"The fire department," he scoffed.

"Call the fire department," Rooks said, and the Captain ran out of the room like a chastised boy scout.

"Maybe we can get Fat Boy to Nellis," Rooks said. "*If* we have until 9 tomorrow morning."

I raised my eyebrows, wondering what and where Nellis was.

"Nellis Air Force Base and Nuclear Testing Site", Rooks added, filling in the blanks. "East of Death Valley."

"Fitting," I nodded.

I tried to think like Shamseen. *What would I do? Or more to the point, what would the corrupt Harrigan Matre have done when his evil plans were about to be foiled by the brave and clever martial arts master Tran Le?*

Harrigan had rigged a trap floor so that when beautiful and sexually stimulating but still virginal Hoa Tuan was freed of her bonds the girl and her rescuers would both fall through the trap panels in the floor into the vats of acid.

"What if..." My thoughts trailed off. After all, these guys were experts. I doubted my illusionary worlds of the silver screen could have much of substance to offer.

"What, Matt?" Rooks urged. "Say it."

"Well, Shamseen is enormously devious. I mean, he doesn't seem to have any guilt at all. I know he's got his reasons, but he's never said what his motivation might be. I'm just thinking...what if he set a trigger to blow Fat Boy if anybody tried to take it apart?"

"Oh, shit..." the man in the rumpled suit said, getting up and hurrying from the room.

The experts working on Fat Boy slowed their progress by a factor of ten, now that they were looking for triggers and hidden mechanisms as well as simply unscrewing nuts and bolts. Their Geiger counters had certified that there was a nuclear device welded in a shallow compartment in the front or base of the cement tub. From the shape they could deduce it was an implosion device. But it was nearly midnight before they found the fail-safe trigger, and it was one o'clock in the morning before it was dismantled.

While Rooks and I sat in Vinnie's huge study, the crew toiled on through the night, swarming like ants around the big yellow-orange cement truck, which had been cabled to several ancient oaks on both banks of the creek.

The news on all channels still had America's Favorite Set in play, with continuous feed and a live shot from a news helicopter hovering a half-mile away. The narrators were speculating at the nature of the virus rumored to be contained in the orange cement truck that had somehow fallen into a creek in the Coastal Range near Malibu. Further speculation was, the virus had to be contained, otherwise the men seen scurrying around the scene would be in isolation suits and masks. Cut-aways replayed shots of superstar Joy Benefeté, who had been rescued as part of the same complicated situation, the seriousness of which 'was unfolding even as it was reported.' Joy's clinging blouse was clearly pornographic, and Matt doubted anyone heard a word she said, not that she was making much sense, either.

"Terrorists," she insisted, "were responsible for the assassination of my agent, Harry Hiatt."

"But," the skeptical newsman asked, "what possible reason could they have for killing your agent?"

"As you know, I am the front runner for a Golden Globe for my work in Intimate Remembrances. I won't mention names, but there are people who think it should go to a foreign actress."

The newsman seemed confused, but Peanuts was getting real mileage out of that thin, damp silk blouse. I was beginning to suspect she had somebody applying dampness to keep the look going. In the presence of America's Favorite Set, Channel 7's late-night anchorman was having as much trouble concentrating as everybody else out there in Southern California, sitting entranced at home in front of their television sets and enjoying the show. And, although it's an old joke, Joy gave a whole new meaning to the old expression boob tube.

For my part, I wanted the bomb to be hoisted up and away so I could go back to Sea Garden Cove to figure out what Shamseen had done with Bertrand and Julia. I figured it was a long shot hope, but it was all I could do.

Rooks interrupted my thoughts, nodding at Joy on the television screen, "You were married to her for what, ten years?"

"The bliss lasted a few weeks…we stayed together for two pictures…about two years."

Rooks gave me a sideways look, "But the news said…"

"We just didn't get around to the divorce."

"And now you're getting back together."

I shook my head, "Not a chance."

"You're crazier than your old man."

"She's great in the sack, alright…" I clicked the mute on the TV set, "Say, what was that stuff about my dad, anyway?"

Halliburton Rook sighed, "It's old business, but I guess you should know. I told your father not to write that book."

"What book?" This was a new direction for me. I'd been talking about the fact that Jack Havoc had known Shamseen. Puzzles were opening to reveal more puzzles.

"Crazyhead," Rooks said. "The one you want to do the movie."

"How much of that stuff was true?" I asked, rolling with the tide. If Rooks was in a talking mood, I was going to listen.

Halliburton Rooks shook his head, remembering, "We were partners over in Nam, and after that, back at the agency. We both knew too much dirt. They called us *Mad Jack* and *Hip Hal*, two guys who went a little over the edge from all the mayhem and the madness. Johnny got disgusted and quit and went away, and he shouldn't have written about any of it. It was the little details, like the green thread they used to mark the corpses that had the dope sewn inside, things like that gave it away. You see, they knew he knew."

"Who is the *they*?"

"Matthew, there's always a *they*. Don't worry, they're mostly dead and gone now. Dead and gone…mostly…"

Rooks gave me a complex look that somehow made me think of sudden violent bloodletting.

"You're saying Crazyhead was a true story? Transporting opium back from Vietnam in dead G.I.s' bodies?"

"Heroin," he corrected me. "That's what you're talking about, right?"

"And somebody killed my father because of it?"

"True enough."

"But..."

"They're all dead, Matt. Specifics, you don't want to know."

"What about Dad's disappearance?"

Halliburton just shook his head, his thoughts seemingly far in the distant past. "Matt, your old man could hold a crowd. I remember him clear as if it was yesterday, standing in the Cherry Bar on Tu Do Street in downtown Saigon, a Ba Muoi Ba in one hand and his other hand waving, showing us just how this little Viet Cong terrorist kid had come at him , waving a pistol that was almost too heavy for the puny teenager to hold.. The great Johnny Havoc always was a storyteller, but there were certain stories that weren't meant to be told."

I hadn't found the answer as to what my father had done to Shamseen Usudman to cause him to seek revenge the way he had, but other mysteries were opening up for me. The real life of Johnny Havoc, it seemed, had been at least as complex as a Berger Royal picture of high action and adventure.

Chapter 24.

The first hint of gray dawn was streaking the eastern sky over the lip of the bowl surrounding Vinnie's ranchette in Malibu when the giant red crane helicopter appeared, riding its own wave of thunderous flapping. There were too many trees for it to land, so it hovered overhead and let down winch lines. It took less than 20 minutes to secure its deadly load.

With the bomb from Fat Boy slung underneath, the S-64 looked like an ungainly stork carrying an unwanted baby. Rooks assured everybody there was plenty of time (actually over an hour to spare) and the people at Ellis were ready and confident. Still, we all sighed in relief when the big helicopter lifted up and away from Vinnie's creek.

Vinnie and Gloria had gone to bed, figuring if Fat Boy was going to go off, they wanted their last night to be something special. When the huge crane helicopter came thundering in, they reappeared, disheveled and sleepy. We all watched it flap away over the hills to the east. I felt more tired than I could ever remember, but I knew I had to get back to Newport Beach.

Rooks reassured me. "We have word Bertrand and his granddaughter are okay."

"I have to get back down there. You need a ride to the airport?" LAX was on my way, and I figured I might get some more information out of him.

"That would be nice," he said.

I knew where the keys were, so I borrowed one of Vinnie's cars, a Ford Explorer. I put it in 4-wheel drive and we bumped through the creek at the upper end of Vinnie's property. But once we were on the road, my fount of information fell sound asleep, and so I didn't learn anything. I left Rooks standing in front of the American Airlines terminal.

"You know how to contact me," He said. "Rooks in the East," I said. He saluted and I tossed him a wave in reply. One terse smile and my father's old friend turned away and walked through the doors and into the busy terminal.

It was nearly seven in the morning when I pulled in to Sea Garden Cove. The window in the guard shack had been repaired, but there was nobody on duty and the gates were again wide open. I drove on up to my condo and jumped out of the car. My front door was unlocked, and a familiar shape was sleeping in my bed.

"Julia!" I said happily. "Oh, Julia, you're here!"

She opened one sleepy eye and looked me over.

"Oh, it's you," she said. "The guy who's getting back together with America's favorite Ice Princess." And with that, she pulled the covers over her head and turned to the wall. This was going to take some persuasive action, but I figured I was up to the task.

I stripped off my grimy clothes and took a long hot shower. After that, I came back to my bedroom. Julia was sitting up, watching me dry off.

"Don't bother putting that bathrobe on," she said. "Come over here, idiot-boy."

"I thought you'd surrendered me to the Ice Princess."

"I changed my mind. I've got something over here that might make you forget her."

"Oh," I said, "what is it?"

"Something you told me was warm and soft and tender and wonderful. Come here and you'll see."

She was right, in no time at all I forgot all about Peanuts. Superstar Joy Benefeté may have been the rest of America's Favorite Set, but she certainly wasn't mine.

I woke some time mid-morning, full of questions. Other than the rising sun, there had been no great light in the sky to the east except the ordinary sunrise, so I presumed the military successfully achieved whatever they'd intended with the part of Fat Boy they had carted off to Nevada.

I cut some John Murrell sausages into small squares and scrambled some eggs. Julia joined me just as the bagels popped up in the toaster. I find you can toast bagels without getting them stuck if you cut them thinner, in four slices instead of in half. The trick is cutting them lengthwise, but with the help of a very sharp bread knife, I'd become good at it. I fixed Julia a café au lait, and grinned triumphantly across the table at her, *the man who had saved the Southland.* She looked sleepy and rumpled in a sweet sort of way. I let her get most of the way through her eggs before my curiosity got the best of me.

"Okay. How did you get away?"

She shook her head. "They just thugs, Matthew. They weren't very bright. They had Grandpa and me in a motel somewhere in Santa Ana. There was one guy with this ugly little black pistol that looked like it could spray a lot of bullets. We had to keep quiet or he would shoot us. Some time late, there was a phone call, and the man said he was going for food, and he didn't come back."

"Shamseen must have called him after he got away from us at Vinnie's place in Malibu," I said.

"Why did you go there?"

"Vinnie parked the cement truck there, the one they heisted from the oil tanker to get some of their money back."

"But the truck had a virus on it." I didn't say anything, and she looked at me. "Matt, what? We saw it on television, your delightful ex rescuing you from two inches of water and hugging you to her mighty breasts, everything."

I had to tell her. Maybe Johnny Havoc had to keep secrets from those he loved, but he was a spy. I was Hollywood Havoc, producer of schlock movies for the King of Schlock, Vinnie Berger. "A bomb, my sweetie pie princess. The truck had a very large, extremely large, huge in fact, bomb welded inside."

"Big as twin towers?" she asked.

"Big as Hiroshima," I replied. We just stared at each other, thinking of what might have been.

It stayed between the two of us. Vinnie and Gloria knew, of course, but we didn't tell Bertrand, who wouldn't have believed us, anyway. There were plenty of rumors and the National Enquirer ran a story that flat out declared it was an atomic bomb, but you know the way that works—with their reputation they did the truth more harm than good.

Vinnie's money source had dried up for our new Carnage Days project, but he was Vinnie Berger, the unstoppable Hollywood force. He went on the warpath for new funding and in no time at all came up with a French banker "formerly of Lebanese extraction" who had dabbled in European cinema and wanted to go Big-Time Hollywood.

"Just a matter of days, now," Vinnie assured me.

Bertrand went to a medical supply convention in St. Louis and I had three days of bliss with Julia before I had to start pre-production on Carnage Days. My sweetie pie princess and her idiot-boy went over to Catalina Island where we rented a small cottage and pretended we were just the ordinary Joneses instead of the splendid and magnificent couple who had saved Los Angeles from nuclear annihilation.

Life was good. A story with a happy ending. And we lived happily ever after, right? Well, not exactly…

Julia and I got back to Sea Garden Cove on a Sunday evening. We were sun burnt and happy from hiking in the hills. I'd almost been run over by a charging buffalo, and Julia was laughing so hard she sat on a bee and justly got stung in the butt.

She gave me a lingering kiss of dismissal, and then headed for Bertrand's.

"Letter taped to your door," she said, talking over her shoulder as she fished in her big purse for the key to Old Gramper's place.

I saw FedEx had tried unsuccessfully to deliver it to three or four places. I probably should have burned it on the spot, or at least kept my mouth shut—but that isn't my style, either. I examined the fat letter, and called after my sweetie pie princess.

"It's for you, Julia. Something from Japan, looks like…"

The letter had bounced its way from her job at the Getty to Bertrand's and finally found itself taped to my front door .

Bertrand had taped it there out of spite. By this time, he'd figured out I'd gotten past first base with his granddaughter, and, at least for the time being, he wasn't speaking to either of us.

She ripped the letter open and her face lit as she quickly scanned it.

"Matt, Matt—MATT! It's an offer to study Zen haiku painting in Japan!"

"Ohh," I said.

"No, this is really something once-in-a-lifetime! Gorji is the last living master—and he's already overdue on his trip to the hereafter. I mean, he's *really* old."

"So, you're going to Japan?"

"Well, not *forever!* Matt, this is fabulous," she bubbled, waving the letter in the air.

I hoped my disappointment wasn't showing; we hadn't really talked things through, but I had thought we were a once-in-a-lifetime chance too...Still, I couldn't tell her that. I knew Julia as well as I knew myself. Any fool could see, she wasn't ready to settle down with me. Julia was eager and ready to fly, she wanted to soar west over the Pacific as badly as she'd ever wanted anything. The California hippies used to say *If you love someone, set them free.*

My mother had been a free spirit, a child who came of age in the 1960s. An old hippie, she'd called herself, and I'd loved her and everything she stood for. I just hadn't realized how much it could hurt, to open yourself up to somebody and then have to help them fly away.

"Yeah, it does look like a great opportunity," I said.

"I can't wait to tell Old Grampers!" And she rushed off, certain he would happy for her, as well. On that score, I had to agree with her. Bertrand would be delighted by anything that separated me from his granddaughter.

A few days later, Julia and I said our goodbyes, promising to write and love forever, and I dropped her off at the airport.

Vinnie still wasn't paying me, but I started preproduction on Carnage Days, anyway. Anything to keep busy, you know? Still, my mind kept drifting back to her...

. Julia, Julia, Julia…*and how many sleepless nights will I spend remembering you, my sweetie pie princess?*

ABOUT THE AUTHOR

During the Vietnam War, John Klawitter was a military intelligence spy with a Top Secret CODEWORD clearance. He worked at a SE Asia branch of the National Security Agency's so-called 'Puzzle Palace'. Back stateside and having been awarded an Honorable Discharge and an Expeditionary Forces medal, he began his career as a cub copywriter at the Leo Burnett Advertising Agency, working on such national accounts as Kellogg's cereals and Nestles chocolate bars. He became a do-it-yourself filmmaker and won many awards, including an EMMY, for his political documentary work. Advancing over the years as a Hollywood writer, producer and Directors Guild of America director, as well as a member of ASCAP and The Authors Guild, he has authored over a dozen novels and non-fiction books, including the highly regarded HEADSLAP: The Life & Times of Deacon Jones, HOLLYWOOD HAVOC: The Trouble With Fat Boy (EPIC Author's Award 2009 for Best Action-Thriller Novel), and TINSEL WILDERNESS (EPIC Author's Award 2009 for Best Non-Fiction Book). His trade paperbacks are available from Amazon, B&N and the rest of the usual suspects.

E-books of his titles are available in all formats from www.double-dragon-ebooks.com. Information on upcoming novels and film projects available at www.johnklawitter.com.